If Wishes Were Horses

by

Jayne York

This is a work of fiction. Names, characters, places, and incidents are either the product of the author's imagination or are used fictitiously, and any resemblance to actual persons living or dead, business establishments, events, or locales, is entirely coincidental.

If Wishes Were Horses

COPYRIGHT © 2019 by Jayne York

All rights reserved. No part of this book may be used or reproduced in any manner whatsoever without written permission of the author or The Wild Rose Press, Inc. except in the case of brief quotations embodied in critical articles or reviews.
Contact Information: info@thewildrosepress.com

Cover Art by *Rae Monet, Inc. Design*

The Wild Rose Press, Inc.
PO Box 708
Adams Basin, NY 14410-0708
Visit us at www.thewildrosepress.com

Publishing History
First Mainstream Women's Fiction Edition, 2019
Print ISBN 978-1-5092-2725-9
Digital ISBN 978-1-5092-2726-6

Published in the United States of America

Once upon a time, she'd run away from Tamarack like her heels were on fire, and now here she was volunteering to step back into the furnace. What was the definition of insanity? Doing the same things over and over, expecting a different outcome. Like if she managed to change, be stronger, be smarter, things would turn out better—different.

It wouldn't be that simple.

Through the windshield of her Jeep, the wilds of the Wind River Range eventually gave way to the high country of Colorado, and soon Emily was navigating the twisting curves where she'd learned to handle a four-wheel drive vehicle in snow up to her backside. Twelve hundred miles on the road culminated at Cutthroat Pass, the entrée to Tamarack. It was hardly the most direct route to the town nestled in the valley below her.

She downshifted the Jeep to slow for the last of the S-shaped turns on the narrow ribbon of asphalt. The road led her past the pretentious granite columns that marked her stepfather's compound. She wasn't consciously holding her breath, but a trickle of fear dribbled down her spine just the same. Her molars ground together in determination. The past wouldn't decide her present, not ever again.

In spite of herself, images of her last day on his estate flashed through her mind like the herky-jerky frames of a child's flip deck animation. Fear sharpened every visual, clarified every word, enhanced every touch.

Dedication

To my daughter, Dia. A truer heart never beat.

Chapter One

Returning to Tamarack had *never* been part of the plan. Emily Converse had sworn the only way she'd ever step foot in that slice of hell again would be to dance on her stepfather's grave. Time and circumstance, however, had a way of intervening.

She was not a woman given to self-pity, but damn, it was tempting. And practically impossible to avoid, considering the litany of crap that had landed in her lap in the last two weeks. She'd never considered herself a glutton for punishment, but on top of all the other things on her list of woes, she was driving cross-country to rescue her brother from financial collapse.

Certainly not the way she'd planned to ring in year number forty. She was *supposed* to be on a plane right now, headed to Playa Del Carmen. She was *supposed* to be floating in water so warm it felt like a bath and so blue it looked like a summer sky. She should have kept the reservation and celebrated her freedom, but no. Instead she reverted to a previous version of herself and did the last thing on earth she wanted to do—drive home to Tamarack, Colorado.

She rocked her head to loosen the tension in her neck and flexed her shoulders. Her hands felt like claws clamped around the steering wheel. She was exhausted. The last few weeks had been pure hell as she rushed to wrap up one life and hit the reset button on another.

Add to that a two-day snooze-fest drive from Seattle, across the flatlands of Idaho, and into the hills of Wyoming. It gave her plenty of time to obsess over the step she was taking.

Once upon a time, she'd run away from Tamarack like her heels were on fire, and now here she was volunteering to step back into the furnace. What was the definition of insanity? Doing the same things over and over, expecting a different outcome. Like if she managed to change, be stronger, be smarter, things would turn out better—different.

It wouldn't be that simple.

Through the windshield of her Jeep, the wilds of the Wind River Range eventually gave way to the high country of Colorado, and soon Emily was navigating the twisting curves where she'd learned to handle a four-wheel drive vehicle in snow up to her backside. Twelve hundred miles on the road culminated at Cutthroat Pass, the entrée to Tamarack. It was hardly the most direct route to the town nestled in the valley below her.

She downshifted the Jeep to slow for the last of the S-shaped turns on the narrow ribbon of asphalt. The road led her past the pretentious granite columns that marked her stepfather's compound. She wasn't consciously holding her breath, but a trickle of fear dribbled down her spine just the same. Her molars ground together in determination. The past wouldn't decide her present, not ever again.

In spite of herself, images of her last day on his estate flashed through her mind like the herky-jerky frames of a child's flip deck animation. Fear sharpened every visual, clarified every word, enhanced every touch. She'd run down the steps, racing for her car. He'd charged after her, smelling of alcohol and fury when he tried to stop her headlong rush toward an unknown future. They'd screamed out their mutual hatred, all the bitter dregs of their time together. She smirked when she remembered getting in the lucky shove that had landed him in a heap on the ground. It had been her first glimpse that Senator Ray Domenico was not the invincible, all-powerful monster she'd known him to be.

A deep lungful of crisp air dispelled the clinging fragments of that memory, and she reached out to flick the stuffed mouse hanging from her rearview mirror. She'd bought him to guard her good luck. The specters grabbing at her from Ray's driveway had only landed a glancing blow, so his silly grin and suit of armor were working perfectly.

Finally, she was in easy striking distance of Tamarack. First she had one crucial stop to make.

The apex of the last switchback widened into a pull off, and she nosed her vehicle into the space provided. The roaring voice of Angel Falls surrounded her, and she felt the power of the Saint Vrain River as it plummeted more than one hundred feet over a massive rock outcropping. From there it boiled and foamed its way to a clear, tranquil lake adjacent to the town. The view was impressive, no arguing that point.

She sat quietly for a moment, gazing at the jagged peaks surrounding the valley. Her seat belt seemed to unfasten itself; she was drawn out of the Jeep as if an invisible rope towed her forward. She found herself on a slim finger of stone overlooking the cascading water. With a shaky breath, she remembered all the times she'd come here to pay respects to her mother.

The cacophony of the torrent below swallowed her greeting. "Hi, Mama. Bet you thought you'd never see me here again. I sure wish you were here; I could really use you right now." She leaned back against the rocks that provided a seat for watching the terrible, beautiful tumble of Angel Falls. "I'm ashamed to say it, but I think you'd be disappointed in me. You counted on me to take care of Ian, and I tried so hard to help him. Nothing seemed to work with him. I got tired and frustrated, and I quit trying. Now, I'm back, and he…well, he's not going to like it."

She took a deep breath of the fragrant air and settled more comfortably on her stone seat. Aspens, tall and white-barked, skirted the edges of the canyon and shivered in the crisp fall air. Their golden, coin-shaped leaves glittered in the afternoon light.

"I didn't do such a bang-up job with my own life either, Mama. The man I finally married? Yeah, so much for him being my hero. Balls of solid brass, though. Can you believe he and his pregnant girlfriend had the nerve to ask me to paint a mural for their baby's room?" The roaring of the falls drowned out her derisive laugh. "The sale papers were already signed, so I figured what the hell and told him exactly what I thought of him *and* the baby-mama. Not my finest hour." She leaned back on the stone. The texture was cold and gritty on her palms, an accurate metaphor for how she felt. "Guess you and I had poor taste in men in common; neither of us could pick a good one out of the herd if we tried. I was a fool for a pretty face and smooth line. You picked power and money. More fools us, huh, Mama?"

Emily studied the drop from the edge. This had been her mother's favorite vantage point, the final thing she saw before she died. This was the spot that had changed all their futures. It looked innocent enough now, just a wide spot in the road. Just a point for tourists to take in the natural grandeur of the falls and the valley below.

Innocent, deadly, and dear.

On a map, the falls were only wavy lines. In her world, they were an indelible marker. One that brushed away her childhood and replaced it with unassailable loneliness and anger. For years, she'd lived with impotent outrage at the twist of fate that allowed her mother's car to sweep off the curve and plunge over the edge with her toddler brother still strapped in the backseat carrier. Locals had proclaimed it a miracle they'd found Sarah's car, let alone the little boy trapped inside. The cold water, they'd said, was the only thing that kept Ian from suffering brain damage. Ian should have drowned, just like his mother. Their mother.

A full-body shiver shook Emily at the horror her mother must have felt during that moment.

Sadness tugged her gaze to follow the course of the Saint Vrain past the falls and down to the mirror finish of the lake. The spillway closest to town poured back into the river and sliced the town in half like two sides of one body. For most of the year, the river was a rollicking tumble of water. Occasionally, like the spring it had taken her mother's life, it swelled to a raging torrent.

She sat forward and dusted her palms on the legs of her jeans. The day was waning. Soon the light would wash the valley in vibrant pinks and soft violets before fading quickly into the crystalline blue of evening. The town, from this vantage, looked unchanged; some of the older landmarks stood out. She picked out the courthouse roof, the steeple of the First Baptist Church, the public library, and a few of the more established businesses, like Blanche's Diner and the Moonlight movie theater. An extra traffic light hung on Main Street. Over the years, new houses had been built up the sides of the valley. Roads cut into the aspen groves. The changes reinforced how long she'd been gone. From this distance, Tamarack was as perfect as a picture postcard, and that was the problem. It wasn't a postcard, all squeaky clean and shiny. It for damn sure wasn't perfect.

"So, Mama, here I am, right back where I started." She swallowed the guilt she still carried over the self-inflicted separation from her little brother. The tough-love approach she'd adopted hadn't worked to keep him in her life. It was a rough and awkward tightrope to walk most of the time.

"Maybe this time will be different for us both. Kinda like that old quote, 'If wishes were horses, beggars would ride.' Remember? You said that countless times. The wishes we made for better times and a happier future were never enough to make them a fact, were they?" She levered herself to her feet and took a last look down into the misty foam below her. Touching her lips, she blew a silent kiss to Sarah Converse and turned toward her Jeep.

She made her way back past the stone barricades at the edge of the road. The rectangular barriers had always reminded her of primitive altars. Their slab tops were thick plinths of gray-and-white, mottled stone that sparkled in the sunlight. Pressuring the state to install the cement and granite guards had been the only good thing her stepfather ever did. Of course, it'd come too late to prevent his wife's death.

She straightened her spine, shook off the melancholy the falls always brought to her, and climbed back into the Jeep. Soon she was rolling down the last stretch of road and onto Main Street. The Cloud to Ground Gallery fell slap in the middle of the business district. Its rustic faux front testified to the town's Old West origins. She'd intended to call her oldest friend, Noni Evans Sears, to announce her arrival but had gotten distracted up at the falls. As she slowed to a stop at the second of Tamarack's three stoplights, she saw two familiar figures standing arm in arm on the wide sidewalk in front of the gallery. They must have had the road into town staked out, waiting for her. If they were trying to look nonchalant, their foolish grins ruined the disguise.

She eased to the curb, and Noni's father had his arms open to her before she got out of the car. A feeling of peace filled her when Sheriff Pat Evans wrapped his big arms around her and lifted her off the ground. His rough voice rumbled into her hair. "'Bout time you showed up, Emmy."

"It's so good to see you, Papa Pat. Sorry, I'm later than planned. I had to stop and talk with Mama. Guess I was up there longer than I thought."

Noni bounced on her toes like a two-year-old on a sugar high. "Oh, my God. Oh, my God. You're here! What took you so long? You shoulda been here by noon."

Pat gave her an affectionate pat and one last

squeeze before relinquishing her to his daughter. "Glad you're finally here," he said and gave Noni an indulgent smile while he rubbed the small of his back. "She's been impossible today."

"Now, Papa," Noni chastised. "You know you love being needed. I've had him running errands for Lois's wedding all day." She patted his arm. "How would I have gotten it all done without you? You're so big and strong."

He just grumbled. "Yeah, yeah. I'm tellin' you, Emmy, it sucks to be the only man in a family full of crazy women."

Emily grinned at them bantering like an old married couple. God, she'd missed them. Independence was no substitute for the familiarity of lifelong friends. Maybe coming back wouldn't be as jarring as she'd feared. She could use a period of quiet and positive interaction with her new/old town.

The gallery storefront beckoned her, and she reached for the door handle. The old brass knob was smooth with wear, and she rattled it when it didn't turn. Her brow furrowed. "I was expecting Brad to be here, foaming at the mouth." She glanced up at the sign above the gallery windows. It could use a fresh coat of paint. At least the glass was clean, and one of Ian's pieces was on prominent display. Disappointed, she dusted her hands and jammed them in her back pockets.

Noni snorted. "Nope. He's in Denver meeting with his lawyer. Said he'll see you tomorrow at the bank to sign the papers." She looped her arm through Emily's. She took a determined step down the street toward Blanche's Diner. "You hungry?"

Emily only resisted for a second. "I'd rather find a

shower and a bed. I've been on the road for days, and I'm bushed." Her stomach picked that moment to gurgle in protest.

"Ha, that's what I thought, and besides, Blanche threatened to whip my butt if I didn't drag you to the diner soon as you got here. Come on, I've got a surprise for you."

Pat huffed loudly but followed along like her long-suffering servant. Noni frowned him into submission.

The interior of Blanche's Diner was unchanged. A veritable symphony of fifties chrome and seventies kitsch with a sprinkling of Western rodeo. Worn Formica still covered the long counter that sported a tall pie spinner. Shiny chrome corrals railed in napkins, menus, and condiments. Brightly upholstered stools lined up like overstuffed mushrooms, waiting patiently for the backsides of regulars and first-timers alike. Booths flanked wide windows, perfect for people-watching and gossip. Their broad depth repeatedly covered, then re-covered in tucked and rolled vinyl. All of it so familiar Emily willed back the sting of tears.

Behind the counter, Blanche Reese stood, her arms akimbo with her bony hands gripping denim-covered hips. A beehive of impossibly red hair still topped her head. Her normally scowling face split into a wide grin when she saw who Pat and Noni hustled along with them.

"Well, I'll be damned if it ain't a blast from the past." The woman's voice sounded like gravel on an old dirt road as she threw open her arms and gathered Emily into a hug. "Honey, you look so much like your mother it takes my breath away. Welcome back." Without warning, she bellowed over her shoulder.

"Teddy! You ain't going to believe who I got here. Come out and say howdy."

Before Emily could say a word, she was grabbed and spun around. This time by the long, strong arms of Blanche's flamboyant son, Ted. "Honey, I can't believe it. Is it truly you?" His expressive bright blue eyes welled with tears, and he dabbed at them with the corner of the apron around his narrow waist. "Now look what you made me do. I got mascara in my eye; that shit burns like fire."

She plucked the cloth from his fingers and took over wiping his eyes. "I've been telling you for years waterproof is the way to go. You never did listen to me, did you, Teddy Bear?"

She stepped back to look them over. Mother and son were still quite the pair. Both unique and unafraid of flaunting convention. Blanche had raised her son on her own, fierce in her protection of the boy who never fit into a traditionally male role. Ted had known early on that his view of the world and his place in it were never going to jibe with the narrow-minded members of Tamarack's conservative older generations. Somehow though, he'd managed to win a grudging acceptance from them. It might have had more to do with the way he loved and supported his mom than maintaining his alternative lifestyle out of town. Of course, being the lead dancer in the most popular drag club in Denver made it tough to ignore him.

"Honey, the days you taught me to use an eyelash curler are so long gone they're gathering dust." He cast a disapproving look down her wrinkled T-shirt and worn jeans. "Looks like you could use a really good meal and a bath. In that order. Want me to fix you up with my latest miracle on a plate? We can catch up while you eat."

Pat clapped the younger man on the back. "That sounds great, Ted, but we'll just have coffee and a piece of Blanche's famous apple pie. If you don't mind." He pulled Emily into a booth. "Y'all can catch up later. I don't want to drag out getting her settled in the apartment."

"*Papa!*" Noni slapped her father's arm. "You just killed my surprise, dang it." Her scowl became a sunny grin. She flapped her hands in excitement. "Okay, okay. I've been keeping this a secret, but I found you a place to live. You'll love it, and you can't beat the commute to work."

"I thought I was staying with you," Emily said suspiciously. Noni, problem solver extraordinaire, had the homecoming bit clenched in her teeth.

"You were, till the kids came down with chickenpox. Didn't think you'd enjoy that, so I came up with the perfect answer. The apartment above the gallery is just ideal for you."

"Oh, come on, Noni. The place has been storage for years. It can't be livable. What have you done?"

"I pulled off a miracle in two short weeks, that's what. You said Ian refused to come back to town, so Cloud to Ground needs a presence. That's you." Again the grin and the shrug. "It's a done deal."

Ted huffed his disappointment. "Well, I see where I stand in the pecking order, so I suppose tomorrow will do just as well. I'll save you a plate of *huevos rancheros* for breakfast, Em. How's that sound?"

"I can't wait, Teddy Bear. Besides, I'm sure Pat can live without our trip down shenanigan lane."

Pat's laugh filled the diner. "Ain't that the damn truth. Parents never want to know all the stuff their kids got away with." He pointed a beefy finger toward the apple pie, and Blanche dropped three wide wedges in front of them along with three coffees.

Emily relaxed for the first time in weeks. For better or worse, she was home.

Chapter Two

To Emily's unending surprise, Tamarack opened its arms and welcomed her home like a prodigal daughter. A regular parade of people "just dropped by" the Cloud to Ground Gallery. All of them curious, some of them nosy, but most simply wanted to touch base—and offer a bit of gossip. Without exception, they wanted to know why she'd left behind a flourishing career as the art director with a big advertising agency to run a small-town art gallery in the mountains of Colorado. She always gave the same answer: too much pressure, too many hours, no life outside her work. It was true, but only the barest possible truth. Fired, homeless, and divorced wasn't the picture she wanted to paint. Eventually, the whole story of her life would be common knowledge. The town would put together the details to make up their own picture of her. For now, what she told them seemed to be enough, and she was glad for that.

Noni was absolutely right. The world's most perfect commute to work was the biggest perk to being back in Tamarack. Only thirteen steps down the stairs from the apartment, and she was in the retail space of the gallery. Her office, studio, and workspace were separated by a few more steps. It beat the hell out of facing the kind of traffic and chaos she'd dealt with every day for the last twenty years.

Sitting at her desk in the space she'd commandeered as her office, she smiled and patted the folder of legal papers that transferred Brad's half of the business into her hands. As if Ian had her on camera enjoying a moment of satisfaction, the phone by her elbow fired up. His face filled her screen, and she blanched. She never knew whether it would be a tirade or an entreaty, and she preferred to avoid both extremes. It was sorely tempting to let it go to voicemail.

He typically tried to bend others to his will using tactics that would make Machiavelli proud, but she was an old hand at dealing with his manipulations. For the most part, he'd been playing nice. He'd called a few times to alert her to impending deliveries and even agreed to end his desert exile to attend the wedding of Noni's little sister, Lois Evans, and her groom, Dillon Prentice.

She frowned at the phone and punched the accept icon. "Little brother." Her tone was wary.

"Usurper." He slurred the Rs in the insult. A background country song brought visions of a dusty cowboy bar. She sighed, loud and long. The prospect of a battle royal with Ian wore her out before it had the chance to happen.

"That's me, the female version of Napoleon. What can I do for you, *partner?*" Dealing with her cross-addicted brother made her want a drink or ten of her own.

"Do me a favor. Don't think sweeping in to save the day makes you part of my career. Get one of your own."

She heard him light a cigarette. At least, she hoped

it was tobacco. Drunk and stoned Ian was a different beast altogether.

"Oh, wait. You tossed that away along with your marriage and your fancy condo, didn't you? How is ol' Ricky boy? His newest toy have the baby yet?" Okay, score one for the snide, hurtful side of her brother.

"You know? It seems to me that if you want to pick a fight so bad, or God forbid, take a hand in running this gallery, you'd pull up your big-boy panties and mosey your butt back to Tamarack." His barbs might hurt, but she'd be damned if she'd let him see it.

"Ooo, shots fired." He snickered into the phone.

"What do you want, Ian?" She tried to keep her tone level, but he knew how to poke at her soft spots better than anyone.

"Gee, now that's a big question. World domination? Worshiping hordes? Ricki Martin?" He snorted at his own joke. "Nothing so epic, sister mine. I'm calling to let you know I won't be staying with you during the wedding this weekend. Teddy made me a better offer."

Poor Ted, still caught up in Ian's web. Was it love or codependence? "Good to know. Ted already told me, seeing as how I've been here two weeks and still haven't seen your face." She paused, hoping he'd jump in with assurances. "It doesn't have to be like this, you know. I guess I hoped things would be easier between us."

He said nothing.

She sighed, defeated. "Okay then, guess I'll catch you at the DoubleTree."

"Yeah, I'll see ya when I see ya."

She waited for the sound of him clicking off or

maybe for a softening in his tone. He might have muttered, "Christ," then there was silence.

"Ian?" Again, silence. "What's going on with you? Can I help?" She couldn't stop the gentling of her voice, although, in the final analysis, it wouldn't do anything more than piss him off. He'd only let her go so far before he started pushing back. She'd done all the protecting and cuddling she was allowed to do when they were kids. When she wasn't sure they'd live to see adulthood.

"Look, I gotta go. The bartender has the sweetest ass I've seen since the last time I was at Teddy's club." He took a long drag on his smoke with the telltale change of inflection as he held it in. "I can't help but wonder if things would be different if..." He blew out his hit. "Never mind. I'm stoned. I'll see you in Denver if I can. Don't let the boogeyman get ya." The phone went dead in her hand.

"Damn it." She dropped the phone back on the desk and took a frustrated breath. The puzzle that was her brother was something she'd never be able to solve. What would make a kid with that much talent and that kind of brilliance forego it in favor of the next high? She'd love to find a way to channel all the effort he put into ignoring his abilities, into one solid year of pouring out his gift onto canvas.

She looked at his paintings gracing the gallery walls. Stunning, exciting, sometimes darkly evocative of yearning and release. He was, in her opinion, genius personified. Unfortunately, he resembled brilliant artists who'd preceded him. She was afraid that if he didn't find the key to unlocking his prison, he'd die inside it. She wished she could ignore that niggling harbinger, but it was like a debt that went unattended. The cost grew like a fungus whose weight expanded until one day, it poked its ugly fruit above the surface.

A garish pink sticky note glared at her from her desk lamp. *Eight o'clock. Dress up. Don't make me come get you!* The note was a perfect example of Noni's idea of reintegrating her into town. One she'd *love* to ignore. The woman was bound and determined that Emily get the heck out of her blue jeans and boots, put on a dress, and show up at the local Mexican restaurant for Lois's bachelorette party. She groaned to herself. She didn't know any of the women who'd be there aside from Noni and Lois.

"God, don't be such an old woman," she said to the empty gallery. "Even if it's a thinly veiled excuse to drink copious margaritas, it's better than sitting here feeling sorry for yourself." Besides, she could still fill out a cocktail dress with the best of them. Why not show these small-town girls how it was done uptown?

****

She smoothed down her skirt and ran a nervous hand through her hair. It was dumb to be skittish about being thrown into a bunch of women younger than her, but she'd never been close friends with Lois Evans. Fifteen years' difference in age was a huge stretch of time in terms of perspective. Even greater in terms of life experience.

The colorful entrance of La Chiminea, Tamarack's only Mexican restaurant, stood out boldly in the darkened parking lot. Tejano music blared from outdoor speakers, and its portico was awash in the colors of the Mexican flag. Enrique, the owner and majordomo, stood proudly at the door to personally welcome all those crazy enough to drive an hour and a half from Denver for a last-minute bachelorette party.

Enrique's heavily accented greeting rang out to her before she made the steps up to the door. "*Buenas noches*, Emily."

"Hey there, Enrique." She blinked up at him, surprised at his enthusiasm. "It was nice of you to do this on short notice. Noni's got a lot on her mind just now. Is everyone here?"

"*Si, si.* In the back dining room. They wait for you." He escorted her up the steps and swept a grand gesture toward the foyer of the restaurant. He tucked his menus smartly beneath his arm and turned to help her with her jacket. "You know the way, yes? Straight past the bar and through the big doors." He patted her shoulder and shooed her into the bar. "Enjoy the night *y muchas felicidades.*"

"Uh...thanks?" Emily wasn't sure why he wished her many happy returns, but it seemed harmless enough. He was probably confused by the whole bachelorette thing. She doubted it was a common occurrence in Mexico, though tourism had more than likely introduced the custom. God knew, many a prospective bride had suffered the effects of tequila and temptation on a trip to Los Cabos. Probably how her favorite brand had gotten its name. *Party in Cabo, Wabo home.*

A waiter guarded the tall double doors leading to the banquet room. It seemed rather odd, but since returning to town, "odd" was a regular occurrence. Odd that her status as newcomer passed so quickly, and odd that she'd been seamlessly reinserted into the flow. Odder still that she'd not seen or heard from the one man she was sure would bar her entry at the gates of the town. Thankfully, her stepfather spent his time in Washington while the legislature was in session. Such a big, important job, being the savior and champion of the American way of life. Veteran Senator Raymond J. Domenico. Icon. Legend. Fraud.

She shook her head. This was supposed to be a party and no time for allowing memories to encroach on her good time. Maybe a miracle would happen, and the bastard would get smeared by a taxi in DC. The thought of never seeing him again made her smile. Perhaps she could find an obliging cabbie in need of a few bucks.

As Emily approached the doors, the waiter stepped in front of her. He flashed a broad smile and held up a hand. "*Esperte, por favor.*"

"Wait? For what?"

"*Si, si. Esperte.*" He turned and rapped loudly on the dark wooden doors, then pushed them open with a flourish.

"Surprise!" screamed the crowd. Lights flashed on, and music erupted. Emily was grabbed and hauled into the middle of the room.

"W-what's all this?" She clapped her hands over her mouth and stood dumbstruck, clutched in a tight hug from Noni.

"It's your birthday/welcome-home party, goofy," Noni crowed above the din and danced her around in a circle. "I got you! I got you good. This is so great. You had no idea, right? God, I'm a master at this stuff. I should do this for a living I'm so good."

"Shut. Up. I can't believe you did this." Emily covered her eyes, trying to keep from erupting in tears.

"My birthday isn't till next week, you crazy wacko." No one had ever done anything like this for her before. A quiet drink, a special meal, yes. But a party—never.

"I know! Aren't I brilliant?" Noni bounced on her toes and pumped her fist in the air, clearly over the moon for pulling this off. "You never saw it coming."

"What about the bachelorette? I thought... Well, aren't you the sneaky bitch?" Emily narrowed her eyes and wagged her finger in Noni's face.

Noni wheezed, trying to catch her breath. "Oh, there's a hen's party all right, just not here. The girls and the boys are whooping it up in Denver tonight. No way I wanted in on that debacle."

A beefy arm landed on Emily's shoulder. "Happy birthday, Emmy, and officially—welcome home." Pat Evans' big voice had no trouble cutting through the rough chorus of "Happy Birthday" that broke out around them.

"Officially? You bring me the key to the city or somethin'?" Emily looped an arm around his waist and gave it a squeeze. "And for the record, you're just as sneaky as your daughter."

"She comes by it honest, that's for sure." He cleared his throat and puffed out his chest. "As I'm 'officially' the county manager/sheriff, I get to make the calls around here. I'm calling this *officially* your homecoming party." He looked very pleased with the way he tied up his argument.

She was pulled into a sea of well-wishers and didn't get a chance at a comeback. Amazed and stunned, she was enfolded by a room filled with familiar faces. Blanche with her boyfriend, Billy Strauss, and an eclectic group of area artists all lined up to give best wishes. Her high school art teacher and the librarian both gave her prim kisses on the cheek. They followed it up with a discreet going over like they might cite her for a too-short hemline. Julie and John Coffee, the quintessential quarterback/head-cheerleader duo from senior year, finished the line. A few gallery customers showed for the free drinks. They all laughed, sang, and clapped like they were applauding a play.

The ringing clang of a spoon against a beer bottle quieted the crowd. Pat's big hands landed on Emily's shoulders. "All right, all right. Settle down," he called. "Everyone, grab your glass. Emily, this margarita is for you." He slapped a frosty, salt-rimmed tumbler into her hand. "Let's all wish a collective happy birthday and welcome home to Emily Converse. Gone too long, home to stay!" The crowd cheered, and Emily blushed.

She was blown away by—her friends. Friends, a concept she'd quashed under the weight of distance and independence. She was surprised, thrilled, and humbled at their willingness to come forward to let her know she'd been missed. Frankly, she couldn't believe— didn't believe—she'd made much of an impression on the town. She'd come to characterize the time she'd been gone as her years wandering in purgatory. Perhaps her focus had been too narrow, always looking inward and forgetting that, like pebbles in a pond, every action had a reaction. Every time she stepped up to defend her brother, waltzed past disapproval, or caused a scene, she'd made an impact on how people saw her. Every time she and Noni embarked on an escapade that brought them into the public eye, she'd planted a memory.

Clearing her throat, Emily swallowed back an

uncomfortable tightness and fought the prickling threat of tears. "I can't believe you've all come here. I didn't expect anyone to remember me or even care that I was back." She swiveled, looking at each person in the group. "Thank you for being here, for…well, for everything. Now, Jesus, let's eat and get really drunk. This is supposed to be a party. Right?"

To her relief, a chorus of "About time!" and "Damn straight!" erupted, and the focus moved to a groaning buffet table. Silently, she thanked God there was no giant, blazing pile of frosting and candles for her to deal with. Not yet, anyway. She just never knew with Noni. Some hunky dancer of Ted's might make an abrupt appearance from stage left. She gave a careful look around. Nope, no one she didn't recognize. That, by itself, was remarkable.

A general surge toward the food sent a sigh of relief through her. No way would she keep anything down beyond more of the excellent, top-shelf tequila in the glass she currently gripped like a lifeline.

She patted Billy Strauss on the back and shuffled out of his second hug. He tended to hold on a bit too long. Not that she was grossed out by his attention, but she didn't want to encourage it.

"You make me miss her. You know?" His eyes were decidedly glassy.

Just how long had the crowd waited for her to arrive at this little soiree?

"What's that, Billy?" she asked, patting his arm from a distance. "Miss who?"

He gave her the one-eyed stare. "Sarah, honey. You're the spittin' image of your ma when she was a young gal." His smile was wistful as he continued to study her.

"Thanks, Billy. That's what people say. It makes me happy to know I carry her with me, you know?" Since returning to Tamarack, her mother was frequently on her mind. Every place in town reminded her of something. Like the little park where she'd played as a child. She remembered the feel of the wind in her hair as she sailed skyward on the swings. She used to laugh and call out, "Higher, Mama!" She could still hear Sarah's voice filled with the simple joy of playing together. "Don't fly away, baby bird," she'd said to her five-year-old daughter. "Your wings are barely dry."

Billy looked down at his feet for a moment, then up at her. "Don't remember if I told you how sorry I was when we found her. It about killed me to find her that way. Still don't understand how she could have missed the turn like that." He paused, shaking his head. "She'd driven that road a million times. Hell, she knew it like the back of her hand." He frowned for a moment and then smiled sadly.

She closed her eyes. He meant well, but damn it, she didn't need any help feeling the loss of her mother. She definitely didn't feel like coddling a maudlin drunk tonight.

He gazed off into the past. "I taught her to ride, ya know. We used to take the trail along the top of the falls and down beside the river. She was a good rider, careful and sure in her seat. 'Member that paint pony she had? I broke that horse myself, but she gentled it to the hackamore. Never would ride with a bit. That's how much she loved that horse." He sniffed loudly and wiped his nose with the faded bandanna that was a perpetual resident of his back pocket. "Them was real happy times."

Emily slipped an arm through his. It was wonderful to know her mother was remembered fondly in the town that had been her home long before the birth of her children. Another reason Emily had been unable to resist the call to return. Her roots here were sunk as deep as the bedrock this town was built upon.

Billy patted her arm. "Don't matter much anymore, but she wouldn't a'wanted either you or the boy to spend your time grievin'. I just wanted to be sure that you knew how I felt." He turned back toward Blanche who manned the beer keg in the corner.

"I'm grateful to you too, Billy. And I do remember, though sometimes I wish I could forget. You were the one who found the car, right? The one who pulled Ian out of the wreck? You were a hero that night, Bill. I remember that." She wrapped him up in quick squeeze before stepping away. "Now," she said, clearing her tight throat, "that's enough sad memories for the night. Go get yourself a beer from that cute redhead over there"—she nodded toward Blanche—"and tell her to put it on my tab."

As she watched him stagger off, she got the feeling there were a lot of things she didn't know about the time Sarah Domenico and a younger Billy Strauss had spent together in the backcountry. Emily shook herself and made a conscious choice to let go of the unhappy recollections that Billy brought with him.

She cut through the crowd and found a table clearly indicated for her by the large sombrero with her name spelled out on the brim. She collapsed in a chair behind it and fended off Noni's attempt to make her wear the giant hat. Instead, she looped an arm around her friend and dragged her down into the seat beside her. "What the actual hell, Noni? I should be totally ticked off at you, but I can't seem to drag up the strength."

Emily finished her first margarita, and Noni replaced it with another.

"You can't be mad. You love me too much," Noni said, a look of smug self-importance on her face. "You've been home two damn weeks, and you haven't crawled out of your shell. This is my little way of shoving my foot up your butt and jump-starting the process. Believe me, this is a lot less painful than the huge party Daddy wanted to throw at the ranch. It would have been a real snooze of a BBQ. Besides, I was afraid the senator might show up, and I knew that would go over like a fart in a wet suit."

Emily made a sour face. "Definitely not a good thing. I consider myself blessed that he hasn't paid a call on me yet. I was really hoping he'd managed to curl up and die while I was gone, but no such luck."

"We couldn't be that fortunate. Besides, the old bastard is too mean to turn toes up. You have plans in that direction you're not telling me about? It would serve him right to finally get the comeuppance he deserves at your hand. Or Ian's. Preferably Ian's."

"Not likely to happen, honey. If there is a God, He'll see to it for me." Emily had long ago stopped looking for new and different reasons to hate her stepfather. The upbringing he'd treated her and Ian to was enough of a reason to detest the man. It was a blessing that he rarely starred in her nightmares anymore. At least, he hadn't until she'd returned to Tamarack. Now the damned things were back with a vengeance, causing her to think twice about confronting the monster in her closet.

"Speaking of your baby brother, I thought for sure he'd show up tonight. I sent him an email, but I didn't get a response. Have you heard from him?" Noni slipped margarita number three in front of Emily while she surveyed the line of thirsty people at the bar.

"He's out of Denver for a while. Painting in the high desert, he says." Emily picked up her drink and looked at it suspiciously. Wasn't it was almost empty a second ago?

Noni snorted, then looked away. "Is 'painting' code for eating handfuls of shrooms and smoking dope till he can't tell up from down?"

"That's hardly fair." Emily heaved a sigh into the rim of her glass. "Though probably true. He was definitely high when he called me earlier. I hoped Brad was just blowing smoke when he got me into this. But…I guess not."

"Can I just say something once?" Noni gave her an aggravated look. "I really hate that you keep signing up to be Ian's scapegoat. Please don't let him pull you down his rabbit hole. I don't think I could take that again." She held up her hand to stop Emily's retort. "You know I love you, but for one of the smartest women I know, you sure can be dumb. Brad, the little rat, totally used you to get out of a losing situation. He's not the love of your brother's life anymore. Ian prefers chemical-induced escapism and sexual diversity, no big surprise there." Noni took on a scolding tone.

Emily cut her off. "Hey, I didn't drag my ass to this party for a lecture, Noni. Besides, you're supposed to at least be sympathetic, not all judgy."

Her friend's mouth turned down at the corners, and Emily cringed. "The gospel according to Noni" wasn't at an end.

"Just another case of crazy for you, my friend. And I know this may not be the right time for a hiding, but I'm telling you the straight facts. You're a big girl; you can take it." Noni took a breath and launched into the rest of her argument. "Now, as to your poor choice in husbands. What the hell were you thinking? Rick the Prick? I mean, come on. The man let his junk dictate his priorities and then had the balls to talk you into using the same lawyer for your divorce."

Emily huffed. When put like that, she did seem to have lost a few IQ points. "Yeah, well, in all fairness, at the time I still thought he was a decent human being."

"Christ." Noni's palm slapped her forehead. "Sorry, hate to say it, but I'm right. He weaseled you out of anything like a decent settlement, and you know it."

Emily laughed. "Damn, tell me how you really feel, Noni. That's harsh." But true. There were downsides to knowing someone for a lifetime. Between them, no secrets.

Noni's face softened. "There is an upside. You're home. You're taking your life back, and I'm stinking proud of you. Maybe now I can talk you into devoting some time to yourself." Noni's voice quivered. She took Emily's hands in hers, and she stifled a sniffle.

Emily patted her friend's much smaller hand. "That's exactly what I'm doing. Don't you worry. I've put the gallery records back in order and set up shop in the studio. It's beginning to feel like the place is mine. I won't let Ian make me feel guilty for doing what's best for me. I didn't have any reason to stay in Seattle. I'm taking this step because, in spite of everything that has happened, this is my home. The gallery is the place my mother loved best; I won't see it pissed away because he can't keep his shit together. How's that for determination?" She squeezed Noni's hands, then released them to pick up her drink. The tart, bright flavor cooled her throat. She blew out a long breath, realizing she'd needed to speak her truth out loud as badly as Noni need to hear it.

She hadn't come back to be a volunteer victim *or* a taskmaster with a whip. Healing her brother wasn't her job. He was the one who had to decide to change his trajectory, but she couldn't pretend his disease didn't exist. She couldn't go on as if Ian didn't count either. He wasn't the bad guy in this scenario.

"That's right," Noni said. "You're a big girl. You get to decide. I'm here regardless. You know that. Just don't expect me to keep my mouth shut if I see you caving in. Okay?" She grabbed the huge *sombrero* and tried to slap it on Emily's head. "I forgot to tell you I saw him at a fundraiser in Denver a month or so ago. Had some boy toy on his arm. Gorgeous, slick, muscles for days. A dancer with Ted's group of reprobates down at Bahama Mama's. What a waste of man flesh. I think those boys need to learn to share the wealth."

Emily ducked the attempted crowning with a slap to the garish, rhinestone-encrusted hat. The change of topic was much appreciated. "Oh, for Christ's sake, Noni. The guys in Ted's troop rarely share. Besides you're a married woman." She gave her friend a decidedly lopsided grin. Her vision did a little swirly thing. How many margaritas had she had? She really needed to remember that nothing was guaranteed to get her toasted faster than tequila at high altitude. It looked like it was doing the job just fine.

"Married, not dead." Noni laughed and smoothed down her mop of dark brown waves.

A shout went up from the bar. The partygoers grouped around Pat Evans and Billy Strauss. The pair had squared off and were settling into an arm-wrestling match. Pat's bulk vs. Billy's wiry strength. The bout was a time-honored contest between old friends. Bets might be laid, but no one really tracked the score. The sight was as comforting as a campfire in the dark.

Chapter Three

Three hours later, Emily cursed the rocky ground as she stumbled across the dark parking lot behind La Chiminea. The mountain air was soft and full of chilly whispers from the trees by the river. Crisp breezes were one of her favorite things about Colorado. They always held promises. No matter the season, the scent of pine was always a reminder that the Rockies were just outside the door.

She slipped into her Jeep, stuck her key into the ignition, slapped it into reverse, and let out the clutch. The vehicle rocked but didn't budge out of the parking spot.

"What the hell?" she asked the guard-mouse dangling from the rearview mirror. She didn't remember rolling into a hole when she parked, but then those extreme margaritas had been calling her name.

For a moment she regretted sending the rest of the party home, all the while swearing she was sober enough to drive the half mile to the gallery. She pushed in the clutch, revved the engine, and popped it, confident that Li'l Red could climb its way out of almost anything. She heard a shout of alarm and felt the bump of her back wheel as it lurched up and over—please God, not a person.

Panicked, she stomped on the brakes and stalled the engine. Hand scrabbling, she groped for the door handle and flung it open. She skidded to the gravel, praying the silence behind her didn't mean a dead body. Guts everywhere. Police. Prison.

"H-hello?" She stuck her head around the back of the Jeep. With a death grip on the spare tire rack, she peered into the shadows between her car and the one next to it. To her horror, on the ground just past her tail light lay a long arm clutching a boot in its fist. Not under the wheels, *thank you, Jesus*.

She eased out around the spare tire and crept past the bumper. Hesitantly, she tracked the length of the man's extended arm to his shoulder and finally to a dark head. He didn't look like she'd run him down. Exactly. His other arm lay folded across his broad chest. He appeared intact, but it was too dim to tell for sure. She swallowed hard.

"Mister?" Closer, another step. "Mister?" Louder this time.

Emily stepped over the outstretched arm with boot attached and knelt to touch him. Blood painted a thin line from his hair to his ear, along his jaw, and onto a truly hideous Hawaiian shirt.

"Oh, shit." She gasped. "Hey! Mister!" She reached out and shook his shoulder. Nothing. "Hey, man! Oh, please don't be dead." More desperate by the moment, Emily pressed two fingers on the artery beneath his ear. She carefully avoided the blood on his neck. His pulse was a slow and welcome motion beneath his warm skin. Okay, not dead, out cold. His shoulder was braced against the corner of a backpack wedged beneath her tire, the evidence of its recent status as a speed bump visible even in the shadows.

Gratitude swept through her. Killing a man was not

the way she wanted to end her evening. Without thinking, she leaned down and whispered in that same ear. "Wake up, handsome." And kissed him full on the mouth.

That was stupid flashed through her mind, but her brain short-circuited when his hands grabbed her shoulders and he rolled her to the ground. His heavy body was in total contact with hers, chest to ankle, and he was kissing her back. She froze stiff as if a spike of electricity interrupted her brain's ability to react.

She got a closeup view of eyes that were open but unfocused. They were the only things about him at all confused about what they were doing. One big hand threaded into her hair. Rough fingers scraped to her scalp and tangled in the strands. He easily held her mouth in place as he moved his lips and tongue on her as though he'd kissed her a thousand times before. His other palm swept down her side and cupped her hip, and he brought her in solid contact with the front of his zippered jeans.

Emily bucked and pummeled. She pushed and swore, but he effortlessly held her hard against the gravel. Then somewhere between preparing to scream and looking for leverage to knee him in the balls, the taste of him seeped into her mind. Maybe it was the tequila, or maybe she'd forgotten how it felt to be caught up in something totally unexpected, but she wasn't afraid. She should have been, but she wasn't. The fluid warmth of his tongue slipped past her lips, and it pulled a gasp from her that was more pleasure than fear. Two things which should have been polar opposites hung suspended together for a moment. Reality blurred.

Until his knee slid between her thighs and nudged one leg out of his way.

The air Emily had forgotten about seconds before rushed her lungs. Adrenaline coursed through her veins, strength and reality returned, and she screamed bloody murder to the empty parking lot. All the details of the moment snapped into sharp, sober clarity. This was no fantasy come to life. This was not only out of control but suddenly, shockingly real.

The decibel level of her scream effectively got his attention, and he flinched back. "Come on, baby. Don't be that way." His voice was a raspy slur.

He burped and swamped her senses with a cloud of booze. Bourbon and a lot of it.

"Don't you 'baby' me, you drunken son of a bitch!" she shouted in his face.

He moved just enough to allow her the leverage needed to jerk her knee into satisfyingly solid contact with his most vulnerable possessions. He grunted in pain and jackknifed into a fetal position. His big body rolled to the side, and he clutched his jewels with both hands. Emily shoved the last of him off her and jumped to her feet. Head spinning and balance wavering, she gripped the side of her four by four. She backed away from her assailant and couldn't stop her satisfied smirk to see her well-placed knee cap was still having the desired effect.

"Christ Almighty, you shit-faced idiot!" Roughly, she pushed her hair back and jerked her jacket into place. "What the hell was that? You think you can just grab what you want?" She gave him a hard thump with the toe of her shoe. "And what are you doing out here hiding by my car—in the damn dark? I nearly killed you, you stupid jerk!"

A deep rumbling moan rose from him. Then a resounding snore.

"Well, aren't you just completely typical." Totally typical of the men in her life. She jabbed him again for good measure, then stomped back around to the driver's door to grab her purse and keys. She beep-locked her doors, and with a huff of angry disgust, she crunched her way back across the gravel lot to La Chiminea's side entrance.

Tinny Tex-Mex mariachi music still filled the restaurant. It was past their closing time. A single table remained surrounded by the waiters and busboys. Emily ran a trembling hand through her hair. Post-traumatic aftereffects, she told herself. She bunched her fingers into a fist and stepped into the dining room.

Enrique looked up and waved cigar smoke from his face. "Hey, Emily—what's wrong? You got car troubles?" He stood from the head of the staff gathering and motioned her in. The other men turned in her direction. They were different shapes and sizes, but all eight of them bore a scary resemblance to Enrique. They were definitely related. Sons and brothers, she'd bet.

She sucked in a calming breath, and though she pretended control, words flooded out of her mouth. "I'm glad you're still here. There's an—uh—*hombre* in the lot next to my car. He's very drunk, and I thought I hit him, but he's passed out, so I don't know if he's okay or not. I mean, I'm sure he's fine, but could you come out and check and call like an ambulance or the sheriff's office or something? I mean he was okay enough to kiss me, but then he passed out and… What if he's—?"

She shut her mouth like someone jerked a string. She'd meant to leave out the kissing part.

"He kiss you, then you hit him with your car, then he pass out?" Enrique's English was good, but Emily had been babbling like a filly spooked into a dead run.

"No, Enrique. I hit him, then he… No, wait, I didn't hit him. I hit his backpack or something. Please just someone call an ambulance or the police. Come out and check him with me. Okay? He's, like, lying by my car!"

The majordomo spat out his cigar along with a string of rapid-fire Spanish. The bartender reached for the phone, and the rest of the men hustled like rats evacuating a sinking ship. Apparently, they were none too crazy about the whole cop suggestion, because before Enrique could grab his coat, the place was empty.

She stared, agape at how quickly they moved. "Hey, how come it takes me ten minutes to get a drink in this place when they have that kind of talent?"

He gave an elegant shrug and slipped on his coat. "Motivation and incentive, *señorita*." A grin lit up his round face. "Come, let us see if your *novio* is still asleep in your car."

"By my car, not in my car," Emily grumbled, grabbed his coat sleeve, and hurried him out the door. "And he's not my boyfriend."

The temperature was dropping fast, and there was a hint of rain on the breeze. The moon, now veiled behind ragged clouds, made the lot dimmer; the shadows between Emily's vehicle and what must be Enrique's truck were very inky.

"Is very dark out here. No?" Enrique whispered. His steps faltered at the halfway point. "Why you park by me and not out front, Emily? There is no light back here. Could be trouble and you would no see it coming."

"The place was packed when I got here. Besides, this is Tamarack, not Denver. I'm not going to get mugged." Oh, wait, she had gotten flipped on her back and kissed within an inch of her life. Did that count?

"I think we need the flashlight. I go get one."

Enrique turned, but she grabbed his arm to drag him back around.

"I thought all you Latin guys were supposed to be macho, take-charge, manly men. What happened to that, huh?" She had a death grip on his forearm; he wasn't going anywhere but across the parking lot with her.

"You watch too many movies." He straightened his spine and shook off her grip, then took several hesitant steps toward the cars. He cleared his throat and called loudly, "Hey, *señor*, you still there?"

Silence. No moaning at least.

"Hey, *hombre*! I call the sheriff." He shuffled a few steps closer and peered into the dark. He fished out his lighter and flicked it open. The breeze caught the Zippo flame, and it guttered higher, just not enough to crack the shadows.

"Christ, you're so fricking helpful." Emily's patience with her macho protector ran out. "I'll go see if he's conscious or alive or something. Just don't leave, okay?" She pinned him with a stay-put glare and cautiously approached the scene of the crime.

Her eyes carried light traces from Enrique's torch,

and she blinked to clear them. She rounded the car closer to the spot where she expected to find Cinderella. He was gone. The area of her foolhardy wake-up kiss was vacant.

"He's gone. Huh. I thought he'd still…" She squinted, then shuffled her feet across his resting place just to make sure. Yup, empty. Emily unlocked her passenger door and flooded the area with light. No body. No blood. No backpack. Just a boot and a hand print smeared in the dirt on her unwashed quarter panel.

Chapter Four

In the Rockies, dawn didn't happen like a switch was thrown but with a slow warming of light and color. The edges of the trees crept into focus as the air crystallized. The gentle building of birdsong joined the light, and the world blended into wakefulness.

Senior Master Chief Michael James McCandlis, USN Retired, came to consciousness with a jerk, aware of two things. First, some asshole was pointing a spotlight straight into his face, and second, his right foot was frozen in a block of ice.

Pain registered next. Everything hurt, from his hair to heels, and his head pounded with every stubborn beat of his heart. He tried lifting both hands to his face; one obeyed. He couldn't feel the right one at all; his left one flopped into motion and landed over his eyes. Darkness was a blessed relief. Slow and careful, he peered between his fingers, and a haze of green seeped through them. Rushing water rumbled in the background.

What the hell? Was he lying on a stream bank?

Time for a more personal recon. If he could move his legs, maybe the rest would follow. Left leg—functioning. His boot sole scraped loose gravel. Right leg—moving but dragging what felt like a giant block of ice. Taking a breath to build up his nerve, Mike heaved hard on his leg. He was rewarded by his instep landing on warm dry stone. Relived, he realized it wasn't ice at all but water so cold it could double for it.

He took another breath, deeper this time, to fight off what he was sure would be nausea-inducing results. He needed to roll left and sit up. Needed to be a man and see if the light trying to split his head open was an aneurysm or a sunbeam. *One. Two. Three.*

Sunbeam, thank God. But Christ, that hurt.

Slowly, he took in his surroundings. His frigid foot bath was a shallow pool on the edge of a rushing creek. He was grateful the drunkard's angel had tripped him up at the last moment and kept him from falling head first into the stream. He swiveled, looking for evidence of how he came to ground. Broken bushes marked his path to the stream. Way, way above him, up a steep embankment, appeared a road of some sort.

Mike located his numb right arm. The twisted strap to his backpack wrapped around his wrist. The pack was damp but miraculously still with him. He dragged it up and over his side, then rested. A muddy, segmented stripe streaked down one side of the black fabric. The marks looked like—tire tracks. Shit, so much for his phone.

His pulse beat a pounding rhythm behind his eyes. Gathering courage, he crawled to the nearest boulder and scared a nearby chipmunk into a berate-filled retreat. From there, he surveyed the damage. His favorite shirt was a mess. Streaks of dirt and blood smeared across the palm trees and beaches emblazoned across his chest. His boot was missing, his sock was present, but a hole allowed the escape of his big toe. Judging from the jagged nail and the scrape to the tip, it looked like his foot had led the way down to the river bank.

Feeling began to seep back into his right hand. He felt for his wallet and found it still in his back pocket. So he hadn't been rolled by—what was her name? "Lisha, Trisha, Trixie, Dixie? Oh, well, you were probably a prick anyway, McCandlis. No wonder she kicked your ass into a freaking gully." He had no doubt the whole scene would come back to him at some point. For now, it was still hazy and formless.

Self-recrimination wasn't his go-to setting, although he detested the loss of control that had landed him in this situation. He had to man up and make some kind of headway. Mike inched his protesting body into a standing position against a boulder. The ground and the green world did a loop around his head; he wondered if a bath in the rapids that swept past his feet might serve to sharpen his concentration. He ruled it out in favor of staying dry. He winced as he pulled his pack over his shoulders and snapped the buckles into place. He would need all hands on deck to haul his sorry butt back up to the road. He hoped his flip-flops were still in his pack. He was going to need them.

****

By the time Mike managed to wander onto the main street of the little mountain town, he was shivering like a malaria patient. He found a sun-warmed bench beside a brightly painted sign: *Welcome to Tamarack: Pride of the Front Range.* Wherever the hell that was, at least it told him something. He slowly lowered his aching body to the convenient seat. The laces on his one remaining boot were broken, so he wouldn't have to cut himself out of it. Good news, because trusting himself with a sharp blade was a recipe for disaster. He looked skyward, said thank you to the man upstairs, and opened his pack to fish out his flip-flops.

He leaned back against the slats of the bench and looked over his surroundings. Hopefully, he could find a pay phone and a cup of coffee. It was Sunday; most places were closed up tight. In spite of a monstrous headache beating a tattoo inside his skull, he had to admit it was a picturesque little town. Clean streets. Shop windows featured bright displays in autumn colors. The place looked prosperous.

Halfway down Main Street, Mike spied a flashing neon sign advertising Blanche's Diner. The small parking lot to its side was packed; the distinct promise of warmth and redemption came from inside. He needed both. Desperately.

His ratty sandals slapped the pavement in a broken stride as he made his way down the street to the diner. The place was jammed, and he was lucky to find an empty seat at the counter.

"Mornin'." He nodded to the woman guarding the cash register. He reached for a laminated menu shoved between the napkin dispenser and ketchup bottle. "Can I get some coffee? And that Western omelet sounds great." He looked up from the menu into her squinted eyes and noticed the necklace hanging around her scrawny neck. He gave her his most winning smile. "Thanks, Blanche."

Her eyes rolled skyward, and she stuck a heavy crockery mug in front of him. "You look like you could use 'em both. Rough night?" She scribbled his order on her pad and stuck it in the window to the kitchen directly behind her. Her voice sounded like she was really familiar with a carton of Lucky Strikes.

Mike took a cautious sip of the coffee she'd splashed into the mug and looked around him. "You could say that. Is there a phone I could use?"

"Phone's for paying customers only. You got any cash under that god-awful shirt?"

She smirked when he pulled a twenty from his pocket. He slipped it under his mug and stared her down.

She sniffed and reached for the cordless phone beside her cash register. "Keep it short."

Nodding, he dialed the only person he wanted to know about his current circumstances. "Jerry? Hey, it's Mike. Yeah, I know, quite a night. Yeah, yeah. Listen, man, I've got a favor to ask. Yeah, that's right, I need you. Shut up, will you?" He pulled the receiver away from the laughter in his ear and tried to ignore the old lady pretending not to eavesdrop from the other side of the counter. "Do you know where Tamarack is? Great, I need a ride. Like yesterday. Don't say anything to the other guys, just come and get me." He paused, his eyes clenched tight, praying Jerry would stop sniggering at his misery. "I'll explain when I see you. Blanche's Diner, on Main Street. You can't miss it. An hour plus? Thanks, man, I owe you." He handed her the phone and turned back to his coffee.

"Well, you feel like telling me the story or letting me make up my own?" She splashed steaming black brew into his cup and swiped a damp rag around it on the bright orange counter. She watched him with undisguised curiosity and tapped a bright red fingernail on the side of the glass pot.

He ran a hand through his hair and turned a bloodshot eye on her. "Sweetheart, I'd love to tell you my life story, but I'm a man about to die from starvation. Can it wait till this coffee takes effect and I get that omelet you promised? Or you just been teasing me?"

"You know, smart guy, my throat's feeling really funny." She made a phlegmy rattle. "But I live to serve. So how 'bout I just scamper back to the kitchen and make sure your omelet is just as *special* as you are?"

"Oh, man," the guy on the next stool whispered. "Ain't no way I'd eat that, if'n I was you."

"Great." Mike felt the strong desire to shoot himself and get it over with. He needed those eggs real bad. He rose up off his stool and called across the pass-through into the kitchen. "Ma'am?"

"Yes?" she answered sweetly from the kitchen. Her voice sounded even creepier with sugar heaped on top of the rattle.

"Ma'am, sorry I was testy. I didn't mean to be rude. Please forgive my stupidity. And please, for the love of God, don't spit on my breakfast." He was still begging when she popped around the swinging door with his plate in her bony hand.

She grinned victoriously and spun his plate onto the counter in front of him. "Now, about that story."

He looked from the plate to Blanche and back to the plate. "Did you forgive me?" he asked, feeling as small as the last time he'd been in front of a pissed-off officer. That hadn't worked out so well, either.

She gave him a self-satisfied smile and shrugged. "Enough to let you eat while you spill the goods on how an adult man can show up at my diner looking like a rented mule who's been rode hard and put up wet. While we're at it, I'd really like to know how come you got no coat over that ugly ass shirt and are wearin' flip flops like it's July, not October."

Spit or no spit, the omelet tasted like manna from Heaven. He took another bite and sighed with pleasure. "I'd like to make it worth your while, but the last thing I remember clearly is a bachelor party for one of my crew. He's getting married tonight."

"Mmm hmm." She twirled her finger in the air in the universal sign for "stop stalling."

He raked his fingers back through his dark hair. He needed a haircut before this afternoon. He doubted Lois Evans would appreciate him showing up at her wedding looking like a shaggy sixties refugee.

"Okay, okay. Bachelor party, right. We started at the DoubleTree, then took cabs to someplace downtown. Mama something? I don't remember the name, but they put on one hell of a show."

"Bahama Mama's?" The guy beside him started to grin. He shoved his coffee closer to Mike and leaned his cheek on his palm like he was hanging on every word.

Mike snapped his fingers. "Yeah, that's the place. Big drinks and some of the tallest women I've ever seen. But man, could they dance."

Bits and pieces flashed back. Jerry waving off a redhead with tits out to here. Dillon kissing some blonde. Then there'd been this brunette on stage with legs that wouldn't quit. She'd been singing to Mike like he was the only guy in the room, and he'd stuffed money into her cleavage and bought her drinks. Her name was…Della? No…Dora.

"Bahama Mama's. Right." Blanche's mouth quirked as she asked the guy next to Mike, "Say, Bill, ain't that the place where Ted works?"

"Why, it is indeed, Blanche." Bill's grin got bigger, and his brows wiggled up into his hairline. "Matter of fact, I believe he's a headliner there."

"Well," she said, "ain't that some coinkydink. Club's famous around here. Everybody knows it 'cause it's the first and the most famous drag club in Denver." She snorted, then coughed and pounded the counter, trying to gulp air around her laughter.

Bill let out a whoop that ricocheted around in Mike's head until he thought his omelet might make a return visit.

"Say, Bill," she continued, "would you please tell Mr. 'Is that a pickle in your pocket or are you just glad to see me' exactly who cooked his breakfast this morning?"

Knowing without a doubt this game-show routine was sure to get worse, Mike covered his face with both hands.

"Better yet, Blanche"—Bill swept a hand out toward the kitchen's swinging door—"let's show the poor bastard who's behind door number one!"

The surprise guest star burst through the opening as though she were entering center stage.

Mike peeled open his fingers. His mouth dropped open and slammed shut. It was her—ah—him. "Dora" from last night, now sans makeup and glittering costume, wearing a wife-beater T-shirt and blue jeans. But the false eyelashes were still there. And they fluttered gaily in his direction.

There was a moment of silence, then the diner broke into howls of hilarity.

"Dora" stepped up, took a bow, and strolled down

the counter toward Mike. He trailed his fingers up Mike's arm, then turned to Blanche. "Mama, look what followed me home. Can I keep him?"

"Son of a bitch!" Mike tried to jump to his feet.

"Dora" leaned on his shoulder and spoke in his ear. "Sugar, if you hadn't been so shit-faced, I would have shown you how it's done." He slapped Mike on the ass, then quickly backed up to avoid the elbow Mike aimed for his ribs. "Now, now, sugar." Dora held up his hands in defense. "Nothing happened. Your virtue was safe with me. Technically."

He danced back a few steps, blew Mike a kiss like Marilyn Monroe leaving the stage, then soft-shoed his way back toward door number one.

"Ladies and gentlemen," Bill called out, "let's have a round of applause for our resident star, Teddy, and his newest apprentice!"

To the crowd's roar, Teddy/Dora paused to curtsy and blow kisses. His smile dimmed slightly as he passed the last booth. The man sitting in the corner glowered and gave a snarl of thinly disguised loathing.

"Senator Domenico, such an honor." Ted smirked at the man, bowed, and flipped imaginary hair over his shoulder. "Your son says hi by the way." He curtsied again and exited stage left.

Mike banged his head on the counter a couple of times. Pushed back his omelet plate, gathered his shredded dignity about him like a cape, and staggered to his feet. The door seemed a long way off, but he set his course and sauntered out like the he-man SEAL he used to be.

Before Blanche's Diner.

Chapter Five

The buzz started just south of Emily's navel and continued down the slope of her belly until it centered on the tightly strung bundle of nerves at the apex of her sex. It hummed and circled, flicked and tickled. A warm wave of comfort, salted with sparkling bursts of energy, forged its way out to her toes, through her fingers, and into her brain. She raised her hand and reached for the tousled head lodged between her thighs. Her fingers grabbed for a handful of his hair, and pulling him closer, she rode his tongue. He obliged her unspoken demand for more by adding questing fingers to the mix. Stroking in, out, and around. He found that interior hallelujah spot, the one that carried her up and over the precipice into free fall. She floated, she swam, she touched down with a languid stretch.

She felt the breadth of his shoulders and his furnace-like warmth. She sensed him. His hooded eyes and a sexy, confident smile on his lips. He was secure in the knowledge of a job well done. She couldn't keep from smiling.

Her own voice dragged her toward consciousness. "M-m-m-m. Thank you, baby."

Then she woke. Damn it all.

Steamy dreams never lasted long enough. The post-orgasmic buzz was sure to wear off and be replaced by the throbbing pain of a killer hangover waiting for her to crack open an eyeball. This was becoming a regular thing. Something she should take a hard look at. Later.

She just wanted to lie there and delay the wages of overindulgence for a moment. Wet dreams didn't come around that often. It was probably some kind of hormonal surge, the result of too many margaritas and too much post-party adrenaline and recrimination. Maybe it was simply afterglow and longing. No, that was just wrong. That kiss had been…wrong. Right?

As she slipped back into the fog of sleep, a hideous shriek blared next to her ear. Her cell phone continued to sound off like an air raid warning as she searched for the blasted case under her pillow. Her fingers finally found the hard plastic of her phone, and she swiped repeatedly at the screen, eventually finding the right spot to quiet the annoying blast.

Noni's voice replaced the shrieking alarm. "Emily, for God's sake. Wake up, I need you."

"Christ, I can hear you, for crying out loud. Stop screaming." Emily slumped back into her pillows and tossed her arm over her eyes. "When the hell did you change my ringtone? It sounded like the place was burning down."

"I thought I might need to get your attention this morning. Sorry if it scared you." Her friend didn't sound the least bit sorry, but maybe that was the hangover talking.

"What could be so damn important that you need to wake me at zero dark thirty?" Emily didn't regret the annoyance in her tone a single bit. After all, it was Noni who had left her to her own devices after all those cocktails.

"I'm making sure you're alive. I didn't realize till I got home that I hadn't actually seen you get into Daddy's car. When I called him, he thought you'd gone with me. I made Bob go back to the restaurant. He said your car was parked on the street at the gallery, so we knew you made it home."

She paused to breathe. "Anyway, I've got a huge problem. Lois called me in the middle of the night, crying her eyes out. Sobbing about her maid of honor, high heels, broken bones, and emergency rooms. My God, I thought they'd had a car accident or something. Turns out that the idiot she chose for her maid of honor, you know, 'Cheerleader Sherry,' picked last night to fall off her shoes and break her stupid ankle. Lois is beside herself, though more about the uneven numbers in the bridal party than about the cheerleader, and she dumped the whole deal in my lap. I've got to find a way to fix it."

In the middle of the tirade, Emily managed to float off into the gauzy darkness, but she snapped back to attention when Noni stopped talking. "Mmm, I feel for you." That should cover most situations.

"You're not fooling me one bit, Emily Converse. You rat, I know you nodded off. And now I don't feel bad at all for roping you into taking the place of the maid of honor at the ceremony today."

Emily sat straight up in bed. "What? Are you crazy? I'm not doin' anything of the kind." She flopped back, jerked a pillow over her head, and tried to burrow into the mattress. "You can't make me."

"No, I can't. But before you deny the girl you love like a little sister, listen to me. Lois needs your help. See, if she asks one of the other girls to step up and take over, there'll be the catfight of the century. She's trying to keep the peace in the wedding party, and I want you to help her."

"I can't. Besides, the dress won't fit, and I doubt she'd approve of me wearing blue jeans. So, sorry. Not happening."

"That's your out? The dress won't fit? Well, suck it up, buttercup. I just happen to have a dress that will fit you perfectly." Noni sounded rather smug. Damn her. "And you can because I have worked really hard to make her wedding day perfect for her. Besides, if they were here, both our mothers would make you do it. So there." She was probably right about that. "Go get some breakfast and haul your ass down to the DoubleTree in Denver. I have hair and makeup arranged for two o'clock, so you have time to recover. Now, do I need to come over there and drag you into the shower or what?"

Emily tried valiantly to find a crack in the mattress to melt into. No such luck. She was stuck. If Lois needed her as a stand-in, she'd do it. She didn't need Noni to twist her arm too hard. She was dragging her feet on principle. Principle and pain-filled eye sockets. She hadn't seen the bridesmaid dresses, but she could imagine. With her luck, there would be a huge butt bow and layers of frilly ruffles in some hideous color. Christ on a cracker.

Her pillow suffered an exasperated slam to the bed. "All right. All right, no need to pull out the mom voice. You and I both know I'll do it. But if the dress is truly abhorrent, I'm coming after you with a butter knife."

"Yes! Thank you. I knew you would if I asked nicely."

She could practically see Noni pumping her fist.

"Now get up, get up. I'll see you in Denver in like four hours. And Emily, it's not all bad. Did I mention that the groomsmen are all Navy SEALs? Ha, don't tell me I don't have your best interests at heart. Love you."

The click of Noni hanging her out to dry resonated in her ear. Damn, but that girl was a master at manipulation and maneuvering other people into spots they couldn't wiggle out of. She came by her leanings quite naturally; her father was the same way. Pat Evans used to marshal all the kids into a work crew when it came time to cut and bale hay. He put the boys to work slinging bales at the back of a flatbed truck. Their objective had been to haul enough fodder for the winter, but their reward was using any girl dumb enough to be wrangled into stacking hay off the truck and into the field. The boys had been so dedicated to their task Emily secretly believed Pat paid them a bounty for a direct hit.

With a groan and a mighty heave, she hoisted her body out of bed and headed for the shower. With any luck, Blanche would take pity on her, and Ted would make it all better with the best breakfast in town.

****

Half an hour later, Emily climbed into her Jeep and cranked on the heater. The morning chill hadn't burned off, and the watery sunshine did little to change that. Her purse landed with a thunk on the seat. She frowned at her souvenir from the night before. The size-thirteen boot resting innocently on the leather seat took up an alarming amount of space. It was both puzzling and infuriating. What the hell had a man like that, with *those* kinds of hidden talents, been doing passed out beside her car? Then, like a twisted variation on

Cinderella, he'd left his not-so-glass slipper behind. If she checked out the "scene of the crime," perhaps she'd get some answers.

It was only a couple of minutes' drive. If she had been feeling more herself and less like a wrung-out dishcloth, she would have walked it. She just needed to look the place over and decide if it was necessary to call the sheriff's department and make a complaint or a statement or anything. It was kind of late for that, but hey, she shouldn't have been driving last night anyway. She certainly didn't feel like a lecture or worse yet a ticket.

La Chiminea's parking lot showed no signs of recent carnage, so that was good. Enrique argued that the guy probably found his way back to his car while she was in the restaurant. She doubted her idiot in a flowered shirt was capable of finding his own ass with both hands, let alone his car. Enrique, however, wasn't interested in her theories. As she thought about it, she didn't remember hearing any sirens last night. She relaxed and forgave herself for her lack of civic responsibility in not reporting the incident. In any case, deputies Whitbread and Oakum, Tamarack's version of a police force, probably had had a date with a late-night donut and wouldn't have been up for a search of the countryside.

She gave the boot on the seat beside her one more glance. "No skin off my nose."

The whole scene was a first for her. Some of it was still really fuzzy, like the fact that it had actually happened in the first place. Or that she couldn't drum up any residual fear regarding the incident. She was one hundred percent certain she'd never been kissed like that. Ever. It still brought goose bumps to her skin and a flush to her cheeks. It had rocked her. Intentional or not, it might set a new standard for future judgment in the foreplay category, though what had happened left out the whole getting-to-know-each-other factor.

Not that there were men lining up to compete. She simply hadn't realized how much she missed the physical rush his strength had caused. Emily ran a hand down her thigh. She didn't have a problem with her body per se. Her curves were all hers, and she owned them, all five feet, seven inches of them. So what if she wasn't a tiny bird woman with a size zero appetite? She was comfortable in her skin and didn't mind the men who watched with appreciation when she waltzed her size-fourteen rump onto a dance floor. She'd learned early to dress for her size and not worry about the labels involved when wrangling her thirty-six D girls into behaving themselves. But when he manhandled her with such ease, it had done strange, butterfly-fluttery things to her sense of self.

She closed her eyes and remembered the feel of his weight above her, his broad palm cushioning her head. The way the hard length of him nestled between her thighs. Wow—her eyes snapped open—had she really felt that or was it the last thirty romance novels she'd devoured leaking into her memories? Probably the books.

She shook her head to clear it and put the Jeep back in gear. She had things to do today. "Breakfast at Blanche's and then I've *got* to find the strength to face an entire room full of bridesmaids on steroids. I definitely deserve a medal for this." She'd have plenty of time to think over her missing, mystery kisser on the way down to Denver.

By the time she parked in front of Blanche's Diner, her mouth was watering. The café was packed with locals. Some headed to church, but most of them were in recovery from the night before.

Emily glanced down the block at the sound of a horn. A big red pickup swerved to the curb across the street. The driver whooped a greeting to the man he'd stopped for. He burned a little rubber as he swerved back into traffic. She watched as they passed her. The driver laughed and pounded on the wheel. The object of his grin remained in the shadows on the passenger side. She caught a wind-born snippet of a cuss word as they sped toward the edge of town.

"Jesus. Idiot rednecks." Emily shook her head at the show of testosterone from the truck. She pulled open the diner's door and promptly forgot the pickup as the smell of greasy goodness and stomach-filling satisfaction slapped her in the face.

The diner was *the* place for most any food-centric occasion, but it was the *only* place to be on Sunday mornings in the cozy, over-fed world that was Tamarack. Hot coffee, home fries, and crisp bacon. It didn't get any better than breakfast at Blanche's. Thirty-five years and still holding on. The place had outlasted hippies, gas wars, and "it's the economy, stupid." A beacon of dogged determination, a haven for lost, lonely souls of all callings.

Billy Strauss patted the seat beside him. "Hey, Em. You're late!"

"Why? It's not even noon yet. Please don't tell me Blanche is out of eggs. I need her help to get through the rest of the day." Emily perused the house and smiled. She knew most the people by name. She'd missed the perks of living in a small town. She doubted her feelings for the town would change; a sense of belonging filled her every time she rolled down Main Street and up to the gallery. Tamarack was still home.

"Shoot, Em, you missed it! Seems ol' Ted found himself a boyfriend and lost him all in the same night." Billy's lopsided grin belied his concern for Blanche's colorful son. "Ain't that sad?"

"Seems to be going around," Emily mumbled as she accepted the coffee mug Blanche dropped in front of her. "Morning, Blanche. Ted got any eggs left? Maybe throw in some sausage and peppers. A couple of slices of wheat?"

"Comin' right up, sweetie." Leaning in, Blanche spoke quietly. "Say, Em, you got them things ready I asked you about? The clock is ticking, you know."

"I should have it all wrapped up this week. How's that work for you?" Emily winked at the woman. Poor Billy Strauss had no idea what he was getting into, namely, Blanche's husband number four. Emily was happy to play her role and provide the design for the wedding invitations. Everybody needed somebody, and Billy definitely needed a strong-willed, no-nonsense redhead like Blanche to keep him in line.

"That works just perfect for me, thanks." She patted Emily's hand and whisked Billy's plate away.

"Hey, I wasn't done with that," he complained.

"Yes, you were. You've been warming that stool for two hours, and you're costin' me revenue. Besides, my ice machine's makin' noise. If you want your breakfast for free, like usual, you'll go work some magic on it before it craps out." Blanche punctuated

Billy's marching orders with a deft flick of her ever-present bar towel.

"All right! I'm goin'." He groused like the henpecked husband he was soon to be. Poor Billy was in for it.

Emily couldn't suppress her grin. "So what's this about Ted? The place was in an uproar when I pulled up."

Blanche rolled her eyes heavenward. "Just some idiot who forgot to check under the hood before he got in Theodore's car, that's all." She laughed. "You should have seen the shock on the poor bastard's face when 'Dora' made his entrance. I guess he was less than pleased when the big reveal happened." She slapped her bar towel over her shoulder. "Hell, you know how enticing my boy can be when he's all dolled up. I swear to you, Em, I thought the guy was going to stroke out right here at the counter."

"Man, and I slept in. Sorry I missed the show." Emily sipped her coffee. "So where's the guy now? He run out screaming or what?"

"Naw, just banged his head on the counter and marched out like he had a flagpole stuck up his butt." Blanche couldn't hold back her grin. "Guess he didn't care for the limelight, because he hustled his butt across the street to a bench. I saw him climb in his buddy's pickup just as you got here."

Aha—the truck full of rednecks. "Big guy, enormous shoulders, god-awful shirt?"

"Yes, yes, and definitely yes. No doubt about the body underneath. It's no wonder Teddy brought him home. Who wouldn't, even an old broad like me?"

The ding-ding of the call bell announced Emily's

breakfast order. Blanche left her to retrieve it and make a refill run for her caffeine-impaired clientele.

Chapter Six

Mike slumped down in the seat of the pickup. Served him right to suffer the slings and arrows of the asshole behind the wheel.

"Shut the hell up, will ya, Jerry? That hyena noise you make is going to make me hurl all over this truck. Then I'll have to kill you. In that order." Mike had endured about as much razzing as he could take from the fool next to him. The one who, as his second in command, was supposed to have his back. Or what used to be his command. Now his team was scattered to the winds. Scattered, that was appropriate. Just like him, Senior Master Chief Michael James McCandlis, USN, Retired.

Scattered, pointless, and with very little reason for—anything.

Jerry Curtis gave Mike an amused glance. "So, boss, you feelin' like sharin' yet, or you leavin' it to me to make up what happened after that dancer poured you into her car?"

Mike growled and glared back at him. He would love it if Jerry would let this whole fiasco go. Didn't look like that was happening any time soon.

"Look, man," Jerry said, "inquiring minds want to know. Besides, I'm betting you won't throw a punch at me while cruising down I-25. Then again, you did get into that dancer's car. A fact, I might add, the rest of us found hilarious last night. Now you look like the south end of a northbound horse, and I feel kinda sorry for you."

"I don't want to talk about it. At. All." Mike fished in his backpack and dug out a ball cap and his sunglasses. He jammed the shades over his eyes and jerked the cap's brim down low on his brow. What a cluster fuck. He was mostly sure nothing life-changing had happened. Then again, disturbing gaps in his memory worried him. No doubt from the whiskey, and God, what was that back taste, Jägermeister? Why. Not.

Why not indeed. Why not prove how unfit he was? Prove he couldn't cut it, couldn't do the job anymore. Prove to anybody watching—especially his crew—exactly why the navy had patted him on the head and shoved him into retirement. Retirement—at age forty-five. He groaned. Even Mike, sober Mike that is, understood the rationale. Younger, better-equipped men were capable of handling the physical requirements of a SEAL Team command. Shit and damn. He was rudderless, stripped of any good reason to get up in the morning. That was a whole new thing for him.

He stared glumly out the windshield. The flat, brown grass landscape to the left contrasted sharply with the spectacular piles of granite and pine to his right. It was an apt setting. He sighed, tired by the constant lack of impetus.

Jerry cleared his throat and draped his wrist over the steering wheel. "Look, man, I know it ain't easy. The transition, I mean. You'll figure it out, you always have."

Mike made a derisive noise. "If you're talking about last night, I got no problem there. If you mean finding some kind of earth-shattering revelation about my 'purpose,' I gotta say I feel like I've been flushed down the bureaucratic toilet."

"Oh, right. I forgot. You're really a *superhero* who was dusted with kryptonite by the evil overlord. You used to be impervious, and now you're human. My, oh, my. Whatever will happen to the rest of us?" Jerry snorted at his own analogy. "That's stinkin' thinkin', man. Fifteen years of hard jumps, cold water, hot sand, and near-death experiences take a toll no matter how superhuman we are."

Mike leaned forward and flipped on the radio. He cranked the volume up till hard, driving rock and roll blasted into the cab. He'd just been called-out on a subject he'd lectured his men on repeatedly. Living through a hundred firefights didn't mean they were invincible. His last mission had proved it when he was slammed by IED shrapnel and choppered out. Truth was, losing focus for one second was a rookie move. And he'd paid for it when pieces of metal dug themselves into his spine. Injuries like his put a cap on his ability to do the job. He knew it; they all knew it.

The US Navy saw it differently. "Thanks for your years of active duty," they'd said. "Let us know if you want to instruct." It'd felt like a handout in payment for services rendered. His years in uniform had been the rack where he hung his pride. Now they seemed reduced to splinters.

Well, no, thanks. Instruct. This.

Jerry turned down the music and punched the tuner till he found a country western station. "You don't feel like talkin', that's fine. Don't fuck with my radio. God, you're like a grumpy old man with a toothache." He settled back in his seat and frowned at Mike.

Grouchy? Well, maybe. The whole fubar situation made Mike's gut clench. "Sorry," he growled. He hadn't wanted to come to Colorado. He'd still be on his surf board staring out at the Pacific Ocean if Dillon Prentice hadn't begged him to be here. He definitely wouldn't be hungover, wondering why the hell he'd let the guys talk him into taking the bachelor party to a sleazy dive in Denver. Should have kept the damn thing at the hotel where the wedding would happen—no driving, no chicks with dicks, no blackouts.

He needed to take his old man's advice and ask for help when he needed it. Stop being so self-contained. Or was it stubborn? "So, since you're such an expert, what do you think I should do? Put my feet up and coast? Become a discount store greeter? Teach snot-nosed kids how not to get their asses shot off?"

Jerry smacked him in the chest with an open hand. "Ha. Now you're talkin'. Mosey on down to the big box store and teach the brats how to hold an M16. You'll look good in that little blue vest. It'll bring out the color in your eyes." He laughed with that annoying honk again. "But right now we have a wedding to get to, remember? So next, we'll stop for gas, then get that ugly mug of yours shaved and trimmed so you look less like you been drug through a knothole. Get a beer, have some lunch, and you're going to stop feeling so *freakin'* sorry for yourself. How's that sound?"

"Don't make me hurt you, Jerry." Mike huffed. "I might even wait till we're not doing eighty miles an hour, but don't count on it."

"Ooo, I'm so scared." Jerry waved his fingers in mock terror. "The way you're looking right now, my grandma could take you."

"Is she here?" A grudging smile crept across his face.

Jerry rarely failed to have that effect on him. The dude had a way of defusing almost any situation with a smart-ass comment. Sometimes they were even funny. It wasn't a trait Mike came by, but it was effective for the high-stress job Jerry was about to take over.

"You got the nod, right?" Mike asked from beneath his cap. His voice was back from sandpaper to smooth. Maybe his equilibrium would resurface as well.

"Yup. Came last week." He was silent for a second. "I know my name wasn't at the top of the list to take over the team. Thanks for the recommendation. I appreciate you speaking up."

"Nobody's a better fit for the job." *Except me.*

"Still and all, it won't be the same without you."

"I sure as shit hope not. You've got your work cut out for you, that's for damn sure. All I can tell you is set your own standards and don't take any shit. Because it doesn't matter how long you've known these guys; they're still sure to make you prove yourself. Be the alpha."

"That's advice I'll take." Jerry cleared his throat. "What's your plan now? You goin' back to California to stay or what?"

"I've got a lot to think over. Now I've got nothing but time to do it." He bounced his skull against headrest a couple of times. "Maybe I'll put my mad skills to work and devise a way to tell a chick from a dick when you're loaded."

"If all of us hadn't been in the bag, we'd never have let that happen. Seemed like you would figure it out, then we saw you give us the ol' one finger salute as sh…ah, you left the parking lot." Jerry's grin crept into his voice. "How'd you get all the way out here anyway?"

"The last thing I remember clearly is the bar, then there's only holes and flashes. Something about adhesive tape, and then I'm pretty sure I threw up. Seems like I fell down a lot, and there was this redhead who called me something weird. Shit…I don't remember. I woke up freezing my balls off in the woods, one foot in a creek, and with a blinding headache. Totally fucking bonehead situation." Mike closed his eyes against the searing turquoise of the Colorado sky and felt every one of his forty-five years.

"You want me to call my grandma? Judging from the chicks you been hanging with, she might be a step back into the light. You know, like away from the boom-chicka-wow-wow dark side."

"Shut up. Again." Mike's smile got perceptibly bigger. "Don't make me bring up that epic time in Manila. What was her name? Hector?"

Jerry barked a laugh. "Yeah, well, at least I didn't get in his rickshaw before I checked the tires, ya know?"

Mike still felt like a class A fool. But hey, fuck-ups of this magnitude made for the best stories.

Chapter Seven

The DoubleTree Hotel in Denver was located way the hell and gone from downtown. Surrounded by miles and miles of nothing but miles and miles, it served as a welcome mat for traffic in and out of the Denver International Airport. During the twenty years since Emily called Colorado home, small foothill towns had congealed into a solid mass of indistinguishable developments. It had become one massive town from Lyons through Golden and most of the way to Colorado Springs.

Really sad. She rolled the Wrangler into the hotel's drive. Human nature seemed to dictate that the last drop of individualism and beauty be wrung from the most stupendously gorgeous spots on Earth. Not that the vertical sandstone faces of the Flat Irons above Boulder weren't beautiful landmarks. Not that the Front Range wasn't still breathtaking in all its towering majesty. But in her estimation, the pristine quality of life had suffered. Especially when viewed across a sea of rooftops instead of the open sagebrush and scrub pine that once covered the foothills.

She cruised into the parking garage and found a spot close to the entrance. She pulled down the lighted mirror in her visor while reaching blindly for her purse and a brush. Instead, she made contact with the toe of Cinderella's leather boot. She glared at its continued presence in her life and summarily tossed it over the seats into the far back. It clunked against the tailgate. Not like she'd have the time or reason to puzzle out that particular mystery today. She had a wedding ceremony and reception to get through. Then she could go home and spend a few satisfying moments reliving The Kiss to End All Kisses.

She checked her makeup, spread on an extra layer of lip gloss, fluffed her hair, and declared herself as good as it got. The peachy lace of her cami gave a glimpse of cleavage beneath a snug navy bolero jacket and flirty little skirt. She felt stylish and comfortable. Or she would be after the shindig wound down and she could peel off her too-high heels. For now, she concentrated on not falling as she negotiated the stairs into the hotel.

The rich greens and deep burgundies of the decor made a pleasant contrast to the rustic granite and fieldstone accents in the lobby. The designers knew their stuff. She climbed the sweeping staircase to the grand ballroom and admired the space from the balcony; it struck the right balance between moneyed classic and Western kitsch.

Emily strolled along the balustrade, enjoying the colors and people-watching. She didn't want to get sucked into the wedding maelstrom until absolutely necessary. A ton of people were in the main lobby below, all dressed to the nines for the wedding spectacle between Lois Anne Evans and Specialist Dillon Prentice, USN. The happy couple would take their vows at sunset with lapis lazuli and amethyst mountains in the background. The reception would follow in the ballroom directly adjoining the terrace where the ceremony would take place. Plus, the hotel promised to accommodate any guest too "overjoyed" to drive home safely. It would be beautiful *and* handy. They should all bow to Noni Sears, practical to the last degree.

"What's a nice girl like you doin' in a place like this?" A deep bass voice rumbled over Emily's shoulder and out into the space over the lobby.

Newcomers below looked up and laughed. She spun and was enveloped by arms like tree trunks. Patrick Evans had lost none of his bulk as his age progressed.

"Well, well…the father of the bride. Good to see you, Papa Pat." She kissed him soundly on the cheek. "'Bout time you married off the last of them, don't you think?" She patted both lapels of his tux and smiled into his broad ruddy face and twinkling blue eyes. Time had been kind to this old rancher.

The Evans family was an odd dichotomy. Colorado cattle had funded the oil business in Oklahoma, which in turn paid for the continuance of the cattle business and now the tech company that was Noni's baby. Five generations and two hundred years had turned the family into old money in Denver society. An American success story if there ever was one.

"Lord knows I've been running candidates past that filly for years. Then she has to go and pick some frogman from California." Patrick pushed back his black Stetson, revealing a wide band of white forehead that seldom saw the sunlight. He was a true cowboy: hat, saddle, horse, and cattle.

Emily loved Patrick Evans like a father, but his tendency to ride roughshod over his unruly girls was legendary. "Seems to me you got lucky with Noni and Bob when you introduced them. What made you think Lois would follow suit? Maybe it's a good thing she ditched those 'candidates' of yours and chose one for herself."

"We'll see how this plays out. Least the boy has a career, and I can't fault his patriotism. What I'm wonderin', though, is how come the prettiest girl here is all by her lonesome."

Emily nodded in the direction of a senior matriarch currently giving them the stink eye. "You mean that saucy little number over there?"

Pat glanced behind him. "Oh, God, no," he hissed and shivered those massive shoulders. "That would be Amelia Stapleton. She thinks we should 'merge' our companies—among other things. I'm countin' on you to run interference for me during the reception in case she puts the moves on me."

Emily barked out a laugh. Pat had been a widower for twenty-five years. His money and looks were surpassed only by his survival skills.

"Oh, yeah? What's in it for me? She looks pretty tough."

The old lady did have a mean gaze. Emily couldn't resist giving Pat a playful tickle to his ear for the woman's benefit. She laughed again as Pat batted at her fingers.

"Stop that. I got my eye on a landscape up at your gallery. Does that count?"

Her gallery. She got a warm glow when she thought about Cloud to Ground being hers. "You mean the one of Bear Lake? Unfortunately, that one only comes as a pair. Can't let them go separately. The artist is a friend of mine."

"That's my Emmy." He laughed and hugged her tight. "Always dealing, ain't you? All right, we'll see how you do keeping that cougar off my tail."

Emily grinned big. Money from the Bear Lake set would go a long way toward taking her first month into the black. "You know, being the civically minded girl that I am, I could see my way toward cutting you a deal. Not a lot, mind you, just a scrape off the top."

Pat gave her a considering look. "You'd best do better than shave off a couple bucks. Ol' Lady Stapleton can be a sneaky, determined broad. Once trapped me in an elevator and tried to kiss me. I barely escaped with my manhood intact. If'n I survive the night, I'll take both paintings and that little bronze thingamajig by the front door too."

She whooped and smacked him on the arm. "Cowboy, you got yourself a deal. You want me to shank her too?"

"Shank who?" Noni slipped her arm around Pat. "Daddy, what are you planning now?" Her head barely reached his shoulder, reminding Emily that her old friend had once affectionately been known as "Short Round." The short part hadn't changed. Now, at forty-one, Noni was a svelte package of energy bound up in the sparkle of happy mom and pampered wife.

An uncomfortable moment of jealousy bubbled up inside Emily. Noni's life wasn't a cake walk, but damn it, how come that kind of luck didn't land in her own lap? Time was moving faster these days. Hadn't it been just a couple of years ago they were students at Northwestern? How had she let the fairy tale life she'd dreamed of get so lost?

"Say, Em." Noni gave a meaningful brow waggle. "You get a gander at the groomsmen?" She patted her father's belly and grabbed her hand. "Come on, chica. This you've got to see." Over her shoulder, she tossed back, "Daddy, the coordinator will come to get you when they're ready to start. Don't get lost, okay? You have an important role to play."

"Go on—git." Pat brushed the girls away. "I'm surprised you ain't tied me to a rail or somethin'. I been through this all before, you know." He harrumphed and turned toward the bar. "And I ain't doin' it again."

"Oh, quit complaining." Noni frowned at him. "Just stay where we can find you. Okay?"

"I'm thinking a stiff bourbon would taste fine about now. Then I'll check on the groom, make sure the boy's toes are nice and toasty. Or I might offer the guy a buttload of cash not to take my little girl all the way to California."

Emily grinned at him. She wouldn't put it past him to give it a try. She stumbled as she was led away. She had enough trouble with her high heels. She didn't need Noni's help to fall off them. The little dynamo hustled her to the elevators leading up to the guest suites.

She tried to pry Noni's fingers off her wrist. "Would you please stop pulling me?"

"Then stop dragging your ass," Noni quipped. "Where the hell have you been, anyway? Everyone's hair is done but yours, and we still have to try on the dress, then do your makeup."

Emily finally escaped her friend's grip. She rotated her hand, and the wrist bone cracked. "Criminy, Noni. You just sprang this on me a few hours ago, and I was too hungover to defend myself."

"Sorry, did I leave a mark?" Noni looked contrite for a second before her face split into a devilish grin. "I've got to show you something, then it's off to bridesmaid hell. I got a gander at the groomsmen at rehearsal, which by the way you got out of. Son of a gun, honey, when I say these guys are prime cut, I mean it. Almost enough to tempt me away from Bobby, and that's saying something. So I thought maybe you'd let me live vicariously. If I can get this damn elevator to move..." She thumped the button a few times. "I'll show you the menu of available eye candy."

Emily breathed an exasperated sigh when the elevator door swished open. "Who are you, and what have you done with my childhood friend?"

Undeterred, Noni hurried her in and punched out the floor numbers. "You wait, you'll thank me. I mean damn, I've never seen the like outside of a male revue, and you know those dancers are either glorified hookers or gay. But these men? They were beautiful *before* they put on their dress uniforms. And then—" She paused to wave an imaginary fan. "—my, oh, my."

"Don't you have better things to do today? Like pseudo-mother-of-the-bride kinds of things?"

"Honey, this is a preemptive strike. You know my sister. She's got herself a stunning bunch of airheads on her side of the altar, all younger than us...ah, you. So I figured what the heck, we'd just get off on the wrong floor sort of by accident. The groomsmen's suite is right opposite the elevator. They're bound to be standing around getting Dillon primed to walk down the aisle. We'll just peek in to see if they need...anything."

"Anything—like coffee, tea, or me?" Emily scowled at her friend and then looked down at her toes.

When had she become the poor, divorced friend who needed help to get a date? She must have missed a sign on the highway that warned her of Noni's plans. *Beware. Matchmaker ahead. Turn back now!*

Crap and double crap.

Chapter Eight

Mike looked around the suite. It was nice, posh even. Two couches, a flat screen, and a dining room table took up the sitting room. The two bedrooms had spacious baths, all done in soothing bland colors, perfect for the use of the groom and his best man. The other four friends were housed in single rooms just down the hall. But on this, Dillon Prentice's wedding day, the entire party was sprawled around the big suite, handing off copious advice on the biggest day of the poor slob's life.

The members of SEAL Team Seven had served together for four long years of continuous deploy/debrief/do-it-again. They were a highly trained, tight, battle-hardened unit. They were also, like a bunch of brothers, capable of riding each other into the ground. All in the name of "because we can."

Mike studied Dillon's face. The kid looked decidedly green around the edges. Dill paced, ran his fingers through his hair, and yanked on his collar as if it were about to choke off his air.

"You okay, Dill?" He felt downright sorry for the youngest member of his team. Ex-team.

"I think I'm going to hurl...again." Dillon swiped a hand down his face and did some deep breathing. "Why is it so hot in here?"

Mike chuckled. The guys weren't taking it easy on

the groom to be. Like it was their duty to razz the shit out of him every time he puked up his guts. Poor Dill, he wasn't hungover like the rest of them; as a matter of fact, it seemed to encourage them to ride him that much harder.

"Rico, Dill's about to blow!" Mike stepped over their tactical expert, Doyle, and grabbed the ice bucket. He thumped it soundly against Dill's chest. He'd said repeatedly that he believed in being prepared, especially when it came to the containment of stomach contents. Dillon made a loud *oof* when the bucket hit his chest. They all laughed except Mike.

"I told him to keep the damn thing with him," Rico, their infiltration specialist, grumbled and stepped out of the blast zone. He flopped on the couch between Jerry and Alec, their linguist. The team was killing time prior to the ceremony by watching the Broncos beat the crap out of the Chargers and cluttering the coffee table with empties from the minibar.

Mike gave the men a hard look and turned back to Dillon. "It'll be fine. Dill. You're just not used to this is all. There's no way you can train for this situation; it's completely different than in the field. We're taught to handle that type of stress. You keep your eyes on the prize and ignore the rest of the idiots in the room."

"Thanks, boss. It's just..." His voice dropped to a whisper. "What if I suck at this whole marriage thing?" He turned his back to the group. "I mean, why would a smart, beautiful woman like Lois hook up with a guy who could leave her a widow at any moment? If I love her the way I should, then why would I put her through that?"

Mike's heavy palm landed on Dillon's shoulder.

"Hey, man, stow that kind of thinking. You're sounding kind of crazy here." He grabbed his jacket and spun Dillon toward the door. "We're walking," he told the other four less-than-helpful groomsmen. "You assholes need to sober up, finish dressing, and find the time to remember why we're here."

"That's right, men," Jerry intoned in his best southern preacher voice. "We've gathered today to lay to rest the historic bachelorhood of yet another SEAL." They all raised their drinks in a solemn salute.

Rico Valenzuela flashed his trademark smile. "Hey, boss, if he's thinking about running—not that I blame him—maybe you should let the expert take him for a stroll."

"Shut it, Rico," Mike growled as he pushed Dillon toward the door. "The whole world knows you're the 'master of going dark.' We're just going for a walk, getting a breath of fresh mountain air. Ain't that right, Dill?" He shook Dillon's shoulder and nudged him forward.

Dillon swallowed hard and nodded. Mike smiled indulgently as the kid jerked his back straight like he was about to face a firing squad.

They stepped into the hall, crossed to the bank of elevators, and stepped into a waiting car. He punched the button for the roof deck. As the door swooshed closed, Mike caught a glimpse of two women exiting the car next to theirs. He got a quick impression of long legs and red hair. Surely the guys wouldn't be ordering hot-and-cold running girls. Not today. Then again, they did tend to check their smarts at the gate when they weren't on assignment. He loved and respected each member of his team, but at times they allowed their little heads to do the thinking.

When the elevator door reopened, the two comrades stepped into a glass-enclosed foyer that led to the roof. Thankfully the place was deserted. A cold wind whipped at their jackets as they stepped to the rail. In the near distance, Denver's skyline sparkled in the glowing afternoon light. The Rockies floated in a gentle haze with a growing corona of sunlight setting the Front Range ablaze like an ad for a vacation getaway. Streaks of vibrant orange, swaths of salmon, and arcs of glowing pink were in the clouds to the northwest. All of it underscored by the sweep and majesty that Colorado was famous for. Mike took it in; he'd always thought vistas like this were photographer's tricks reserved for postcard racks. He and the kid pulled in simultaneous deep breaths.

Dillon leaned on the rail and rested his head on his tightly clenched hands. "Shit, Mike, I feel like such a pansy ass. There's no training to fall back on here."

"You're spending too much time in your head. You're already seeing Lois as a widow. You know that shitty kind of thinking only increases the odds of it coming true. Stay in the present, man; don't project the what ifs."

"Yeah, you're right. I know you're right." Dillon straightened his stance and shook his head. "But getting my heart to understand what my brain knows is true is a whole 'nother thing." He was a sharp kid who regularly envisioned problems before they became apparent to anyone else. Mike sometimes forgot the guy was only twenty-five. He wondered if he'd ever been that young.

"Look at me, Dill." He waited till Dillon's worried brown eyes met his own. "Lois is exactly the kind of woman who can handle anything life throws at her. She's a successful businesswoman. She's got to be tough, emotionally and physically, to do her job well."

Dillon turned away from the mountains and found a bench for his backside. "Yeah, she's incredibly focused. Smarter than me, that's for damn sure. And she picked me—I still can't believe it."

"Of course she picked you. Those aren't good-conduct medals on your chest. You earned every ribbon and insignia, starting with your Trident. So don't tell me you ain't got what it takes, man. I know different, and so does Lois."

"Yeah, well, regardless of that," Dillon said, "guys like us have a rotten record with marriage."

Mike gave a quiet huff in agreement. "Finding the balance of career and home is our hardest job. God knows the numbers prove that well enough. But from what I can see, success is pulled from a set of realistic expectations. If you go in knowing what the hurdles are and expecting to compromise, you've got a leg up on the statistics. Lois is savvy. She's done the research she needs to be prepared for your deployments. She's already made contact with support services and is doing everything she can to be duty ready. Just like you do. In my book that makes her part of the team."

Dill took in another deep breath and let it out slowly. "Thanks, boss. Your opinion is important to me. If I never made that clear while we were active, I'll say it now." He stood and squared his shoulders to his former team leader. His salute was sharp and took Mike by surprise.

He snapped to his feet and returned it.

Dillon thrust out his hand and grasped Mike's. "It

has been my distinct honor to have served with you, Master Chief. I'll miss your mug on each and every mission."

An unexpected surge of emotion clogged Mike's throat. "The honor has been mine. You're a credit to the navy and to this team." He cleared his throat and gave Dillon a warm smile. "I think it's about time to get this party started. And if you need me to handle your razor for you, I will. We wouldn't want you to damage that pretty face, today of all days."

They were still laughing when they reached the room. Damn, this kid was more like a son to him than he'd realized. They were all like his kids and his little brothers. Their bond had been forged in battle, but their lives were lived stateside. They did their best to sweep all thought of home into a corner of their hearts when they were on assignment. Sharp focus was hyper-critical to survival. But when they got back to their lives at home, separating themselves from the twenty-four-hour intensity of the mission flipped them all upside down.

Dillon's fear was real. So was the dread Mike felt at building a life outside the cocoon of his team. He had to keep reminding himself to stop the pity-party routine and find a way to transition into a new way of being.

Chapter Nine

"Damn, Noni. I cannot believe you," Emily said as they stepped back out of the elevator on Lois's floor. "You are one crazy hooker, you know that? Where did all this man-ogling, covert-cougar junk come from?"

Noni snorted. "I think it's a survival mechanism. I developed it around the time my husband decided to quit being gainfully employed and work from home. I never thought I'd miss the smell of the newspaper on his clothes, but damn, the man is under my feet these days." She pushed Emily down the corridor toward the bridesmaids' suite. "Besides, as I said earlier, I'm married, not dead. And if you'd shake loose the stick up your butt, you'd bow down to my mad hookup skills. Wasn't that Rico gorgeous? Every dark-roasted, Latin inch of him? And the quiet one, Doyle, he's something out of a romance novel; he's all yes, ma'am and no, ma'am with his Southern drawl. Then there's Jerry, the smooth one. Yum. Who was the quiet, muscly one? Alec, right? He reminded me of that English actor—oh, man, what's his name from *This Means War*? Tom something."

"Tom Hardy," Emily supplied. She had to concede the groomsmen were quite a sight. All that testosterone packed in dress blues. "Okay, I admit it, you were right—they're snack-able. But, Noni, so freaking—young."

"You're not dead either, you know. Just because you have, historically, had the worst luck with men, doesn't mean every swinging dick out there is a bad guy. So there's no reason I can think of that's stopping you from seizing the opportunity to do a little 'education' of the nation's impressionable youth. Somebody's got to do it. Why not you?" Noni wiggled her eyebrows lasciviously.

Emily burst into laughter at the ridiculous idea of picking up one of the groomsmen. "Yeah, well, I'm pretty sure they're more likely to teach me a thing or two. But you're right, I'm not dead. I'm also not into robbing the cradle, so can we just move this roadshow along? Let's see if I can squeeze my fat ass into that dress you so mysteriously happen to have on hand." She looked down her nose at her shorter friend. There was something seriously suspicious about the whole "Gee, the best friend of the bride just broke her damn ankle, and the only one on the planet to fill the role is you." The odds of that happening were like a gazillion to one. "What did you do, pay someone to push the cheerleader off her shoes?"

"That's ridiculous. I was with you all evening. Besides, Lois would kill me. Though, if I'd had the time, I might have looked into it. Seriously, that Sherry girl is a big-time pain. How she and my smart little sister ever got to be besties is beyond me. Reminds me of a yappy little purse dog—all hair bows and teeth. 'Look at me, ain't I cute.' " She poked her finger into her mouth and pretended to retch. "Lois was panicked there'd be a catfight for the slot, so I had to come up with the solution. And as to the dress, I swear there was a screw up by the dressmakers; they made one of the dresses in fourteen, not a four. It was like fate or something, and you were *the* perfect choice."

"You mean I was the only choice," Emily grumbled. "All right, show me to the dungeon. I'm ready to take my punishment. You know you're the only one in the world I'd do this for. Right?"

Noni smirked, swiped the key card for the suite, and threw open the door. "Saint Emily, our lady of mercy and goodness." The room rang with the raucous blast of hip-hop and laughter. A wave of hairspray and lavender chiffon washed over them. They waited for a break in the music and stepped inside.

A tiny blonde clutching a bottle of champagne wobbled forward on her crutches and toppled into Emily's arms. "Um-m, hi," she hiccupped into Emily's chest, then surged upright. With difficulty, she focused on her rescuer. "You lost?"

"Nope." Emily stepped back to avoid spillage as the blonde struggled to hold onto the bottle while remaining upright on her supports. This had to be the supplanted cheerleader. "You must be Sherry. Sorry about your ankle. I'm your stand-in, Emily Converse."

Sherry looked her up and down with squinty eyes; her focus had clearly deserted her. "Oh. My. God. You're the sister's friend? Honey, there's no way you'll fit—" She gestured down Emily's body and hiccupped again. "—into my gown. Bless your heart. It's just not happening."

Noni stepped forward to snatch the bottle from Sherry's hand. "That will be enough of the bubbly for you, Frisky." She walked Sherry backward into the room, depositing her on the nearest couch. "Sit. Stay. Good girl."

Emily burst into a fit of tear-inducing snickers. The whole purse-dog analogy was such a dead-on characterization of the tiny little blonde; the urge to bark at the woman was nearly irresistible.

With a roll of her eyes, Noni grabbed Emily's hand. "Come on, there's no time to fart around with this. The hair and makeup people are in here." She dragged Emily toward one of the bedrooms. "First you've got to try on the dress. Thank God, you've worn the heels I got you because I forgot about your shoes. Oh, and by the way, I got an email from Ian. He said he'll be here with a plus one, whatever that means. It's about time he made an appearance, don't you think? Maybe we'll finally meet the mystery boyfriend."

Emily bit her lip and looked aside for a moment. Sometimes the weight of responsibility she'd taken on was overwhelming. Couple it with her failure to drag Ian back on board, and it was enough to buckle her knees. "He actually called me yesterday. I'm glad he confirmed with you. I wasn't sure he'd follow through." She drummed up a smile for Noni. "Christ, sorry. I get nervous when he hides out, and it drives me crazy the way he ditches the gallery. He's going to have a cat fit when I hit him with my ideas for changes at the gallery. If he cares at all, that is." The balancing act was exhausting. Care—but not too much. Reach out—but don't fall off the cliff and enable him. "He's been level for the last couple of years as far as I know, but that last stint in rehab was rough on us both. Now, when he slips, he goes right back down the rabbit hole."

"I know, honey." Noni ushered her to a garment bag hanging from one of the closet doors. "It's hard to know how much to do. Instinct tells you to sweep him up and protect him like you did when you were kids. But he's not a kid anymore, so your rational mind tells you to let him find his own way. Then there's all the unresolved shit the senator put him through, and you're right back into protective mode. It's like a die-hard version of the push-me-pull-you situation." She opened the bag and shook out the skirt of the dress.

Emily sighed, thinking about Ian. In and out of rehab programs for years, he couldn't stay clean for any meaningful length of time. It hadn't stopped him from flying around the US doing exhibits at different galleries and dropping in unannounced on her in Seattle. He never stopped long enough to deal with his life. Maybe that was his tactic; keep moving and life would never catch up. Put as much distance between him and his past as possible. Pretend it never happened. Deal with it by not dealing with it.

Gee, that sounded uncomfortably familiar.

Noni cleared her throat loudly. Emily dragged her thoughts away from her brother, and her eyes widened as she took in the dress dangling from Noni's fingertips. Stunning was the word for the soft lavender of the fitted bodice and the drape of delicate fabric that fell in a gentle sweep of chiffon. The color flowed ever darker along the length of the skirt, finally reaching a deep amethyst as the hem dusted the carpet. Beginning at the straight, strapless neckline and continuing along the entire length, tiny crystals were sown in sweeping patterns of leaves and vines.

"Oh, Noni, it's beautiful. I...I didn't expect this. It's just so, well, gorgeous. Are you sure you want me to do this? What if it doesn't fit or...or my boobs fall out or something? You know I can be a terrible klutz.

What if I spill something on it or rip the hem? I'd feel terrible and..." Emily stumbled to a halt as all the foreseeable catastrophes of pairing her up with this beautiful creation swept her confidence right out the door.

"Nonsense, it's like fate had you in mind for the occasion. The color is perfect with your shade of auburn, and the style is right for you and your tatas. Your girls will stay in place if we have to use superglue. There's no way you're gonna mess this up, so stop worrying. Now strip and let's make sure of the fit. Then it's on to the torture chamber. Come on, chop-chop." She shook the dress at Emily. "I've got to make sure the kiddies are sober enough to get down the aisle, and check on Lois. I stashed her in the suite next door so she didn't get overwhelmed by the fumes. I swear there's enough hairspray and perfume in the air to choke a crow."

An hour and a half later, just in the nick of time, Emily was declared fit to call herself the maid of honor. In her personal opinion, compared to the children that formed the rest of the entourage, she should change the title to matron. Seriously, she had at least ten years on the rest of them, and she was feeling every day of it in her feet. The heels were perfect with the wonderful dress, but her toes were already barking, and the party had yet to start.

Noni was like the proverbial killer bee. She flashed back and forth from Lois's suite to the bridesmaid lair in a blur of fevered detail checking. The last trip included pouring cheerleader Sherry into one of the beds in the dressing room and tucking her in for the duration. Emily hoped that was the case because the annoying little shit was getting on everyone's last nerve. The final straw was her crying jag because mean ol' Noni wouldn't allow her to wear her "butifull purrple pwincess dwess."

Finally, Noni dragged Emily down the short hall to the bride's island of quiet. She ran her key through the slot, pushed open the door, and stopped in her tracks. Lois stood wrapped in white organza and pearls. She was so beautiful Emily's heart faltered.

"Oh, honey, you're stunning," Noni whispered and sniffed back a tear. She ran a gentle finger beneath Lois's chin. She wrapped Lois in a tight hug, careful not to smudge her makeup or crease her veil. "I wish Mama was here to see this."

The bride's chin began to quiver. "Is it okay? Do I really look pretty?"

"Yes, baby, you're perfect. Mama would have been so proud. And jealous. Her dress looks better on you." Noni fanned away her tears.

"You don't think she'd be angry that I had it redone? All those layers of crinolines just swamped me, and the sleeves were way long."

Lois's voice reminded Emily of when the girl was around nine years old and struggling to accept that her mother couldn't come to see her win the science fair. Cancer was beyond her understanding. It still was.

Lois sniffed and turned her eyes toward her sister's best friend. "Oh, gosh, Emily. Thanks so much for doing this, and you look lovely." Lois gave her a hug and a watery smile.

"Dillon is a very lucky man." Emily slipped an arm beneath the veil and squeezed Lois's shoulders. "Don't you worry about making over your gown. Givenchy never goes out of style."

"That's right, and neither does tradition," Noni declared. She dug into a hidden pocket in her skirt and pulled out a delicate gold locket. Its soft patina glinted in the lamplight as she lovingly drew the chain around Lois's neck. "I'm only letting you *borrow* this, get it? When my daughter gets married, you can let her *borrow* it back." Noni clasped the chain beneath the bride's hair and smiled at her in the mirror. "Mama wore it the day she married Daddy. I wore it with Bob. Now you'll wear it on your day. Tradition, see?"

Noni pulled a tissue from her sleeve and discreetly blew her nose, then stepped away to grab her phone. "I'll check that everything is good downstairs, and we'll head out." She punched an icon on the screen and spoke quickly, then gave the bride a thumbs up. "Emily, would you collect the bridesmaids and get them into the elevators? We'll meet you downstairs. 'Kay?"

Orders were orders. Emily preceded her friends into the hall.

****

As predicted, the Rockies provided a royal velvet backdrop for the flower-covered arch that framed the altar. Lining the aisle, candles in hurricane globes lent a warm highlight to the union of Dillon Campbell Prentice and Lois Elaine Evans.

The wedding planner marshaled the phalanx of bridesmaids into order at the doorway of the wide-open terrace. The cool twilight breeze rustled layers of gossamer chiffon and teased the hair of the bridal party. Noni's four-year-old twins, the flower girl and ring bearer, fidgeted like unruly puppies. Noni paused to give them the mom look; they quieted long enough for her to turn her back. With a pat to her husband's shoulder, she broke ranks and stepped back to whisper in Emily's ear. "We missed one."

"What are you doing?" Emily hissed at her. "Get back up to the head of the line, and let's get the show on the road."

"Wait till you see the best man. How a guy that size got past me, I'll never know. I mean, holy crap, he's gorgeous. The tie-me-up-and-cart-me-off, hunky kind of gorgeous."

Noni's grin was so wide Emily feared the woman's face might crack.

"Would you stop? The last thing I need is you playing matchmaker with some poor defenseless sailor. Go. Do your thing and stop being so freaking crazy." Emily turned her friend around. "I swear to God, if you do anything to embarrass me, I will kill you dead."

Noni laughed and wiggled her butt at Emily. She sauntered to the head of the line and allowed her husband to lead them all into the ceremony.

With a surprising degree of decorum, Noni and Bob made it to their seats. The music swelled, filling the air with the soft strains of Pachelbel's Canon in D. Emily watched as the wedding coordinator held the shortest of the bridesmaids back, waiting for the proper musical cue, and then signaled her forward. She couldn't help but smile into her bouquet of lilies and orchids. The tightly wound coordinator's role, at this point, was that of a nuptial crossing guard. And thank God she took it seriously. Otherwise, it would have been a stampede to the altar.

As her turn approached, Emily breathed a sigh of relief. She cast a glance behind her at Pat Evans, a glowing Lois at his side. He gripped his black Stetson in one hand, and with the other, covertly wiped at his eye. Welling emotion tightened Emily's chest. God, she hoped Lois knew how very lucky she was; the love of a father was a wonderful gift.

A loud *pssst* from the crossing guard jerked Emily back to attention. It was finally her turn to promenade. She took a deep lungful of air, let it out slowly, and stepped carefully through the door. The twins, with their dark brown curls, preceded her. The little girl, Meryl, or Early as most people called her, blithely tossed big handfuls of petals into the air. Many just happened to land on her brother, Lasiter. To everyone's delight, he grabbed a fistful of bright floral confetti from the basket his sister carried and dropped it accurately on her head. The guests all laughed. Noni's head popped out of the front row, and the twins fell obediently back in line.

Concentrating on her feet, Emily watched the comedy in front of her. The end of the aisle finally arrived, and she prepared to step up on the raised dais. She looked up, and her gaze was caught by the dark blue eyes of the best man. Her step faltered, and for a frightening moment, she thought the prediction she'd fall was coming true. The catastrophe was averted when his broad palm gripped her elbow. She hadn't even seen him move.

"Easy there, beautiful." His voice was deep and quiet. Perfectly gravelly.

Embarrassment burst into full bloom on her cheeks. "Sorry," she whispered. "I tripped on my hem." His hand remained steady beneath her arm as she glanced up at him and then back to her flowers. He smiled conspiratorially and handed her up into her place next to the pulpit just as the first notes of Mendelssohn's wedding march pealed through the crowd. She was spared further scrutiny as all eyes swung to the bride and her father.

The groom murmured, "Wow, isn't she incredible? I can't believe she picked me."

The groomsmen all chuckled into their ties. The best man cleared his throat, and they settled back to attention.

Lois *was* incredible. Exquisite. And about a hundred other adjectives. She seemed to float toward the altar. The only thing that belied her nerves was the death grip she had on her father's index finger. Emily was once again swept into the past. A memory of Lois as a tiny child beside her mother's grave, clinging in the same way to her father's finger. Pat had been just as stoic then as he was today. He was focused on the job of getting through the ceremony and would deal with his loss privately. Emily reminded herself to pay special attention to him in the coming hours. He was going need some TLC.

Vows were read and repeated. The couple joined in holy matrimony. There was a round of applause from the witnesses as the bride and groom turned from the altar for their introduction as man and wife.

Emily didn't hear a word of it. She made the mistake of making eye contact with the best man. The look of focus on his face stole her concentration, and for a moment she was riveted. She forced herself to look away and counted her breaths. Heat rose from her chest into her cheeks. It held the same fire that stung her arm when he'd touched her. It didn't mean anything other than she was embarrassingly clumsy, right? That and it had been an excruciatingly long time since a man touched her, even if it was only to keep her from face-planting on the altar steps. Confused, she swallowed hard. She felt foolish to need it and grateful to have it in the same instant. Just because need and desire surfaced together didn't mean it was a smart idea to act on it. And that alone was a good reason to discourage Noni's attempt to set her up for another undoubtedly spectacular fail.

She was making headway convincing herself of that when the man responsible for it stepped forward and offered his arm for the recessional.

"Come on, beautiful. What do you say, want to race to the bar?" He turned on the power of a full megawatt smile. Maybe he thought it was a sure winner when it came to the ladies.

Not this time. She refused to be the woman in his crosshairs. She returned his smile with a polite upturn at the corners of her lips and a cool look down her nose at his glib comment. "I'm pretty sure we've got some stuff to do," she whispered as she slipped her hand into the crook of his arm. "Just get me down the aisle without killing myself, and we'll consider it a win."

He stiffened slightly, and she felt bad for coming off as stuffy. Ordinarily, she enjoyed the banter, especially with gorgeous men. He damn sure was that. Every broad-shouldered, dark-haired, uniformed inch of him. What she didn't appreciate was the "ain't I a knockout, resistance is futile" attitude pouring off him.

No. Just no. Not this time.

Chapter Ten

The scent of flowers filled the ballroom, transforming the huge space from impressive to ethereal. Gauzy drapes festooned the crystal chandeliers. Flickering candelabras adorned each sparkling table. Centerpieces of bronze orchids and glitter-spangled mums in a breathtaking array of fall colors topped snowy, linen-covered tables.

A band set up to the side of the head table. They would remain in background mode until it was time for the dancing to start, and the party would go into full swing. Personally, Emily couldn't wait. She figured a drink or two wouldn't hurt anything, especially if she got to sit down and take her shoes off. For now, she was stuck in the receiving line. The only upside was the tower of muscle standing next to her. She might be resistant to his come-ons, but she didn't manage to remain completely unaffected.

The tower bent toward her and snagged her hand. He casually looped it back through the crook of his arm. "What? My arm was getting cold." He shrugged and unleashed that smile again, and oh, God…dimples. "Michael McCandlis, US Navy, Retired. At your service, Miss…?"

Emily leaned away just enough to let air back into her lungs. That cocksure grin was one powerful weapon. "Emily Converse. Stand-in maid of honor and not looking to get taken for a ride on your boat."

"Ship, ma'am. We don't have boats. Only have ships." He grinned. "It's all about the size, you know."

"Let's not do the 'size' thing. Okay, sailor?" Geez. Apparently, this guy thought she was some kind of clinging bimbo, all aquiver with anticipation and longing. "Besides, if we play nice and don't cause a ruckus, we can get the heck out of here that much quicker. Sound good?"

His arm flexed beneath her fingers. "I'm all for getting out of here, but I think it'll have to wait. Here comes the horde." He nodded at the line of guests currently queuing up to her right. "I've never done this before. What's the protocol?"

Emily smiled to herself. It seemed as though Mr. Perfect was just a little nervous. Cute. She should take pity on him, she really should. But where would the fun be in that? "Simple, you shake hands with the women, kiss the men. Rinse. Repeat. You'll get the hang of it after the first fifty or so."

He gave her a squinty-eyed look. "Pretty *and* a smart-ass." He stood a little straighter as the guests approached. "A combo I find hard to resist," he said out of the side of his mouth.

Holding the number one slot in the order of attendants, Michael and Emily found themselves on the end of the line closest to the bridal couple, separated from them by Noni and her husband, Bob. Pat held down the anchor position as the father of the bride. He was all smiles and solicitude, proudly introducing each guest to his new son-in-law.

The line seemed to stretch on forever. Emily rocked from foot to foot in a vain attempt to lessen the ache in her toes. She wished desperately for an end to the throng of well-wishers. Her counterpart, however, seemed unaware of her discomfort. She could swear he was taking sadistic delight in chatting amiably with every single skirt who waltzed by them.

She was just about to play the bathroom card when a voice brought her heart to a shuddering halt. Like a vanquished ogre come back to life, there he was pouring his corrosive presence back into her present. She'd been foolish to think he would lay down his weapons and let her return to Tamarack unscathed. His need for control was as pervasive as her need to destroy the vestiges of its hold on her. He'd almost cost her everything.

It had been half a lifetime since his shouts battered her ears with threats. Since he'd attempted to crush her race to freedom before it had a chance to begin. Her mind filled with the images of their final vicious tug of war over how her life would play out. The fight had been the final straw that stripped her bare of every childhood dream and slicked her in a thick coating of pure hatred.

His words were acid-etched in her memory.

"You always were a stupid kid," he'd railed at her. "The only thing you were ever good at was stirring the pot and causing trouble, just like your whoring mother. The only thing she got right was to die and save me the indignation of a public divorce. She couldn't even give me a son that was worth a damn. I should have known better than to take you on when I married her. You're just like her. Glib. Stubborn. Never looking at what's important, or who really matters in this world. You think you're so grown up, little girl? You think you can make it on your own?"

"You got that right, Ray. On my own. Without you," she screamed back at him.

"You'll get no help from me, and you can kiss your trust fund goodbye. I'll see to it your money is tied up for years. You'll waste what little you have on lawyers before you see a red damn cent. You can bet your sweet ass on that," he'd roared.

The Right Honorable Senator from the great state of Colorado, Raymond J. Domenico, her stepfather, moved forward in the line. Emily ceased to breathe; every muscle froze in place.

Michael reacted to the stiffening of her body. His hand swept down her arm and flashed across her as though prepared to push her out of harm's way. Instinctively, she leaned toward him as he stepped forward to shield her. She forced herself to meet her stepfather's gaze directly.

"Emily," the senator said in his most politically correct tone. "I was told you were back in town. I'm surprised you haven't come to see me."

Her lungs finally reinflated; she shook herself back into the present. All the years of separation and self-analysis that should have saved her deserted her in favor of the lost, angry kid she had been the last time she'd seen the man. Wasn't it enough that he'd stolen her mother, changed her brother into something unrecognizable? What cosmic law allowed the bastard to hold any sway over her? All it took was "I'm surprised you haven't come to see me." A single sentence and the years of pain, fear, and anguish came sweeping back.

And it pissed her off.

She ignored the shiver that crept across her skin and stiffened her spine. The little girl he had frightened and cowed retreated into the corner of Emily's heart, and the adult stepped forward. She drew a centering breath, raised her chin, and glared at him. "It's a small-town, Senator. I figured we'd run into each other eventually." Her voice was smooth, not a quiver to be heard. She glanced up at Michael and was surprised to find him scowling at her stepfather. At that moment, she liked him a bit more than was comfortable. "Allow me to present my date, Navy SEAL Michael McCandlis. This is my stepfather, Senator Ray Domenico."

Michael swung a surprised glance to her. He relaxed his stance fractionally and reached a large palm out to shake the man's hand. "Senator."

Grateful that he was willing to play along, she slipped her hand around his bicep as she watched Michael's hand dwarf the senator's. She felt the swell of strength applied and got a secret thrill knowing his grip was a touch stronger than necessary.

The senator retracted his hand and flexed it. "Another SEAL, huh." He flicked a dismissive glance at the gold trident on Michael's chest. "I noticed the groom had quite the contingent on his side of the altar. We thank you for your service to this great nation, son." Emily's stomach soured as her stepfather effortlessly slipped back into electioneering mode.

"It's an honor to serve, sir," Michael answered levelly. "I'm familiar with your service, as well. Are you still active on the Armed Services Committee? I understand there have been some changes lately."

Emily looked up at him, surprised he had any

knowledge of her stepfather, let alone anything about his career. She loved that Ray's habitual influence-peddling ways forced his resignation from the committee. It pleased her even more that Michael disliked him on sight.

"I've taken a less-public role for now. One never knows what the future will bring. Does one?" The senator turned back to Emily. "You look lovely." He gave her a once-over from hair to shoes and back again. "You remind me strongly of your mother just before we lost her. Such a tragedy and so many unanswered questions. The kind that leaves you with a lifetime of wondering. Don't you agree?" He paused. "I hope your return to Tamarack is a good move on your part. But as I said, one never knows." He gave her a smirk that passed for a smile and moved off into the crowd.

She knew the bastard was fishing, trying to see if she'd come home to cause trouble.

She tried to relax as the distance increased between them, but her effort morphed into a full body shudder. The tremble started in the hand that clutched Michael's arm and worked its way down to her knees.

"Okay, that was intense," Michael murmured.

She glanced up at him and fought to control her rapid breath. She'd been a hair's breadth from slipping into fight or flight mode until Domenico slipped away. A tingle of appreciation leaked through her fear as she remembered that Michael's gut reaction had been to protect her.

Michael watched him retreat. "I think I've had about all of this meet and greet I can stand. How 'bout you?"

When she gave a shaky nod, he leaned out of line

and caught Dillon's eye. He gave a lift of his chin toward the bar and slipped his arm around Emily's waist. Dillon nodded back and whispered something to Pat Evans. Pat scowled down the line as the senator disappeared into the crowd, then looked at Michael and gave him a grim smile.

"C'mon," Michael said. "I could use a drink, and I'm betting you could too." He tucked her into his side and walked her into the virtually empty bar.

She slid onto a bar stool and lifted a hand to the bartender. "Maker's Mark on the rocks and don't be shy about it."

She closed her eyes and took a calming breath. The welcome tinkle of ice in crystal landed in front of her. The drink was halfway to her mouth when she felt the warmth of Michael's body at her back. Strange how a girl could miss something that had never been hers. She looked up, caught by the steady steel-blue of his eyes as he watched her in the mirror behind the bar. Her face, her whole body was tense. He stood close, a solid presence behind her. She could swear he was breathing her in. She was suddenly caught up, wishing fervently for more than a brief moment behind the safety of his presence. A sojourn in the quiet where someone else chose, someone else picked up the pieces. It had been ages since anyone had been on her side, considered her first. She pushed back a surprising wash of longing.

"Can I buy you a drink, sailor?" As openers went, it was pretty cheesy, but she couldn't drum up the wherewithal to be brilliant.

"That's my line, beautiful." His voice vibrated up her spine.

"I saved you a seat." She gestured to the line of

empty bar stools beside her. Apparently, the buffet held more interest to the guests than the alcohol. *More fools they.*

"I can see that." He took the stool next to her and ordered a Corona. "Now you want to tell me what the hell that was with the good senator?"

She sucked down half of her drink, then took a breath. "Nope." She shook her head. The very last thing she wanted to do was talk about the past. That man had spent too many years living rent free in her head; he didn't rate one more iota of consideration. But Michael McCandlis looked like a very determined guy.

He narrowed his eyes at her. "Okay…so not talking about the elephant. I can do that." He paused for a moment, then said, "Want to discuss the weather or the Broncos? How about the fact that you smell incredible and are hands down the most gorgeous woman here tonight?"

His unwavering gaze made her heart beat faster and brought goose bumps to her arms. "Ha. Smooth transition. I can see you're an alarming, charming man, sailor. Thanks again for playing along with being my 'date.' " The stealth attack by her childhood's worst nightmare was inevitable, and it scared her shitless. She employed her fallback position and threw up a wall of bullshit. "See, I thought I had my bastard-repelling force field all tuned up; apparently, it's got some holes in it. Looks like I'll have to go back to Jedi school for a refresher." She held up her hands in a fair imitation of Luke Skywalker. "Can you feel that?"

Michael's chuckle was a deep rumble. "I feel something all right. I'll have to reserve judgment until I've had a chance to analyze it." He turned toward her and laid his gold-braided sleeve along the back of her swivel seat. Leaning in, he took a deep breath of her perfume. "Mm-mm, Cool Water. My personal favorite. There's something else beneath it, though. Something purely you."

Not bad for a distraction. God, that voice did good things to her. Gooey things. She returned the gesture, taking a long sample of his scent. "You smell like—fresh air. How is that possible?"

His one-sided smile was pure deviltry. "Clean living and pure thoughts."

Emily snorted and slapped a hand over her mouth in chagrin. The bourbon was clearly having a hasty effect.

He burst out a full rolling laugh. "You snort-laughed, I love it. I'll make it my mission to gather as many of those as possible tonight." He looked down at her bare shoulders for a moment, then let his gaze wander over her face. His blue eyes sparkled with interest. "Man, you're pretty. Skin like cream and raspberries." He studied her, his head cocked slightly. "You've got an intriguing face. Expressive eyes with a few happy lines at the corners." His gaze moved to her mouth. "You smile easily but not in a fake way. I get the feeling you're a 'take me or leave me' kind of girl. What's that like? To just breathe in and out, and do your best to roll with what comes your way?"

She frowned down at her empty glass, uncomfortable with his scrutiny, and signaled the bartender for a refill. "If you only knew, sailor." She cleared her throat. She needed to clear the air of unanswered questions before she was tempted to flirt her way out of being honest with this man. "I probably owe you an explanation about my stepfather's little display of character. Huh? We don't get along, and I didn't think he'd be here. He wasn't on the guest list, so he took me by surprise. That's all."

"You don't owe me explanations, Emily. I don't like bullies. Never have. Some of them are exceptionally good at hiding who they are. I've got my own version of your bastard-repelling force field. It's not very subtle or sophisticated, but it gets the job done."

She glanced down at the large hand that flexed on the edge of the bar. "Where were you twenty years ago, sailor? I could have used some backup."

"That's a big question, Emily Converse. One best left for another time. Right now, I think it's a waste of a great night and a gorgeous dress to hide away in this bar. So I'm wondering how you'd feel about a dance. I hear the band is pretty good, and I for one could stand a night to concentrate on the beautiful woman in my arms. Maybe I'll even show you a few of the moves I learned in Dubai."

Emily snorted again. Michael's grin snapped back into place, and his eyes twinkled with amusement. This man had a way about him that teased her inner hussy to the fore. He liked to spar and play. She was just the girl to accommodate him. Perhaps Noni knew what she was doing after all. There was definitely something liberating about spending time with a handsome man. It reminded a girl that, regardless of the snakes lurking in the grassy margins, all possibilities were not lost. She believed that as long as this man's arms were around her, there wouldn't be anything else snapping at her heels tonight.

"Dubai, huh? Now that would be extremely interesting," she said and slipped a finger beneath his lapel to peek inside his jacket. "You got veils hidden under your uniform?"

"I don't like to brag or anything, but I've got a lot of stuff going on under this uniform." He ran his finger down her arm and took her hand. "Wanna see?"

She laughed and looked him up and down. Maybe this time it would work out differently. Maybe this time, she could find...what exactly? Probably nothing more than a few hours of hot, sweaty belly rubbing. Nothing wrong with that, right? A little steamy stress relief? Meaningless, mindless, messy. And then what? Go home alone, crawl back into her safe little hole. Now there was an enticing image.

Emily's smile dimmed. "Down, sailor." Hadn't she decided not to do this again, no more bending to the pull, right? Because this was how it started. She'd recognized the glint in his eyes; she responded to it. Spontaneous attraction. It set her up for an inevitable slide into disappointment. It was how she'd managed to get married, shoved aside, divorced, and damn near broke. She gave herself a mental slap to the libido.

She slipped her hand out of his and reached for her recently refreshed glass. Obviously, drinking didn't help. She pushed it back. Alcohol and orgasms, the alpha and omega of scenarios guaranteed to rob her of the ability to make genuinely good decisions. "Look, I appreciate your willingness to step up and protect me from the monster in my closet, but don't look at me as a pushover. Especially if the direction you're pushing is toward your mattress."

"Damn, you're prickly. *And* all over the map."

Michael frowned back at her. "Look, I'm trying to distract you, that's all. I'm not trying to push you in any direction you don't want to go." He looked down at his beer and brushed a broad thumb through the condensation lacing its surface. "Dang. It used to be easier to flirt a little and sweep a woman off her feet. But I'll be damned before I give up the fight so easily." He hesitated, studied her for a moment. A determined frown brought a crease to his brow as if he was prepared for her to shut him down, but dead set on the risk. "I'm just gonna lay it out there. Okay? I feel some kind of connection to you. I don't know why. Don't really care. I'm only in town for the wedding, and then it's back to California. I'm not looking for anything other than a pleasant evening, a little fun, and a few moments with you. That's not so bad, right?"

Emily sighed. He was so tempting, and he was right. She *was* blowing hot and cold. "Sorry for being so touchy. I guess it wouldn't hurt to unfurl a little and see what the evening brings. Besides, Lois and Dillon deserve more from their chief attendants than a scuffle over who comes out on top. Verbally, that is."

He unleashed not only his smile but those adorable dimples. "See? Now there you go, getting all double entendre on me. Keep it up, and I'll think you're toying with me."

Oh, Christ on a cracker. She could feel the call from the deep end of the obsession pool. It sounded suspiciously like that siren's song was coming from the man sitting on the bar stool next to her. She downed a swallow of her drink and cocked an ear toward the ballroom.

The sound of a John Denver waltz filtered into the

bar. That would be the first dance for the bride and the groom. Emily didn't want to miss it. Besides, if Mr. Perfection in Dress Blues could handle something as lyrical as "Annie's Song," he could probably make it through the bunny hop. Maybe even manage a segue into the Lambada or something.

She enjoyed the look of relief on his face when she folded her hand around his and slipped off the barstool. With a glance over her shoulder, she drew him toward the dance floor. "C'mon, Salomé. Let's see those moves you're so proud of."

Chapter Eleven

The guests formed a rough circle around the dance floor. Emily led Michael along the wall at the front near the head table, found a gap in the viewers, and stepped to the edge of the floor. The bride and her father completed their turn around the space. As the music moved into the second verse, Pat handed his youngest child off to her new husband for the remainder of the song. It was the same music he and his wife Anne had danced to when they married. She saw the weight of memories lying heavily on the father of the bride. He and Anne had been together for too short a time when cancer took her. At times like this, Pat probably felt her loss like icicles in his heart.

Unexpectedly, the sting of tears blurred her vision as she watched the young couple turn and circle through the beautiful song. The lyrics spoke of wishes fulfilled, longing soothed, counterparts sought and found. It was truly the perfect wedding song. So much hope was packed into its words. So much love.

She jumped when Michael's arms drew her back into him. She didn't try to keep from sinking into his embrace. He felt like a favorite blanket wrapped around her. She was only mildly surprised at how much it filled an unrealized need.

The song ended with Dillon performing an elegant dip with Lois arched over his arm. The crowd applauded, and Dillon's face flamed as if he'd forgotten there was an audience. Lois, however, curtsied to the gathering and planted an audible smooch on her new husband's mouth. Emily had never seen anyone so completely, blindingly happy. It brought another stinging rush to her eyes. She flinched when a hot, wet tear splashed on the skin above her bodice.

He tightened his hold on her waist, and his lips brushed her ear. "Don't, beautiful. They'll be fine. Dillon is a good man, and he loves her more than the air he breathes. You don't have to worry."

"I'm happy for them, I really am. I wish them smooth days and warm nights." Her voice was wistful. "It just…it's been my experience that when you're that much in love, life has a way of stealing the sparkle more quickly than we expect." It was hard not to be jaded.

"Shh, none of that." Michael gave her a gentle squeeze and a nudge forward as the music moved into an easy rhythm. His voice was all silk and dark chocolate. "I believe you lured me out here with the promise of dancing. Don't leave me hanging."

Her sigh was filled with wishes. "I did, didn't I? And you fell for it. I'll try not to step on your toes." She turned in his arms and backed them onto the dance floor. *Oh, what the hell. A little dancing never hurt anyone.*

He laughed and spun her around. "I can take it. SEAL. Remember?"

One dance turned into several. Finally, just before the band moved to a break, they played a smooth sexy salsa. Those moves he had bragged about poured over her as he tugged loose his tie and pulled her tight to his body. There was a visceral quality in the way he handled her body. Practiced. Easy. Sexy as hell. She loved the way he tucked each available curve into contact with him. Emily's misgivings dissolved in his heat, and she stopped resisting the urge to just…go with it. She gave in to the feeling of the music and the man. Surrendered to his artful, careful blending of lover and partner.

****

It had been ages since Michael had taken the time to enjoy the flirtation of the first meeting with a woman. One who didn't spend most of her nights cruising portside bars looking to make points with a SEAL. A guy forgot after a while there could be anything else.

He loved the way she flowed along with him, smooth as glass. She responded to his every move as though they'd danced this close, this intimately, for years. The tightness in his shoulders relaxed, only to be replaced by another deeper need. Maybe this was real, maybe not. Maybe he should stop thinking and just…go with it. Because beneath the hand pressed to his chest, his heart rate had picked up. The half-mast in his pants pressed intimately against her thigh. She smiled up at him, and he gave her a low-lidded smile in return. He felt aware of every pore of skin, every flex and release. They seemed promisingly different somehow. He realized suddenly that he wanted this more than he'd thought possible.

Intricate steps didn't confuse her; she moved flawlessly with him. He raised his arm, turned her into a spin, and stopped her rotation with the strong grasp of his hands at her hips. The fabric of her dress wrapped her in silky layers of softness, but he could feel the heat building underneath. Her pulse fluttered in her throat, and her chest moved rapidly. She pulled in cool air and pushed out steamy responses to his every touch. Suddenly, the dance changed to a different kind of choreography. They were no longer simply finding enjoyment in the music or the fleeting touch of dancers in concert. They'd moved into a new awareness of an age-old chemical reaction...attraction.

He pulled back slightly and studied her face. Her cheeks were flushed, lids slow to react as she studied him back. The tip of her tongue moistened her parted lips, and her teeth caught the fullness.

Michael swallowed hard. "I think you better stop that," he growled, "or we're in serious trouble here."

She smiled and lowered her eyes to his mouth. "You think too much." She threaded her fingertips through the hair at his collar. "Let's just dance. I love the way I fit against you."

"Is that what we're doing, Emily? Dancing?" he asked, pulling her even closer. He felt her warm breath all the way to his soul.

"For the moment, Michael, for the moment. We'll figure out the rest as we go." She pulled his cheek to hers and did a subtle swivel that took him from half-mast to full-salute in the breadth of her sigh.

The world and the dance floor retreated into a haze. He felt the strength of his own arms, the softness of her breasts pressed against his chest and the music. She relaxed control, granted his right to lead. A focused awareness crackled in the touch points of their bodies with a willingness to up the voltage. The rhythm, the music slipped into the background. It became secondary to the movement of blood in his veins. Nothing existed outside of the space of their entwined arms and mingled breath. Subtle changes of position and direction ebbed and flowed from his body to hers, seamlessly communicating his building desire.

The music warmed and spread like honey over them. Her muscles became fluid at each brush of his fingers along her body. The fine hair on her arms seemed to become sensitive, alive and seeking his next stroke. She was malleable, accepting, awash in his focused attention. It was overwhelming, exciting, and…welcome. He couldn't remember ever having this kind of reaction. Not to his first lover, to any woman, ever. It was as if she were a gift conjured by a wish. Impossible, improbable, unlike anything his past had led him to expect or deserve.

When the music ended, he didn't release her. The spell that had swept them up remained as firm as his arm behind her back when he draped her over his thigh in the last notes of the song. Time hovered for an instant before reality came back to him.

Emily grasped his arms, took a deep breath, and struggled to stand. "Wow…that was…" She stammered to a halt. She looked up at him, her gaze confused.

He needed to get them out of here, off this dance floor, and someplace more private. "Yeah, it was." His voice was a raspy whisper. He cleared his throat. "You want to get some air? Because I need to cool off a minute."

Michael began to lead her toward the terrace doors. He was never more grateful for the length of his formal jacket. Not that it made walking any easier, just less embarrassing.

Son of a bitch, was he some horny recruit on his first shore leave?

Apparently yes, yes, he was.

Chapter Twelve

Michael's hand clasped Emily's firmly as if he feared she'd escape. Perhaps that would have been the smartest course of action, but her sense had taken a temporary leave of absence. She tripped along behind him, out the doors of the ballroom, and into the soft darkness of the open terrace. After the press of people and the crowd of guests, the cool quiet was a balm to her skin.

He led her across the broad flagstones of the open-air space to a raised firepit well away from brightly lit doors. The flames provided a flickering highlight to the inviting space surrounding it. Deep benches and cushioned chairs beckoned them to share the heat of the fire.

"Hey, sailor, slow down." Emily tugged on his grip. "A girl could break an ankle in these shoes. I'm not sure coming out here is a good idea, anyway."

In answer, he stopped, dropped her hand, slung an arm around her back. His other arm slipped beneath her knees, and he scooped her up against his hard chest. "We can't have any broken bones, now can we?" His voice vibrated through every cell of her body.

She squeaked in surprise and then laughed at his caveman antics. He handled her body as if she weighed less than a feather. She was swamped in delight; the undeniable desire to giggle like a teenager on her first date escaped up her throat. Damn, but the man was more than she'd bargained for.

Before she could staunch the laughter, he crossed the terrace and slid her slowly down his body till her toes touched the stone. He leaned her back into the railing of the balcony and erased the rest of the space between them. He pulled her tight against his body, all strength and determination. Emily smiled a knowing answer to the question his dark eyes asked.

Would she let him kiss her? She answered by sweeping her thumb across his bottom lip. He nipped the pad with just enough force to let her know what he had in mind wouldn't be slow or gentle. Then he took her mouth with power and command that robbed her of her ability to do anything but feel. He licked the seam of her mouth, and she opened to him. The deep slide of his tongue left her with the knowledge that he would be just as thorough and hungry for all her secret places. That strange fade of surroundings swept over her again. The air she panted between the slide of lips and the mingling of sensations seemed in short supply.

She pulled him in with equal desire, willing him to take her past the edges of her emptiness and fill her with his potency. She was glad that for all the strength and skill he poured into the kiss, there was still care. He could have ravaged her. She'd anticipated that, almost relished the thought. She wanted to be lost in the first heady mingling of air and touch, but she sensed in him a need deeper than simple heat and want. He took the time to taste her, savor her, push her toward his goal without forcing her to relent. At each turn, before he went further, he asked consent through touch and hesitation.

Did she like kisses along her jaw? She hummed her pleasure. Her chin lifted, and her head tilted, granting access to the sensitive skin behind her ear. Did nuzzling the fine hair behind that ear cause the goose bumps that traveled up her arms? She shivered her answer and ran her hands down his broad chest to feel the warmth of the shirt beneath his jacket. Her palms flexed over the hard pecs she found there. They shared murmured sounds of approval. His deep in his throat, and hers a whispered, "Yes."

Her belly did an enticing rub against his hardness. She slipped her arms around his waist. The flat of her hands pressed him into firmer contact with her. He tightened his grasp on her hip and shifted in response; she was reassured she wouldn't be disappointed in the gift he had for her. It felt as though he put his all into the way he held her, touched her, made certain she knew he wanted her.

Emily soaked it up like rain on parched earth. Her hands found hot skin beneath the cotton of his starched shirt, and she wanted...more. More skin, more contact with the hard strength of him, the demanding graze of his teeth on her neck. More of the taste of his mouth, of the rasp of his beard as it roughed her cheek. She breathed in his clean, male scent. Tested the flat disks of his nipples, the ridges of his abs, and the rounded swell of his wide shoulders. Desire, fierce and hot, pulled her along. She flipped open the last button on his jacket and finally managed to push back the heavy wool. There was too much fabric between them. His tie was next, then the stiff buttons of his shirt.

He dropped a trail of kisses on her lips, her eyes, her collarbone. His hands ran down her back and up over her rib cage. His thumbs grazed the underside of her breasts and brushed over the pucker of hard tips straining for release. He paused to run matching circles around the tight buds, then slipped his fingers into the fragile fabric at the edge of her bodice and pulled the neckline down to expose her breasts. His lips blazed a trail down her throat. He tasted the junction of her neck and her shoulder and then the valley between the soft mounds.

Emily managed to breathe out his name between gasps and whimpers of heart-pumping pleasure. "Michael."

"You taste like citrus and...you." He sounded like he was searching for words. Somehow his jacket had left his body, and his shirt was open to his waist. She smiled against his hair. And dug her nails a little deeper into the triangle of curly hair between his pecs.

His hand slid down, around the full swell of her ass, and gathered the fabric until he found the seam of her panties. His fingers slipped inside the silk to brush hot, damp flesh. *Yes.* He delved deeper, and she lifted a taut thigh, encouraging his access. She couldn't stop herself from moving closer to his center.

Oh, God. The size, the feel of him was nearly her undoing. Was she really going to do this? If she let this man past her newly constructed barriers, was she doing herself harm, or was this only meaningless indulgence—stress relief? She needed to slow this down. Think logically. If only it didn't feel so damn good to be touched, wanted.

"Michael." Her whisper was rough. "I think..." She trailed off as his tongue swept the edge of her nipple. She felt the fractional release of her zipper.

"Don't think. Thinking is overrated." His mouth found the other hard, beaded tip beneath her neckline. His teeth grazed it just hard enough to bring a quivering intake of her breath.

Her voice was a tiny bit clearer now. "So is public nudity," she said into his ear and took the lobe into her mouth, then released it with a nip of her own.

He leaned back from her and blinked several times. His nostrils flared, and he breathed deeply. Could he smell the onslaught of her apprehension? "You have a gift for robbing me of my good intentions, Emily Converse." He raised his hand and threaded his fingers gently through her hair. He closed her zipper and adjusted the hem of her dress. Somehow it had worked its way up to expose the length of her thigh. "I came out here to cool off, and look what happened." His smile was uncertain. "If you need an apology, I plead temporary insanity."

She glanced up at him through her lashes and pulled her bodice back in place. Then she noticed his unbuttoned glory. She took a beat to appreciate the hard-packed ridges on his abdomen, then began to re-button his shirt. She laid a palm along his jaw and pressed a soft kiss to his mouth. His eyes were heavy-lidded and luminous in the moonlight, his skin flushed with desire. His full lips were swollen and glistening from their kisses. She smiled shyly. He was the most heart-stopping, desirable man she'd ever seen.

"No, I like your brand of apology. Call me crazy, but if you apologize any better, we're going to need a change of venue." Her voice was husky, warm honey and whiskey.

"Hmm, that could take all night long, beautiful.

I've got a room, assuming none of my guys has appropriated it. What do you think of that? Will you take a chance on me?" He searched her face for a moment. A flicker of uncertainty brought twin lines between his dark brows. "I can see your mind working. Tell me, what can I do to convince you?"

"God, I'm so tempted to say yes." Emily rested her forehead on his chest. This glimpse of his honorable side pushed her closer to going with his version of how their night should end. The decision was hers. "I'm just not sure it's a good idea."

She *really* wanted to say more than that. *Take me. Throw me over your shoulder and carry me up those stairs. Toss me on the bed and help me remember what being wanted feels like.* At the same time, the stubborn voice of reason reminded her of the promise she'd do things differently. She couldn't afford to act like a horny teenager racing to an anonymous hotel room with the quarterback. Where, in the name of all things holy, was the smart, well-reasoned woman she had been just an hour ago?

"Michael, listen…"

His grip tightened on her hips, and he nestled his body against her. She felt every inch of him.

He gave her an unrepentant smile. "Just a reminder of what you'll be missing if you change your mind."

She pushed away from him a fraction.

"What's going on, beautiful?" His warm breath stirred her hair as he placed a kiss on top of her head. "Crap, I hate second thoughts."

"Yes… No… It's just… This is not who I am anymore, not who I want to be anyway," she said into his chest. "I don't get what happens when you touch me. It's like a switch flips, and I stop thinking. All I want is more. It's crazy how much I want you."

Could he possibly understand? Would he? Or did she seem like the worst possible cliché, a tease? There wasn't a nerve in her body that hadn't fritzed out on this balcony under a dark canopy of starlight. The man seemed to know what she wanted before she recognized the desire for a shift of hand or change of angle. She'd willingly tossed any kind of restraint right into the fire and welcomed the burn. Damn.

Michael chuckled darkly. "And strangely enough, that's okay with me." He kissed her lightly. "Look, neither of us are children, and you're definitely no late-night pick up." He cleared his throat. "I want you, Emily. I feel a connection to you; I don't understand why any better than you do. It's like a curtain drops around us, and everything outside it fades to gray. Weird, huh? Damn sure nothing I've ever felt before." He stood straighter. "But if you need to back off the intensity, it might kill me, but I'll do my best to understand. It'll have to be all right with me."

"Pretty sure they call what we're feeling good old-fashioned lust. I'm no stranger. It's just that… Hell, I'm in recovery." Yeah, that was mostly accurate. Wasn't there a twelve-step program for survivors of the Divorce Wars? Step one: admit you have a problem. Step two: pray for deliverance. Step three: turn over making decisions about partners to God, because sister, your picker is broken.

His body stiffened. "Seriously? Like the Sexaholics Anonymous kind of recovery? Shit, wouldn't that just figure. Man, I can't seem to catch a break." He pushed her from him gently. "I don't know much about it, but this can't be the way to keep your chip or whatever."

"No, you idiot. I'm not addicted to sex!" She pushed him back. Geez, had she come on that strong? Surely not, please God. "I meant I'm recovering from a lifetime of stupid choices and an incredibly shitty divorce. I shouldn't be even considering this. But you—you're all the things that get me to toss my common sense out the window, right along with my panties. And then I do stupid things. I don't even have liquor to blame it on." She sighed, her shoulders drooping in disappointment. "I think it's time to call it a night and just chalk this up to poor timing." She turned and took a step toward the lights of the ballroom.

"Whoa, Emily. Don't run away from me. I…" He hesitated. "I thought we clicked, and I didn't think much past that." He turned her back around, letting his hands rest on her upper arms. "I know you have a life beyond this bubble of ours. I have my own shit to deal with. But here's the thing, I'm not usually the guy who acts on impulse and sweeps a stranger, no matter how beautiful, into the darkness of a party to make out like a horny kid. I'm in command most of the time. That's what I do, who I am. Or it used to be anyway. It's just, well, tonight you took me by complete surprise, and I let the reins loose a little." He kissed her forehead and then her cheek. "Please don't leave. We could just sit and get to know each other. You know, watch the fire, keep our hands to ourselves, tell our stories. How does that sound? Will you take that much of a chance on me?"

"What's the point? You're only here for a short time. I'm here till who knows when, and that's unlikely to change. Let's just chalk this up to a giant slip in my program." She studied his face in the light of the fire.

He seemed sincere. His expression betrayed no hint of anything other than determination and a fierce focus. It made her want to pause and listen with more than her ears. Hope dug stubborn tendrils into the walls she'd constructed around what was left of her heart.

"Let's not." A stubborn frown wrinkled his brows together. "I don't know why you're pushing back, but I'll listen if you need me to. Doesn't mean I'll give up trying to get to know you, whether we do that vertically or horizontally. It does mean I can be patient. My time is my own. If I decide to stay in Colorado for a bit, then that's what I'll do. Would that be so bad? You can teach me to fly fish or show me where you hid out as a kid. I just want to take the time to know you. That's a good thing. Right?"

She gave a derisive laugh. "That's not what you were looking for when you dragged me out here. And frankly, I don't think starting something with you is good for either of us. You really should look elsewhere for what you need. I'm just not—"

She didn't get to finish her rejection. Michael smothered it with his mouth in a kiss so thorough and drugging that it swept her right back to the brink of…a looming cliff. Her hands were back in his hair, on his thick, hot neck. His tongue robbed her ability to do anything other than relinquish what remained of her control and common sense. She knew nothing beyond the feel of his hands, the fresh taste of him, and the sound of the blood roaring in her head.

She almost missed her best friend's voice behind her.

"Em? What the hell?" Noni's voice climbed an

octave with each word. "Seriously?"

Emily was gathered closer to him, if that were possible, and spun away from the tornado that swept through the ballroom doors. His sudden movement shocked her into consciousness, and she broke their kiss with a wet release of suction. Her head popped up over his shoulder, and she struggled to focus in the direction of Noni's voice.

"Noni?" Her voice squeaked like a child desperately trying to avoid taking the blame for the forbidden cookie in her hand. The very last thing she wanted was for Michael to bear witness to being raked over Noni's proverbial coals. Wait—wasn't it Noni's idea for her to let go tonight? Hell, yes, it was. She glared at her friend. "What's going on?"

"Look, I know this is awkward as hell, but you two need to break up this love fest. Your brother needs you in the bar." Noni paused for a breath and then shook her finger in Michael's face. "You, hot stuff, need to get your men under control and out of the bar before all of you end up in jail."

"Ian? He's here?" Emily was having difficulty keeping up. She disengaged Michael's hands from her waist and stepped around him. "What's he got to do with trouble in the bar?"

"Christ Almighty. What did I just say? Yes, he's here, and I don't know what happened, but there's a lot of shouting. Daddy will have a fit if you don't go straighten this out. Lois will have a coronary, and her night'll be ruined. So move it!"

"Oh, my God. Okay."

Emily swept a trembling hand down her dress and found the hem had again been rucked up around her thighs. Her bodice was in serious danger of revealing an embarrassing amount of the girls. Her hair was in a wild tangle around her shoulders, and she was missing an earring. Michael hadn't fared any better. His shirt was untucked, half unbuttoned, and looked as though he'd slept in it. His tie and his jacket were missing. Even more disturbing, his belt was hanging open, and the button at the top of his fly was undone. Damn, how long had they been out here? And more importantly, how close had she come to giving it away in public? Her hands fluttered, uselessly trying to pull her dignity back together.

Michael cleared his throat. "Give us a moment, will you, Noni? We'll be right behind you, I promise."

His voice was calmer and more reasonable than Emily felt. What the fuck had she been thinking? Nothing, that was the problem. She hadn't been thinking at all. Her body had been doing all the decision making and none of the consequence considering. As usual. This really had to stop. Now.

"Yes, Noni. What he said. Just give me a minute to put myself together. Okay?"

Emily gave her friend a pleading look. There was no way in hell Noni would ever let her live this down. Even if the whole "pick up a sailor" *had* been her idea in the first place. Damn and blast. Now she would have to find a graceful way to dump the most perfect...well, everything her imagination could conjure. And to top that off, she had to do it in favor of cleaning up yet another scene her little brother had doubtlessly brought about all by himself.

Noni drew her five-foot, two-inch frame up with a huff of irritation. "You bet your ass you'll be right behind me, 'cause if I have to come back out here looking for you, it won't be pretty. I can promise you that!" She stomped her foot and turned on her heel.

Emily was in the process of shaking out her skirts and trying desperately not to look up at him, as Michael turned to her.

"Hey." His fingertips lightly swept a stray strand of hair behind her ear. "It's too late to ignore me, beautiful. Look at me."

His voice caused goose bumps to rise on her skin. "I can't. If I do, what's left of my volition will evaporate. We'll end up in another lip lock, and Noni will kill me." Her voice was the shaky whisper of a woman who intended to do the right thing regardless of her desires. "I'm chalking this up to hormones and stupidity. Gonna go find my damn brother and get the hell out of here."

She ran an exploratory hand through her hair and discovered that more than half of it had tumbled out of her sleek up-do. Nimbly, she plucked out the remaining pins and shook the cascade free. Only then did she look him in the eyes.

Michael studied her for a moment. "I could say that I'm sorry I put you in this embarrassing position, but I'm not." He paused in the act of tucking in his shirt and reached for her hand. "Frankly, and I know this sounds like a line, but I would have done just about anything to get you out here. Emily, I wasn't expecting you. Didn't think there was anyone on this planet that could draw me in the way you have, and you haven't even tried. I can tell you're not out there fishing for a man. In fact, from what you've said, you're doing just the opposite. I find that to be one of the most attractive things about you."

He slowly drew on her fingers till he could grasp her wrist and then reeled her against his chest. She came flush against him.

"Now that's more like it." He took a big breath and slowly let it out into her hair. "I swear you're like cool water on a sunburn to me." His grasp on her wrist relaxed, and he held her hand pressed against his chest. The heartbeat beneath her fingers returned to a quieter pace. His shoulders loosened, and his breathing slowed.

"Michael…we've got to go." She buried her forehead in the hollow beneath his chin. "This isn't real. This is just lust and champagne and atmosphere and opportunity. That's all." She felt him tense. All for the better, no one needed to get hurt here. "This always happens to me. I get carried away and mistake lust for l…well, other stuff. Then I get hurt when it falls to shit. Let's just call this quits and move on." They could part as just a bit more than casual acquaintances. She could resume her "new leaf" plan, and he could go back to California or Miami or whatever ocean he lived on, and they would both be fine. Just fine. No harm. No foul.

"You'll have to explain that to me because I'd be amazed to be wrong here. I've got a résumé as long as my arm when it comes to women and what they want. I've managed to stay single for a long time by using that hard-earned education." He pushed her back to arm's length and studied her face. "You're barkin' up the wrong SEAL if you think I don't know the difference between honest passion and spontaneous lust. So just drop the 'I do this all the time, and it doesn't mean anything' shit. I'm not fooled for a second."

Emily contemplated him for a moment, assessing his words, and then slashed a mental hand through them. There was no way in hell this could be anything other than the obvious, no way in everlovin' hell. She also knew she was past being able to draw a rational conclusion. Especially while he was touching her. Discretion being the better part of valor and all that, she shook off his hands and retreated several steps. She wasn't valorous. She was easily swayed. She knew that. This simply wasn't the time or the place for figuring out the truth of the two of them. If there was the two of them.

Time to strike an end to their little interlude. "Look, I don't mean to dent your feelings or impugn your long, impressive list of credentials where women are concerned, but right now we both have a situation to deal with. For better or worse, we'll have to table this, better yet forget this. My brother needs me, and your men apparently need you. Let's just go take care of the real world and move on. Okay?"

"Oh, really?" He growled a harsh whisper, and she was suddenly in his arms. "Well, forget this, beautiful."

His searing kiss branded her lips. It drugged her senses and swamped her body with a want so deep, so sure that when he released her and stalked through the doors into the light, all she could do was stare after him.

Chapter Thirteen

Ray popped a plump shrimp in his mouth from the sumptuous spread on the buffet tables and sipped his third glass of champagne. He congratulated himself on two fronts. One, he'd surprised the hell out of Emily and sounded sufficiently ominous doing it. Two, he'd managed, in the ensuing time, to leverage his attendance at this boring reception into boosting his reelection coffer by securing several large donations. The latter accomplished while simultaneously distracting said deep pockets away from the disgusting display of poor judgment on the part of his stepdaughter. It had been a profitable night. He gave himself a hearty pat on the back.

He was reaching for another prawn when he caught a murmured conversation over the shoulder of a woman standing behind him.

"Seriously, Shirley. I thought they were going to throw down, right there in the bar. I mean, I'm all for equal rights and all that, but do they have to display their personal...proclivities for the world to see? And he was clearly on something too. I mean, honestly, it was embarrassing. The son of a senator—shocking. Just shocking."

Ray froze with the shrimp halfway to his mouth, his hearing tuned for her friend's reply.

"It doesn't surprise me a bit. Didn't you see his

daughter a while ago? She had that hunky SEAL slobbering all over her out there. If you ask me, the apples don't fall far from the tree. The senator's got quite the reputation of his own, you know. He hasn't been what one would call chaste since his wife died. So much for his tired old campaign slogan, 'Flag, Family, and Future.' Yeah, right." The woman laughed at her own wittiness.

Ray dropped the shrimp and tried to contain the anger that surged up his spine. If Ian was indeed showing his ass in public, as he'd done so often in the past, then Ray needed to slice that bud off clean before it had a chance to blossom. Suddenly, it felt like he'd been stuffed in a blender just before the puree button was pushed. His public image, carefully crafted and protected for better than three decades, was fragile enough these days. He didn't need it assaulted by random gossip brought on by the two people from whom he'd thought he'd managed to distance himself. Recent events had shoved him back under the magnifying glass of public scrutiny. Perception was everything in politics.

For a moment, he considered dumping the contents of his glass over the sprayed-in-place hair of the women. Instead, he placed his flute carefully on the table and closed the distance to his detractors. "Excuse me, ladies."

His voice, only loud enough for them to hear, made the gossips turn. Their mouths dropped open on a collective gasp as they recognized him.

His condescending smile was a cruel flattening of his lips. "My mother used to say that gossip is like hot grease. You never know what damage it will cause or how far reaching the effects may be." He gazed down on them, enjoying their discomfort. "If I were you, I'd pass on the shrimp. They're decidedly fishy." He shrugged. "But maybe you enjoy that kind of thing." He left them sputtering out an apology as he turned on his heel toward the bar on the other side of the ballroom.

****

Mike barreled through the doors leading from the terrace. His entire body was lit up from the inside out. He wasn't certain why he was so charged up; it was either unsatisfied need, or he was just plain pissed she'd shut him down. The things he'd said to her sounded suspiciously like begging, but what the hell. She'd pulled more feeling from him in the last couple of hours than he'd experienced since Fallujah. Feelings that weren't mixed with terror and failure. He simply wasn't ready to give up the ghost and let her go.

He'd had her right there, ready and willing. With a bit more time, she would have been in his bed, spread out warm and wet beneath him. Sure, she'd had misgivings, but damn, he was a convincing guy, a good guy. He respected her. She wasn't an easy lay by any means. She was smart and funny, beautiful and a little wounded. She'd felt so right in his arms, everything he didn't know he was looking for. And just when he'd been about to overcome her last objection, the fucking world had to intervene in the form of her spitfire friend. Goddamn it.

The guests in the ballroom parted before his onslaught like waves split by a power boat. He plowed across the dance floor and came up against a wall of curious backs. A crowd of gawkers clogged the barroom doorway. They craned their necks and stood tiptoe, trying to get a look at the scene inside. As though they were a minor inconvenience, he made short work of them. He pushed past them and to the edge of a donnybrook about to erupt into a full-blown battle. His gaze swept the scene in assessment. His guys were bunched behind Rico, who had a death grip on the shirt of a smaller man with long red hair. Hair the same exact color as Emily's. Ian, he was betting. Behind him, Dora/Ted, dressed in a bright plum-colored suit, was hauling for all his worth on the back of Ian's jacket.

Mike started forward just as Rico cocked his arm and plowed a ham-sized fist into Ian's face. Blood spurted in a spray of crimson.

Ted's shriek split the air like a claxon as Ian toppled to the floor. "Oh, my God! What have you done? He's bleeding! You fucking prick, you broke his nose!" Ted started to lean down to Ian, but in a fit of pure fury, changed his trajectory and rammed a fist into Rico's unprotected solar plexus. The big man rocked backward into the team. A chain reaction of imbalance took over, and the whole lot of them toppled to the ground.

Mike stepped forward to push Ted away from the fray that was about to erupt. Ian reached out and jerked Mike's ankle out from under him. Mike went down on the blood-streaked floor, and Ted shrieked again. The bartender backed into the shelves behind him with such force that the top layer of expensive booze wobbled and did a spectacular dive to the floor.

Ian crab-walked backward away from Mike's flailing feet. Ted grabbed him under his arms and heaved him upright. Blood still poured freely down Ian's face.

Chaos erupted as the members of SEAL Team Seven came up swinging at each other in true brotherly fashion. Fists and elbows, knees and shoulders connected with whoever was closest. Most of the blows glanced off, no true harm intended. Some landed with such force a fleet of ambulances was sure to be needed.

Mike pushed off the floor. "Stand down," he shouted. "That's enough!"

He picked a small shard of glass from his palm, another from his hip. So much for his uniform pants, not that he'd be needing them. Unless he had to testify at the tribunal sure to follow the news story about this debacle. Christ, could anything else go wrong tonight? Lose the girl, lose the fight, lose his freaking mind.

"Somebody better be telling me what the hell is going on here. I thought this was a wedding celebration, not Saturday night in a dive bar." His hawk-like glower swept the room. Time in command over younger idiots in uniform coated his words in authority. "Where the hell do you get off brawling like green recruits?"

The men did their best to stand to attention. Ted and Ian tried to look the part of innocent bystanders, like that would pass for real. Mike gave a silent grunt of amusement. The boys had done an impressive amount of damage in a short period of time. There were a couple of split lips, a few swelling cheeks, and more than a few bloody noses, including Emily's little brother. Ted Reese had even managed to get his festive purple jacket ripped at the shoulder.

A voice boomed from the crowded doorway to the ballroom. All the men froze like statues in a museum.

Senator Ray Domenico pushed his way into the bar. "What the hell is the meaning of this?"

****

It took Emily a moment before she followed Michael through the ballroom to the back of the crowd. She hesitated. The sound of the senator's voice raised in angry rebuke rang out over the whispers of the people between her and the scene of the crime. Adrenaline propelled her body forward. None too gently, she pushed her way through the gawkers.

The senator stood, feet spread, his back to the door, facing off with her brother. "Answer me, boy. I asked you a question."

"Senator," Ian said, wiping ineffectually at his face. The blood had slowed, but his shirtfront was soaked. He was a gruesome sight.

"It seems some things never change, boy," Ray said coldly. "Always stirring up trouble. Even, it seems, in settings as special as the wedding of your friend. Can't you manage, one time, not to bring embarrassment to our family?" His voice dripped with disdain and censure. "Christ, you're a mess. Go clean yourself up."

"Senator." Emily gasped. *Here we go.*

Ian didn't move.

The senator raised his hand, pointing to the restrooms, and he snapped his fingers as he would to a misbehaving dog. His voice dropped to a harsh whisper tainted with rage. "Do it now, boy, or I'll do it for you!" His face had gone past red, verging on purple.

"Don't speak to my brother that way." Emily breached the crowd and stepped around him to Ian's side. "You okay?"

He nodded as she placed a cool hand on his swollen face. His nose dripped blood onto her wrist.

She stared at the streak of red and remembered the times she'd had to clean up "accidents" as a girl. Years had passed since the last time, but her reaction was the same—instant mama bear.

She glared over her shoulder at Ray Domenico. "Did you do this?" Her hatred of this man ramped up like a pending explosion in her chest.

"Don't be ridiculous." His chin rose, all self-righteous indignation. "The only one responsible here is your sorry excuse for a brother."

Emily stumbled aside as Ian stepped toward Ray. Michael was there to catch her.

"Ian…" She knew that look. He was about to make this so much worse. "Calm down everyone."

Ian drew in a lungful of air and spit blood onto the floor. "You know what? Not this time." His voice was low, a barely constrained vibration of anger. "Screw you, old man. You gave up the right to call me son when you knocked my ten-year-old butt down the cellar stairs and locked me in till I admitted to breaking your precious dueling pistol. Bet you remember that, don't you, Dad? Or maybe not. It sure as shit wasn't the first time you raised your fist to me. Wasn't the last either."

The senator stepped forward, bristling with indignation. "Shut your filthy mouth, right this minute. This is not the time or the place. You're drunk, or dear God, are you high? Is that what caused this?" The gawkers in the doorway behind him gave a collective gasp, and he sputtered to a stop. He jerked down on his jacket and straightened his shoulders. "I'll have no more of this nonsense. You need a doctor and a rehab program. Now do as you're told." Like a bull, he stepped forward.

Ian took a hesitant step back.

Emily tried to step between them. Michael held her in place.

"Senator…stop. Don't do this." She was shaking, her knees actually knocking against one another. "Ian, leave it. What he says doesn't matter anymore. We need to get you to a doctor."

"That's right, listen to your sister," Ray spat. "You always hid behind her skirts. Why change now?" He reached past her to shove Ian.

She slipped Michael's grasp and shouldered the senator away from her brother. "Get away from him. He's suffered enough from you."

Shock registered when she met with a stiff arm to her breast. Ray neatly bounced her back into Michael's chest.

"Don't you touch me, you asshole," she shouted. "Tell us what to do again, and I promise, you won't like what happens. I'm not scared of you anymore."

Michael's hard grip clamped down on her biceps. The situation was spiraling out of control, but she couldn't muster the focus to stop it. Years of abuse and helplessness swept her forward, presented her with the ultimate choice. To end this charade for good. "In case you haven't noticed, there are witnesses. That makes a difference, doesn't it? Wonder what the papers will have to say in the morning. I'd watch my poll numbers if I were you, Senator."

Ray moved closer with each statement. He raised a hand, intent on laying a brutal slap to her face. "You ungrateful little bitch. You'd be nothing without me. I have given you everything!"

Critical mistake. Ian reacted like a threatened

snake. He made a sound that froze everyone watching. In a blur of movement, he struck Ray with the heel of his hand. The meat of his palm came into solid contact with the center of the older man's throat.

The senator teetered for a moment on his shiny dress shoes. He tried to suck in a harsh breath and failed. His eyes bulged in a gross parody of his previous anger. His arms flailed; he tumbled backward.

She watched in horrified fascination. The raging, ugly, and frightening ogre from their childhood morphed into a crumpled heap at her feet. She gaped at him, remembering the last time she'd seen him fall. Had they the power all along to stop the stinging rebukes or the tirade of vitriol and abuse? Were they so conditioned that they believed it would never have any effect?

Senator Raymond Domenico lay like a turtle rolled to the back of his shell on the barroom floor. Shards of glass had done nothing to cushion his fall. Somehow, he'd avoided the upright stem and foot of a wine glass that would have provided a permanent end to the argument. As it was, his head had bounced against the litter, lacerating his scalp. The pain was sufficient to force his lungs into operation. He spewed out a bellow.

Ted was galvanized into action. He grabbed Ian's arm. With tender care, he moved him at a steady pace out of harm's way toward the crowd in the doorway.

Ian dragged his feet enough to catch Emily's look of horrified sadness. "I'm sorry, Em, I'm not taking this anymore. Tell him to leave me alone. Make it stick because, if he comes after me, I swear I've got all the evidence I need to make him regret more than his big mouth tonight."

She didn't know what to do, recoil from his lashing temper or gather him into her arms as she had after similar bouts with their stepfather. The old bastard was always looking for a punching bag. The primary difference being that Ian was no longer a cowering child. His bravado was a stunning change. Believing it would last came harder. He seemed stripped bare by it, pushed to the edge of his endurance. She'd never seen him publicly willing to confront Ray. Privately, it was a different story. Ian had no problem putting a face to the root of his issues. He'd mastered the art of laying the blame for his addiction squarely at the feet of Ray Domenico. As much as Emily believed that to be true, she knew Ian had never actually taken personal responsibility for his choice of roads out of the pain.

She stepped to his side, grasped his arm, and spoke quietly into his ear. "Let it go for tonight. Please." They had things to discuss if he really was ready to take another step toward ending Ray's reach into their lives. "Go with Teddy, and I'll talk with you about this tomorrow."

"Sure, tomorrow."

He rocked, unsteady on his feet, and she realized he wasn't sober. His eyes had a glassy look, and the pupils were blown wide open, the normal startling green color of the irises shrunken to a narrow halo at the edge. As she watched, a single tear gathered on his long lashes and rolled into the blood smeared across his cheek.

"I'm so done with this, Em." Ian's voice came out on a sob, and his body began to tremble.

"My God, Ian." She tried to speak calmly, steady her voice. "Why take him on now of all times? You know how he is in public. It just makes things so much worse." She'd tried all her life to find safe ground between father and son. When that proved impossible, she'd substituted her body for her words. There were more than a few healed fracture lines in her X-rays to prove it.

"I'm not going to fight with you too," he cried. "I want out of this, permanently. I can't take it anymore."

Casting Emily a sad glance, Ted wrapped an arm around her brother. "I'll take you home, sugar. Don't you worry about a thing. Teddy will take good care of you." He hitched Ian up like a rag doll; the crowd parted to let them through.

Pat Evans stepped from the edge of the crowd. "Let them go, Emily." He ran a hand down her arm and cast a stern look at Michael. He gestured to the bar with his chin. "Get this mess cleaned up. I'll get the senator to his ride and talk to the management. Maybe we can salvage what's left of the festivities."

"Yes, sir." Michael did everything but salute the older man. He turned to Emily who stood frozen, watching her brother make his exit. "Em, go with Noni till things settle down." He spoke quietly. "Then I'll come find you."

His words, though kindly meant and privately spoken, were too close to being an order for her. The very last thing she needed was a virtual stranger making decisions for her or stirring the brew of emotions swirling around inside her. He was probably used to people jumping at his slightest request. His crew was doubtlessly accustomed to this kind of situation. Secure the bad actors, handle the upheaval, and sweep up the noncombatants. Textbook crisis management for Team

Seven. Well, she wasn't a member of his team, nor was she in the mood to be handled.

She lifted her chin and gave him an icy glare. "You kidding me, sailor? Don't order me around. I'm not one of your crew. I don't need you to fix my problems or my fucked-up family. Just butt out." Her sharp elbow connected with his arm as she stormed around him toward her stepfather.

"Calm down there, sweetheart. I'm just trying to help." His grip reclaimed that same elbow and spun her around. "Let the senator get the hell out of here. Okay? I'm sure there are plenty of photographers to get his mug on the front page. You can take him apart to your heart's content later." The pressure on her elbow lessened. "Besides, there's enough glass on the floor to really do some damage. I don't want to have to take you to the emergency room too. Unless you'd like to ride along with Domenico. I'm sure there's room in his town car."

She looked over. Pat was making certain Ray was steady on his feet. Blood leaked from a cut on the back of his head; a dark stain gathered on his immaculate white collar.

"I'm not going anywhere with him. He can bleed to death for all I care." She jerked her arm free and pinned the senator in place with an indignant glare. "Haven't you caused enough pain in his life, Ray? When is it ever going to be enough for you? Can't you just leave us alone?"

"Shut it, Emily," he hissed, "or I'll have that little asswipe hauled to jail for assault. I may do it anyway. Neither of you've ever been worth a shit. Worst mistake of my life, taking you on." He lurched toward the rear of the bar and glared at Pat Evans who had his driver in tow.

Those left behind stood in strained silence as he took his leave. It was like watching a terrible accident from the other side of the highway. They knew it was bad by the wreckage but were past it too quickly to see the real damage.

Like the rest, Emily watched him leave, but she wasn't stunned at his level of contempt. She slumped into herself, exhausted and embarrassed. The cliff notes of her life had been strewn like trash across the barroom floor. She glanced up at Michael; another casualty of her personal blast zone. "Welcome to my world," she said. "I'll…I don't know, go apologize to Lois and Dillon, I guess. Besides, once the management gets a load of what your guys did to their property, you'll have your hands full."

She turned to the crowd. "I'm sorry you all had to see that. Sorrier than you can imagine." Her voice broke on the last word, and she hurried through them.

Noni was hot on her heels.

Chapter Fourteen

Emily slipped through the crowd, then paused to survey the ballroom. She searched the room. Ian was nowhere to be seen. Ted, ever her brother's keeper, was doubtlessly looking for a way to talk him off a ledge somewhere. She had to admit she was relieved not to have to deal with the aftermath of the battle in the bar. Guilt for feeling relieved clogged her throat with fruitless emotions. Her brother, regardless of the senator's corrosive presence in their lives, had once been a bright light. She'd refused to let his schooling slide and forced him, sometimes bodily, to attend classes until he graduated. Naively, she'd believed her job as a surrogate mother was done, and she allowed them to crawl off into their respective dens to lick their invisible wounds. She hadn't been there to witness him turning into the hollowed-out version of himself she'd seen tonight. Based on what she'd just witnessed, Ian's wounds were closer to the surface now than they'd ever been.

Noni's quiet voice brought her back to the present. "You okay, honey?"

She jumped, her hand pressed to her chest to keep her heart in place. "Darn it, where'd you come from?"

"I'm just making sure nothing else blows up around you." Noni's smile was a thin attempt at relieving the tension in the room.

"Yeah. Well, I think I'm done for the night. No more gory war stories for the entertainment of the general populace." She nodded behind them. "I need to apologize to the bride and groom. What a terrible way for the evening to go. I…didn't expect any of it. Didn't see it coming at all." Her voice was unsteady. "How did Ray get in here anyway? I know you didn't invite him."

"I guess he came as a plus one for Amelia Stapleton. She's always been a mover and shaker politically. The bitch loves nothing better than to stir up trouble, then sit back and judge the crap out of those who get sucked into it."

"Really. In that case, your dad was smart to ask for protection from the old biddy." Emily forced a semblance of a smile, remembering the show she'd put on for the woman's benefit before the wedding. Given the events of the night, the profit for the gallery had evaporated. There was no way she could charge Pat for the pieces; her "family" had effectively ruined his daughter's wedding. She'd end up bankrupt at this rate. Shit. Regardless, she still had things to do before she could leave. "I need to try and reach Ian, though he probably isn't interested in talking to me." Her shoulders slumped with fatigue.

Too many razor-edged emotions had washed through her tonight. They sucked away all her strength and left her with a weight the size of Red Rocks on her shoulders. Defeat was a bitter taste in her mouth. She knew without a doubt that Ian would be salving his injuries in the only ways that worked for him, isolation and self-destruction. He definitely wouldn't want to see her, not with the evidence of his problems splashed around the country in such a raw, brutal way. And they would be, come the morning. There was no way in hell the story wouldn't get out. Not that she gave a rat's ass about the effect it would have on Ray Domenico. Ian had always been a victim, and the public was a harsh judge when it came to assigning blame. Sure, they might feel sorry for the child he'd been, but they would punish the hell out of him for being unable to break free of the situation as an adult. What's more, they would point an accusing finger at his lifestyle and sexual orientation, shine a harsh light on his most private places. The hardest thing was not being able to do anything to stop it from happening.

Noni laid a comforting hand on her arm. "First, Lois and Dill don't need an apology. They're so wrapped up in each other they probably didn't notice the slugfest. Second, there is *no* need for you to jet off after Ian. Ted is capable of taking care of him. It's pretty obvious he's used to filling that role. Your brother needs to nurse his hurts for a night, sleep it off. You can catch up to him in the morning after everyone is sober and calm. I'll check with the hotel, and we'll find you a room so you can do the same. Maybe take a hot bath, pour yourself a glass of wine, and put this stupidity behind you."

That was Noni, always making a plan to handle any situation.

"Thanks. The way the evening has gone, I'd probably manage to fuck it up anyway. Right along with my car, so well…thanks."

"Christ, self-pity does not look good on you. Just chalk it up to unresolved crap and try to let it go for the night. There'll still be plenty of stuff to obsess over in the daylight. Right now, scoot. Go up to Lois's suite and change your clothes. I'll get the bellman to bring you a key." Noni stared her down until she nodded her acceptance.

Twenty minutes later, Emily swiped her new room key through the reader. She was surprised to find herself in not just a simple hotel room, but a suite. Warm light pooled on soft-looking navy couches and spilled onto deep burgundy carpeting. The place was welcoming to her abused senses. She sighed in relief at the quiet and kicked off the shoes that had morphed into instruments of torture.

One of two bedroom doors stood open to reveal a huge white bed. It beckoned to her like an oasis to a thirsty man. She scrunched her toes in the deep carpet, hoisted the shoulder bag she'd had the foresight to bring, and walked barefoot into its arms. Or more accurately, face-planted on the duvet. Its high loft wrapped around her like a soft, warm hug. She was tempted to stay just like that and ignore the bath Noni recommended. But her friend was absolutely right. She would feel better once the tightness leaked out of her muscles. Wine would help her sleep.

If only Ian…nope. No more thinking tonight. No rehashing, no wondering, worrying, or obsessing. This was Emily time. She rolled to her feet and made for the bathroom. She purred with pleasure at the sight of the deep jetted tub and sent a note of thanks to the goddess who'd thought to design it. It had to have been a woman who thought of its sumptuous luxury as well as an endless supply of hot water to fill it. She turned the tap, and the spill of water reminded her that part of Noni's prescription for recovery had been a glass of wine.

By the time she returned from a visit to the mini bar in the living room, the tub was full. The only thing left to do was strip off her clothes for the second time in less than an hour and lower herself into the steamy depth of the water. She perched a hip on the lip of the deep tub and upended the contents of the bubble bath provided by the hotel into the water. The spicy fragrance of lavender and vanilla filled her senses, and she pushed the button on the side of the tub to start the whirlpool jets. She trailed an idle hand through the foaming wash of water.

The rumble of the jets almost obscured the ringing of her phone. She slapped the control button and reached for the cell with a soapy hand. Ian's face filled the screen. Good, it saved her the trouble of tracking him down.

"I'm fine, thanks for asking." His voice sounded rough like he'd sucked down a pack of cigarettes in the last couple of hours.

"You read my mind, little brother. Where are you? And what the fuck were you thinking, huh? Your timing really sucks. You know that. Right?" She was incapable of keeping the chiding note from her voice.

"I've never been able to get that down, you know. The timing. I'm always in the wrong spot at the worst time. Tonight just proved it." She heard ice clink into a glass. "Anyway, I thought you might want to know that I won't be back in Tamarack anytime soon. And before I go, I wanted to be sure I gave you something."

"Oh, no, you don't. You can't just stir up shit and leave me to deal with the aftermath, Ian. It's not fair, and you know it." She cringed at the thought of the bruhaha the news organizations would make their family drama. They'd gobble it up like a juicy steak tossed to a pack of jackals.

He huffed derisively. "Yeah, well, you'll think of something. You always do. Tell 'em the truth if you want. Just be ready to deal with the fallout. You'll have to decide for both of us which path to take. I'm too screwed up to choose anymore."

His words were halting, and she got the feeling he was reading from an old script, mouthing the words she expected him to say.

"That's an old song, Ian. Play me something new. Tell me you're going to put that glass down and actually do it. Tell me you're not using again. Tell me you're coming back to town with me, that you remember what it was like when we stuck together instead of running away like you've been doing." He wasn't the only one exhausted by the years of waiting for the other shoe to drop. "Tell me that, and it won't matter what happens in the morning, because we'll handle it together."

He swore, and there was the unmistakable sound of glass smashing against a hard surface. "Damn, now look what I've done." He muffled the receiver, but not completely enough to obscure Ted fussing in the background. "I can't get anything right tonight… I ca—" His voice shuddered, and he stifled a sob. "I can't stand the thought of the things they'll dredge up. You…you only know part of—" He stopped mid-sentence like he'd said more than he intended.

She froze, the bubbles rolling down her arm icy on her skin. "Really? What don't I know? That he beat us, humiliated us, locked us in that godforsaken hole in the barn? Tried his best to break us, make us hate each other?" Her throat closed up, and she couldn't breathe; the tears she'd been holding back pushed past her defenses.

"Aww, Em. Please don't cry. I can't take any more tears." Pain was a palpable knife in his voice. "Wish I was strong enough to win this fight, I want to be. But I'm just too tired. It's been too long, too many years, and too many losses. I've wanted him dead for so long it's part of me. I tried to kill him, did you know that? I planned it anyway. Wanted him to die in the water just like Mom. But when I got the chance, I just didn't have it in me to put an end to him. I wish I had."

"You…you what? When was this?" Despite herself, she felt a little prickle of pride that he'd had the balls to make an attempt at something they used to pray for.

"That first summer when I bolted from Richmond Academy." He paused and swallowed heavily. His flat tone brought chills to her heart. "They tried to turn me into the perfect little cadet, and all I wanted was revenge. I was self-righteous and so stupid. Thought I was a super soldier. Thought I could go all covert ops on him. I planned it all out. Ambush, rope him like a steer, and drag him to the falls. I was too dumb to realize he'd know everything, that he'd be waiting for me. He made me pay for that."

He was muttering now, and she had to listen closely to understand.

"Oh, Ian. What did he do?" she asked softly. Her imagination didn't need any help to run wild with the possibilities. Ray was very creative in his torture. He found ways to hurt them without leaving a mark, usually. Like killing the squirrel they'd found and raised while he was in DC or the forced marches or the bread and water meals or the cold nights in the dark of The Hole.

"It doesn't matter anymore," he mumbled. He whispered something to Ted about going back to bed. "Look, 's not the reason I called you. Before I go—I got to tell you so you'll have what you need. You're strong enough to use 'em."

God, would this ever stop? Her voice was sharp with frustrated impatience. "Stop playing word games with me, Ian. What are you talking about?" She waited while he swallowed several times. The glass had become the bottle apparently. She clutched the phone the same way she wanted to grab it out of his hand.

He rambled ahead, lost to the effects of the booze. "The diaries. They're still where we hid them. You'll have to go get them. 'Member? He never found 'em. He—he'll try to stop you though, so be careful."

His words were so slurred she realized he'd moved past drunk into blackout insensibility.

"Oh, Christ, Ian. Stop this. Diaries? They're long gone, honey."

He wasn't making sense; the notebooks were probably mouse nests if they still existed. He was delirious. There wasn't any record of their past surely.

"You're not thinking straight, honey. Let Teddy take care of you tonight, and I'll see you in the morning. We'll work it all out tomorrow. Just go to sleep now." There was no use talking anymore. Her brother would be out cold soon. Ted would have to watch over him. Same shit, different day.

"'Kay, love you, Em. Sorry 'bout tonight, 'bout everything."

The phone went silent in her hand. She was sorry too.

Emily looked longingly into the bath. Escape, her siren's song. Before she could talk herself out of it, she shucked her clothes and stepped into the bubble-covered water. The silky liquid soothed skin stretched tight by the tension of the last few hours. Nothing would be accomplished by continuing to beat a horse she'd lost control of long ago. She sucked in a lungful of steamy air and ducked under the surface. For the length of her air, she floated in the quiet echoes beneath the water. Burning lungs forced her back to the surface, and she pressed the switch that turned the gentle lapping of the water into a foaming paradise of relaxing currents.

****

Michael stretched long and loud just as the elevator doors swept open in front of his suite. At least he hoped it was still his. The crew had made quick work of the clean-up in the bar. He'd managed to convince the blowhard senator that discretion was the better part of staying out of the papers. Jerry escorted him and his driver to an inconspicuous spot in the parking garage. His car would take him to his personal physician's office.

The asshole never stopped making noise about what a loser Ian was. "Drug-addled, no account, junky fag" were the terms he used to describe his only son. He moaned and groaned, limping like a pro had doled out his damage. He even swore retribution against the team and promised that Mike's CO would hear about the way he'd been "hustled like a sack of rotten potatoes down the back stairs." As far as Mike was concerned, it seemed they'd made quick, efficient work of the whole situation, and the old man could shove his attitude where the sun didn't shine. Besides, he didn't have a CO anymore. Not that he'd informed the self-important prick of that fact.

Michael found his mind wandering to his beautiful Emily.

His? Odd concept to pop into his mind. But somewhere between the last moments of their dance and the stricken look on her face as she watched the showdown between her brother and stepfather, he'd begun to think of her in those terms. He had to laugh at himself for the fool he was because there was no way in hell he'd ever have more with Emily Converse than the brief taste he'd stolen. She was probably home by now and burning up the phone lines looking for her battered brother. One thing for sure, she hadn't waited for him to find her before she'd cut and run.

Of course, he could find her. Convince Pat Evans to tell him where she lived. Just sort of show up tomorrow, kind of casual like. All smooth and stuff. He blew out a scoffing breath. Christ, what an idiotic fool he'd become. There was no way she'd be interested in a broke down, unemployed jerk like him. What was he supposed to do? Ask her to give him a tour of the mountains? Teach him to cast a fly into water cold enough to freeze his dick off? She didn't look like the kind of woman who'd be remotely interested in slimy brook trout, let alone a man so tragically uncreative he couldn't figure out what to do with his life now that he was permanently stateside.

Foolish, stupid, or desperate? All three, more than likely.

He searched for his key card and slashed it through the slot till the little green light signaled approval. The suite was clean, which was nice. No empty beer bottles, half-eaten pizza, or Twinkie wrappers. His men were such kids. He had to force himself to remember he'd been that young when he survived Hell Week. Four of his five guys had seen fewer than six years in the teams. Jerry was the only one even close to scraping ten years, then there was Dillon at only three years with a trident on his chest. It made Mike feel old, and that was just sad. Pretty soon he'd be searching for his false teeth. If he could remember where he'd put them.

His jacket made a soft thump on the back of one of the couches, and he made his way to the wet bar in the corner. He found an empty wine bottle small enough for a single glass and smiled to himself. You couldn't fault a housekeeper for taking advantage of an unguarded mini bar, but leaving the evidence behind? That could get a person fired. He tossed it in the trash and turned toward the bedroom. Light shining beneath the door to the room that had been Dillon's surprised him. Another strike against the maid. He reached inside to flip it off and stopped with his hand on the switch when he heard the jacuzzi rumbling in the bathroom.

"What the hell?" Was one of the guys making himself comfortable in upgraded accommodations? No sweat really, they'd shared stench-filled Humvees. Adjoining rooms wasn't a problem, but it never hurt to rag on them when the chance presented itself.

He grabbed the door handle and threw it open. "Hey, asshole! That's my bath…" His voice stuck in his mouth when creamy skin rose out of the froth like Venus from the sea.

"Hey!" Emily froze in place, shock and disbelief on her face. Then she grabbed the soap and lobbed it at his head. "Get out of here. This is my room, you pervert."

He had no problem ducking her missile, but that was the only part of his body that seemed to be functioning. His feet were glued to the floor, and his mouth hung wide open. His brain, however, registered her skin and the soft pink flush from the hot water. Coral nipples stood at attention and pointed straight at him. He made a valiant effort not to skim the rest of the picture before him, but he failed miserably. His body engaged on a steam-laden gasp, and there was no doubt the object of his daydream was sexier than his imagination had conjured. He took a single step closer to his objective.

Never miss an opportunity. That's what the navy had taught him.

"Wrong," he said, "this is my room, beautiful, and that's my tub you're standing in. Want some company?" He couldn't help the smile that twisted up the corners of his mouth. She was just so goddamned gorgeous. And so slippery wet.

Her next projectile was a soaked washcloth, and it caught him right between the eyes.

"I said get the hell out of here, or I'll start screaming down the house." Her voice was high and outraged. He had no doubt she'd do just that.

He raised a peacemaking hand and pulled the dripping terrycloth off his face. "Okay, okay. I'm going. If you're sure you don't need any help." He grinned broadly as her furious screech followed him out the door. What the heck, she had to come out eventually.

****

Emily fought to control her heart rate. "Right," she grumbled to herself, "get out of the tub, find a towel, try not to freak out. You're naked, not dying. It's not the first time you've been seen in all your 'glory.'" Nothing like getting caught with her pants down—or missing—to raise a girl's heart rate. She'd felt like a bug in a jar, on display while that overgrown ass took full advantage of the situation. She looked down at the bug in question. At least she'd managed to remember to shave all the pertinent parts, and the rest of her was, at the very least, not abhorrent. She took a deep breath and wrapped the fluffy white bath towel securely around her body. She had no reason to run and no place to hide.

"Okay," she said into the foggy air, "you need to get the hell out of this bathroom and call that hussy, Noni."

The woman had lost her damn mind if she thought putting Emily in the same room with Michael McCandlis was going to spark some kind of miracle recovery from the craziness of this night. Or more likely, her idiot friend figured she was finishing up her duty as a yenta. She'd shove them together by arranging a spontaneous little love nest for the people who, just a little while ago, couldn't keep their hands off each other. That thought brought a small smirk to Emily's lips and swept a shiver of awareness across her wet skin. He did have great hands, long tapered fingers, carefully trimmed nails, and he definitely knew how to touch a woman to get the desired reaction. Damn it.

Emily swiped a brush ruthlessly through her hair, hitched up her towel along with her courage, and strode back into the bedroom on the other side of the door. She paused, somewhat surprised Michael wasn't stretched out in all his bounty on the big white bed. She wasn't disappointed, not even a scosh. Really, she wasn't.

And she'd keep telling her belligerent body that until it got the message.

She dug through her bag for the comfy yoga pants she had planned to wear home from this fiasco of a wedding and pulled on the same cami she'd worn in the door. She categorically refused to cower in this room like she was afraid to show her face. She'd already showed the rest of her; the face shouldn't be an issue.

Michael was sitting on one of the deep couches, drink in hand. The sleeves of his white shirt were rolled to the elbows, showing off impressive forearms with a wonderful russet-colored tan. His long legs were splayed out in front of him. He stared blankly at a television whose screen projected a lifelike fire. He looked comfortable and…tired. Emily could relate. It had been one hell of a night.

"Hey," he said cautiously, looking at her over his shoulder, "I called the front desk. They're booked solid, no other rooms to be had. I can bunk down with one of the guys, but every single one of them snores like a freight train. Please, Emily, don't let that happen. I need a night's sleep real bad."

Really? After that scene in the bathroom? She would be crazy not to insist, at least make an attempt to teach the cocky bastard a lesson about messing with her. But…oh, hell. She was as tired as he looked, and that was saying something. Emily stepped forward and slid down onto the couch, a cushion away from his hard thigh. She hadn't noticed the glass of wine on the table in front of her.

"This for me?"

"Yup. Call it a peace offering." His voice was deep, warm honey with a little grit underneath. Soothing but with the promise of some unforeseen doggedness below the surface.

"Thanks." She kept her gaze on the flickering flames playing on the flat screen. She took a sip of the wine and relaxed back against the cushions. Raising her glass, she made a slight turn toward him. A small smile slipped past her guard. "I guess, in the spirit of détente, you can stay. We are adults, right?"

"Yeah, well, I was here first. But given the fact that you're a prettier sight than the naked butt of one of my guys, I've got to say I appreciate your largesse."

"Ooo, big words. I thought SEALs were known more for brute force than brains." *Well, that sounded snarky, Em.* "Sorry, that was rude. I should be thanking you for, well…everything. You know, downstairs and all."

"Not necessary." He waved away her gratitude. "We SEALs are actually better known for our abilities to assess and handle situations quickly. From everything I saw, it looked like that argument was a long time coming. Want to spill the background, or have you already rehashed it a million times?" He didn't sound placating, more as though he was genuinely interested.

"You're right about it being a long time coming. Like, oh, thirty years or so. You're also right about my rehashing. I've only been back in Tamarack a couple of weeks. I started to hope, because I hadn't seen either of them, that there was a treaty in place. But I was wrong.

So I'm stuck in the middle again. Story of my life to date."

He swiveled his big body toward her and cocked one leg onto the cushion between them. "Not contacting the senator, I noticed."

"No chance in hell of that." As a matter of fact, that was at the very bottom of a long list of things she refused to consider. "No love lost there. I guess you could tell, huh. What with your powers of observation and all."

"You mean the threats? Jesus, I wanted to deck the prick myself. I hear he got kicked off the Armed Services Committee. There were lots of rumors floating around base about it. He was quick enough to cover that up with bullshit."

Her cheeks heated a bit with the memory of the bastard during the "battle of the bar." Christ, she'd named the incident. "No surprise there. He likes to be the big fish with all the minnows doing his bidding. Every time he gets reelected, I lose a little more faith in the system." She sipped from her wine. "I've made it a mission to keep my mind off him for all the time I've been gone. He did his best to screw up my childhood, so I decided I wouldn't let him star in my adult years. But you know how it goes. The more you pretend the crap isn't on the rug, the smellier it gets. His real beef is with Ian, always has been. I was the lucky one who got to stand between them. I'd love to do something to change that." Emily shifted her body as well, mimicking Michael's position. Her knee lay against his. Just a few square inches of contact, but it calmed and warmed her all the same. "I'm sorry you got dragged into it. Still and all, I'm glad you were there."

Michael shrugged casually as if it were commonplace. "It's what we do."

Time for a change of subject. "Speaking of what you do, you said you just retired from the service. What's next for you?" Was that too personal a question to ask? She didn't think so; the man had practically stripped her bare in public mere hours ago. Her girly bits still tingled with the memory.

"Damned if I know." He looked vulnerable for a heartbeat. "I'm still trying to find my feet with that. I never bothered to think much past the teams till I got injured. Now it's like this huge blank spot, and I'm drifting. It's not a comfortable feeling after so many years of focus."

"How many?" She watched him steadily. "And you were injured?"

"No big deal." He shrugged. "I joined up when I was twenty and was in BUD/S five years later."

She held up her hand. "Buds? Like the beer?" She smiled.

"No," he said, smiling back, "not like the beer. Unless you want to count our second favorite pastime. It stands for Basic Underwater Demolition/SEAL training. It's only part of the training. The hardest part physically. Something like eighty percent of the guys that are accepted never make it past the BUD/S phase."

"But you did. Obviously."

"I did." He nodded and looked away. The bright flames on the TV screen reflected in his dark eyes. "Anyway, that makes fifteen years active on Team Seven. It's pretty much been my only plan." He slumped slightly, more a caving in of his shoulders than a release of tension. "The navy did the right thing. Even if I believe I could go back to duty, they can't afford to take the chance that my injury might endanger the members of my squad. Neither can I, so it's the highway for me."

A frown gathered between his brows, and Emily felt a deep sense of empathy with him. She was in the same boat really. Plenty of experience to draw on but a shaky framework in which to apply it.

She reached out and placed a warm palm on the knee that touched hers. Compassion welled up in her for this big, virile man. He talked a good game, just like she did. But when it came down to putting a plan into action where their lives were concerned, they seemed to suffer from the same lack of direction. God knew she'd never seen herself running an art gallery, let alone coming back to the mountains to do it. Sometimes she had to search for an answer and other times it just dropped in her lap like fate reached out and handed it to her.

"Then the future's wide open for you," she said encouragingly. "Don't let the big picture swallow you up, Michael. Just do what seems right, and things will work themselves out."

He surprised her by taking her hand. She expected him to let go. He didn't.

"You're too far away." He tugged on her hand, and she only held back for a moment before allowing him to pull her flush to his side. Her head fit perfectly into the notch of his arm and shoulder. He dropped a kiss on the top of her head. "That's better. One of those things that just feels right."

She could feel the smile in his voice and the rumble of his words in the depth of his chest. Mm, lovely.

From the wide expanse of windows flanking one side of the suite, the blue flash of lightning illuminated the curtains, and Emily's own smile lifted her lips. She loved the snap and the fire of a thunderstorm. It always reminded her of her mom who used to gather Emily and Ian on the couch in their big living room. They would watch the storm light up the ridge tops surrounding the valley. For heart-stopping moments, the granite skyline would be bathed in shimmering blue fire. Then it would disappear, blasted away by the crash of thunder so loud it shook the rafters of their huge house. She always felt a blend of sadness and longing during a storm, but she loved it all the same. Just like her mother.

"Turn off the lights, Michael. Let's watch the storm."

He complied with a stretch of his long arm. The suite plunged into darkness interrupted only by the flickering of the flames and the light show. The storm moved down the eastern slope of the Rockies and swept across the plains toward them. Michael held her closer, one arm behind her. His big hand lay firmly beneath her ribs; his thumb made lazy sweeps she felt all the way to her toes. His other hand played idly with a strand of hair that lay across his chest.

She snuggled deeper into the space between him and the couch back. "This is the most relaxed I've been in I can't tell you how long."

"Mm, 's nice. Don't be wiggling, though. You feel too good against me. Besides, you know what happens to my good intentions where you're concerned. And believe me, it wouldn't take much to push me into taking up where we left off on the terrace." His lungs expanded and released a long exhale of warm air into her hair.

"I wasn't wiggling, just getting comfortable. Don't be such a horndog." She poked him in his side, and he shivered. "Oh, my God, are you ticklish?" She poked again experimentally, this time with a little squiggle of her fingertip.

He coiled up like a cat and grabbed her offending hand. "Don't even think about it, beautiful." He used the arm behind her to slide her from her comfy nest and lay her on top of him. He held both her wrists in his calloused grip. "I have mad skills when it comes to wrestling. Don't make me prove it." He gave a rise to his hips and slid her up his body, aligning all their most interesting body parts like puzzle pieces. She knew he was going to kiss her before he moved to take her lips.

He tasted of bourbon and wildness buried just below the surface. Like lightning in a bottle. Ready, waiting for her to pull the stopper. She was willing to ride the tide of need if he was. Her inner warning system whispered she shouldn't be doing this—it could only end bloody. She ignored it in favor of nipping his lip, then sucking away the sting. She was rewarded with a growl of pure male enjoyment. So she did it again and followed it up with a sweep of her tongue into his mouth.

He met her move for move, all the while punctuating each change of angle with a surge of his hips. She felt how much he was enjoying their closeness. His massive erection swept along her cleft and pushed her closer to the edge of something a lot more intimate. The heat gathered in her core. Soon he'd be able to feel it through her clothing unless he found her with his fingers first. Now there was an idea. Maybe she could push one of his hands in that direction. Was this pure avoidance behavior? Yup, and she didn't care a whit. She wanted—needed—to feel something that was hers alone.

As if he'd read her thoughts, his hand slipped beneath the waistband of her yoga pants to palm her ass cheek. His strong fingers squeezed and released her flesh, traversed the globe of her butt and found the crease in between. She'd never been so grateful for spandex in her life. Free access granted with little effort on either part. God, it felt good to be touched.

A rush of want so deep it swamped her had Emily opening to him like a flower. His hands, as intimate and demanding as a long-time lover, moved slowly over her, into her. Places secret and forbidden, he made his territory. His touch was insistent but delicate at the same time. She was embarrassingly slippery, ready to welcome any invasion he had to offer. Heady stuff for a woman who could barely remember the last time she'd been desired for herself alone.

His focus was intense, and she lost herself in it. Cool air touched her back as he pulled her cami off over her head. He ghosted the pad of his thumb over her nipple, then followed it with a sharp plucking twist. She gasped in surprise. The effect was like rocket fuel to her body. Suddenly she pushed past languid enjoyment and became hyper-aware of each breath, each scent. She luxuriated in the rasp of stubble on her neck as he chased each slow kiss with a nip, then laved it away with the wet warmth of his tongue. Breathing? She tried to remember to do it but was barely able to manage. The current and the fireworks going off in her body swallowed her world whole.

He moaned low and deep. The hard length of him pressed tightly to her core. He rocked upward, again and again, driving the span of him from the swollen bud of her clitoris all the way to her navel. She wondered fleetingly if she would be able to take all that length inside and live. Her worry about survival disappeared with his next thrust. Frankly, she didn't care if she died. She was fine with it, as long as he sheathed every inch of that big, hard column of flesh inside her.

"Come with me, beautiful." His voice was a graveled gasp pressed to her lips, his arms wrapped around her, and he pumped another time.

"Now? Oh, yes, God, just keep doing that." She ground herself helplessly against him. Then she felt his smile against her mouth. What? Had she misunderstood? Not come with me, but... "Uh—oh, come with you." Her helpless giggle nearly undid them both. "I thought you meant—well, you know what I thought." She flushed hot as she realized she was bare to the waist and wrapped around his body like a second skin.

"Jesus, you're amazing." He kissed her, lingering over the swollen softness of her lips. "For the record, I'm totally in favor of your coming." He sucked her bottom lip into his mouth, then held it for a heartbeat in his teeth. "In fact, I want you to come. Over..." He bent his head and took her breast's beaded tip into his mouth, then gave its twin the same treatment. "And over..."

The simmering charge of an impending, explosive orgasm rippled up her spine.

"And I want my mouth on you when you do."

Oh, hell, yes, she was completely on board with that plan.

He gave her a wicked pirate grin and sat up with her draped across his lap. "I need room to maneuver if I'm going to get better acquainted with what causes those sexy noises coming from you. It's making me ache to lick you till that noise turns into a scream." He stood, grabbed her hand, and led her to his door.

The room was a duplicate of hers, the bed just as big and inviting as the one across the living room. But this one smelled like Michael. Fresh air and ocean breezes. It must be a combination of the man himself and those things he took comfort in. The scent pulled her into him and would ever be the one she associated with him. She could imagine, years from now, being able to find him in a room full of strangers.

Oh, damn, not again, not this soon. She gave herself a mental slap.

Could she survive another round of disappointment when he left? Yeah, she could. She wouldn't enjoy it, but she could. She also couldn't fathom walking away from him. Not until she knew the feel of him driving into her and the sound of him as he spent himself inside her.

Michael did away with his white shirt and reached for his belt buckle. He drew the belt from its loops in one smooth slide. She wet her lips and focused on his fingers as he unbuttoned the waist and pulled the zipper down. She swallowed hard when his pants and briefs pooled on the floor. He stepped to her and made her clothing disappear in the same magically efficient manner, then he pushed her back onto the soft white duvet.

In a quick maneuver of her own, she pulled herself forward, her mouth level with the darkened purple head of his penis. It jumped as she reached out one finger, barely touching the velvet skin. She ran it around the base of the hood and back up its supple groove to the slit. Looking up, she held his gaze as she wrapped her hand around its girth and brought him to her lips. "Please God, tell me you're clean because I'd really love to taste you too."

"As a whistle, beautiful. And you? Are you clean, protected? Would you let me take you bare?" His voice was a whispered grate of words.

"I am, and I'm glad you are because I'm allergic to latex." She tightened her grip and pumped her hand down to his base and back up. His growl of pleasure brought a smile of pure feminine power to her lips. She ran just the tip of her tongue up the same path her finger had taken, then dipped into the opening. She tasted his salty, spicy flavor, and pleasure murmured deep in her throat.

His hands opened and closed; they trembled as he searched for control. He watched her open and take him inside the hot cave of her mouth. "Oh, God, go slow Emily. If you're not careful, this will be over way too soon."

She backed off, let her tongue linger, and smiled up at him wickedly. Then she took him whole, right to the back of her throat.

"Shit," he breathed out. He shivered as a spasm rocked him and drew his body taut with anticipation. "Oh, honey, that feels so damn good. Do that just one more time."

She did and let her hand wander lower, adding a

come-hither movement with her fingers that rolled him in her palm. The movement almost sent him off the cliff. She could feel it. She increased her suction and drew him a little deeper into her mouth, then swallowed.

His hands tangled in her hair, and he pulled her back with a groan. She resisted, increasing her suction; she thought for sure he was a goner.

"Stop, stop," he breathed. His grip tightened on her hair. "Not. Yet. I want to come inside you. I want to feel you come apart around me."

She whimpered and grasped him more tightly. She indulged in greed for a moment but relented.

His hands relaxed when she let him off the hook. He reached out and stroked a fingertip along her jaw. "Is this a hallucination?" he whispered. "Maybe I'm still lying in the dirt outside Fallujah. Are you real?"

"Michael..." She encouraged him with a wistful smile and studied his eyes. There was a flash of something beneath the layers of desire and excitement. Insecurity? Not sexual. More the "I can't believe I feel this way" kind of awareness. And the "how is this possible" kind. The "should I risk this" kind. His vulnerability was clear, and she understood it was uncharacteristic, unaccustomed. "I can't believe we're here either." Her voice was textured, rough with pleasure.

Her palm slid slowly up the back of his hand. He flexed his fingers and tightened his hold on the mass of hair he'd gathered at the back of her head. It was a primitive move, and she enjoyed the feeling of possession that played through her mind. Her hand caressed his wrist; her fingers splayed wide and searching as they traveled the corded column of muscle that roped his forearm. She was fascinated by the silken glide of her skin against his. Her fingertips mapped a warm trail of desire as she traced the contours that flowed into the rounded fullness of his bicep.

She marveled at the contrast of their skin colors, his a deeply tanned reddish gold and hers as pale and luminous as the moonlight. She stretched to follow his arm up over his shoulder and down onto his chest. She paused to comb her nails through the smattering of dark hair between his pecs.

She rested her hand gently on his sternum and over his rapidly beating heart. "Come and lie beside me," she whispered as she scooted away to make room for him.

He eased down beside her and drew flush to her body.

She kissed him softly. "Let me show you 'real.' "

Chapter Fifteen

"This is one of my favorite spots." He ran the tip of one finger slowly down Emily's side to the dip at the join of her waist and hip. "I never realized how much I like spooning until this moment."

"Hmm..." Her voice was husky with sleep and satisfaction. She rolled to face him and snuggled up against him. Her hand swept his stomach to brush the soft run of dark hair below his navel. "And this is one of mine." She smiled into his chest. *God, I feel so good.* Every joint was loose, every inch of skin supple and sensitive. The voice in her head murmured about morning breath and funky hair. She studiously ignored it, though she couldn't help but acknowledge that this feeling of contentment and peace was temporary. She cracked open one eye. Her smile was soft.

"As a matter of fact," he whispered as the one finger caress became a warm palm brushing across her breasts, teasing them into attention, "I like all your parts." He was quiet for a moment as he studied her face. "Emily?"

Her hand wandered its way to his impressive hard on. "Shh, I'm concentrating." She smiled again when he rocked slowly inside the ring of her fingers.

"Concentrating? I can't think at all when you do that." His breath came faster, and the speed of his hips picked up when she tightened her grip.

Without letting him go, she pushed him onto his back and rose to straddle him. She lifted one knee and slowly rubbed the velvet head along her slick cleft. "I can't seem to get enough of you, sailor." She lowered herself till just the tip slipped inside, then she backed off. He groaned, and she did it again, a little deeper, then deeper still until he was buried to the hilt. Her breath caught on a moan as the pressure of him swelled against her cervix. God, she was grateful they'd had the protection discussion. She loved the feel of his hot, silky length as it rubbed the walls of her passage. It was dangerous, addictive, and drugging. She loved the sweaty scent of their loving, the power of being above him like this. Loved the look of satisfaction on his face when he made her moan.

His hands at her hip bones, he held her still, keeping her in place, then slowly he took over control, directing the speed of her movements. He lifted her, held her suspended above him, then drove up, fully gloving himself in her liquid heat. They groaned their pleasure in the same voice.

Emily braced her palms on his shoulders. "I should be tired of you, but I'm not. You've set up a craving in me."

She gasped as he pumped upward again and drove her down at the same instant. She gave herself over to his charge and relished the building, roaring desire that filled her. Again and again, he pumped into her and forced her down onto his shaft. Her breath came in gasps and pants. Her heart beat a blinding tattoo, sheening her whole body with sweat. Light exploded behind her eyes, and she cried out as heat spiraled out from their point of contact. She splintered into shiny, glistening pieces and relished the deluge of another sizzling orgasm.

What strength she had left deserted her, and she didn't resist when he pulled her down to his chest. His arms held her perfectly still. But she smiled into his chest as the rhythmic waves of her internal muscles gripped him and worked unbidden to milk his climax from him. The sound of Michael's heart thundered through his chest and into her ear as she relaxed against him. He sucked in breath after breath, and she suddenly realized he was struggling to pull back from his own release.

A wicked thought flashed through her. *We can't have that now, can we?* "More please." She gave a tiny nip to his pec along with a slight roll of her pelvis.

He growled into her hair. "Don't be mean, beautiful. I'm hanging on by a thread here."

She laughed a satisfied, breathless sound and forced her head to rise until she could gaze down into his eyes. Her mind blurred for a moment, and she swore she felt the groundwork of her future beneath her palms.

"Like I said, craving." She felt like purring. "You feel it too, don't you? This is just as new for me as it is for you, Michael."

He rocked upright, grabbed her calf, and wrapped her leg around his waist, then did the same with her other. She gasped and then gloried at his depth inside her.

"You fit me just right, Em," he rasped out. "So tight, so wet. I'm going to fill you so full you'll taste me for a week."

She knew it was true and gave him her mouth. She

rocked back to watch his face as he moved inside her. "I won't stop wanting you even then," she whispered.

His eyes were so dark she couldn't see any color other than desire. His strength amazed her, thrilled her. He handled her as if she weighed nothing. It made her light-headed and dreamy. She was, in that instant, fully connected to her femininity. Every cell of her aware of that essential core self, the one that yearned to be possessed and protected, taken and satisfied, wanted and valued. He did all that and more. She witnessed it in the way he watched her, carefully gauging her expressions and reactions to each touch, each movement, each swivel that stirred him against her interior walls. He seemed to have a sensor for finding her G spot, and his shaft brushed it with every move.

His hand left her hip, and his thumb found her clitoris, rubbing with the same demanding, rocking rhythm of his body. He circled it harder, faster. "Come with me? Come for me again?" His mouth found her pebbled tip, and all his movements synchronized. Everything moved in concert: the pull of his mouth, the slick friction of his thumb, and bottoming out of the rock hard column inside her.

Emily welcomed the bright current of electricity as it gathered inside her and blossomed to an interior nova. "Yes, Michael. Yes, do it, make me come again, fall with me. I love it. Swell inside me. Fill me up. Oh, God. Now, please, now!"

Michael pressed hard on her clitoris, and her body erupted in contracting rhythmic spasms. She screamed out her orgasm as he took her mouth. She relished his hot flood as it poured into her, and he roared out his release against her lips.

Her head spun as Michael rolled them both to the mattress, and she gave herself over to the delicious, satiated darkness.

Chapter Sixteen

It seemed like a second later when the insistent beeping of Michael's phone signaled the moments until they would have to face the rest of the world were short; he wished they could stay locked away like this for the rest of the day. He didn't want to lose the connection he felt to this surprising, warm, funny, kinky, wonderful woman. Not yet. It was so good, relaxed and familiar with her curled against him.

In a zinging moment of clarity, he realized that she was the only thing that had gone right for him since he'd left the base. The only good thing that had happened to him in a long time. He felt stunned, as though the oxygen in the room were fading. He couldn't remember ever feeling comfortable enough with a woman that he'd let her take the time to snuggle. Usually, he was only too happy to blow past these slow, sensual moments and run like hell for the finish line. But this felt different. The first instant he'd tasted her mouth and swallowed her gasp of pleasure, things had changed. He'd lost the ability—the *need*—to disappear beneath his duty or his uniform. He was well and truly naked in more than just his body.

Soon they'd have to end their interlude in fantasy land and return to the real world. It also meant he'd have to tell Emily about his streambank awakening in her hometown, though he knew she'd probably find it funny. Still, he was embarrassed about the loss of self-control that got him dumped on the roadside. He wanted her to think the best of him. He needed her to give him the chance to show her he was worth her time. In more ways than those horizontal. He reached for the phone and silenced the alarm.

Emily stirred and smiled from her pillow. "Is it time to face the morning after?" She stretched and groaned. "I'm so sore... You worked me over last night, sailor."

He watched her flex and felt his own painful aftermath. He winced at the twinges of muscles that hadn't had a workout in longer than he cared to admit. God, if there was a way to bottle the rapture and effervescent euphoria she'd drawn from him last night, he'd be a billionaire in a heart-damn-beat.

"Is hiding here all day out of the question?" she asked.

"I'm afraid so. That doesn't mean we can't take a shower and get some breakfast. I know you have to catch up with your brother and deal with the fallout from that. But let me ask you something. Will you have dinner with me tonight or maybe tomorrow? I mean, I know you've got a life here but—but I'd really like to see you again."

"Careful, sailor." She rolled toward him and kissed his pec. "You may have to drive me off with a stick." She laughed a happy, husky sound. "Wait." She snorted. "That won't work. I like the stick you've got way too much."

"Now you're just making stuff up." He enjoyed the flattery too much for decency. Of course, the things they'd done in the last few hours could get them arrested in several states. Decency had little to do with how pleased he was with himself and the armful of woman currently cuddled against him. The way the night had turned out, he was beginning to believe in the power of circumstance. Ordinary attraction was a pale comparison to the things that Emily pulled from him. Rationally he knew the power of the "new and different," but the allure of this woman was way off the scale of his experience.

****

Thirty minutes, one long soapy shower, and two more orgasms later found Emily wondering just how many positions two people could invent in so short a time. She stood in her recycled underwear, considering how she was going to make it out of the hotel without scandalizing the staff. She dug through her bag and held up the skirt she'd worn into town, and it strongly resembled waded-up tissue. The jacket was no better. If she'd thought about it, she'd have at least folded the damn things. Huffing out her irritation, she wondered if she could scrounge a shirt from the man who was currently scraping the stubble off his square chin. At least it would cover her ass in the yoga pants that she'd need to wear home. Besides, if she picked one of his favorite shirts, he'd have to come to Tamarack to get it back. It would, at the very least, be a small insurance policy to ensure he kept his promise to see her again.

"Michael," she called through the door to his room, "can I rummage in your closet for a shirt? I'll cause a riot in the restaurant if I go in like this."

"Ahh, sure." He hesitated. "I'm kind of embarrassed for you to see what's in there, though, but...go for it. Just don't judge me."

"Oh, yeah? Do you have, like, frilly tutus in there or something?"

"No, smart-ass. I have a thing for *manly* Hawaiian shirts. Each and every one of them is a classic. They're collectible, wearable pieces of art. That's my story, and I'm sticking to it."

Emily froze with her hand on the knob of the closet door. Memories of parking lots, dark kisses, and terrifying excitement flooded her brain. She turned to him and started to ask the question. "Michael? Have you ever been to—?"

The room filled with loud, insistent pounding on the suite door. Pat Evans' voice boomed through the wood. "McCandlis? Emmy? It's Pat. Open up."

Before she could answer, Michael was at her side, his warm hand clasped around her wrist. "Just a minute, Mr. Evans," he called back, then spoke more quietly to her. "Let me grab some pants, okay?"

He jerked off the towel around his hips, and she was momentarily struck dumb. The man had a seriously beautiful body. He stepped past her to reach into the closet. She'd had her hands all over his back and felt the changes in the texture of his skin but hadn't seen his back in the bright light before that moment. It was covered in the red tracks of recently healed injuries. Some of them resembled the puckered edges of eroded potholes. Others had a network of spidery lines that lead to deeper, broader scars still showing clear suture marks. Her breath jammed up in her chest. She placed a careful hand on the worst of the marks, a large cluster of dimpled, angry flesh along his lower spine.

She kept her voice as careful as her touch. "Michael? Wh-what happened?"

"Stupidity," he growled. "I'll tell you some other time. Okay?" He snatched a pair of jeans and a T-shirt off a shelf, a colorful shirt off one of the hangers. He thrust the shirt into her hands and stepped nimbly into the jeans. The T-shirt slipped snugly over his broad chest and covered the shocking evidence of combat on his back. He avoided her eyes as he strode to the door. "Come in, Mr. Evans," he said as he jerked it open.

The older rancher, hat in hand, stood uncomfortably in the hallway. "Mornin', Mike," he mumbled as his eyes caught sight of Emily standing in one of the bedroom doors. She clutched a bright swatch of cloth in a white-knuckled grip. "Emmy." He nodded in her direction, then cleared his throat. "Sorry to interrupt this…whatever this is." He gave Michael a disapproving glare as he took in their wet hair and the scent of soapy steam in the air. "I just got a call. It's Ian. He's in the hospital."

She frowned in confusion and jerked the garish flowered shirt over her shoulders. "Why the hell didn't anyone call me?" She rushed to the couch and grabbed her purse. She fished out her phone. The battery was dead. "Shit. What happened? When?"

Pat's face softened. "I don't know the details. Teddy left a message with the desk, and they called me. I talked with him a few minutes ago. He said Ian overdosed. They took him to Denver Health late last night or early this morning; I'm not sure. He wanted me to find you and tell you to come quick as you could. Might not be as serious as it sounds, you just never know with Ted. He can be pretty dramatic."

"O-overdose?" she whispered. "But he's been clean for…well, I don't know how long." She tried to calm her racing heart. That word—overdose—sounded so clinical, so accidental. She knew, as surely as she had the first time it had happened, that this was no accident on Ian's part, and she knew what sponsored it. Ray Domenico was now and always would be a trigger for Ian. The cork to his bottle, the needle to his vein. If Ian wanted out of his pain so badly that he'd try to take his own life, she was certain Ray was at the root of the wound.

"It'll only take me a second to grab my things." She ran into the second bedroom. A moment later, she was back with a small duffel and her shoes in her hand. "I've got everything."

She paused and glanced at Michael. He'd finished dressing and was waiting with his hand on the doorknob.

"You don't have to come with me. I'm sure you've seen enough of hospitals." She was clearly referring to his back injuries. He frowned at her, making her rethink her effort to leave him behind. "Or not. I just meant I don't know what to expect, and I don't want you to feel you've got to come along."

"Yeah? Sounds to me like you could use a driver at the very least and maybe some backup. So how about we get a move on and sort out the rest later?"

"I'm perfectly capable of driving." She regretted the tone as soon as it left her mouth. Michael wasn't her enemy. She knew very clearly where that designation lay. If anything happened to her brother because of Ray fucking Domenico, there wasn't a place on this earth where he could hide.

Pat spoke up. "Don't be stubborn, Emmy. You don't know what you might need. Accept the help and quit getting in your own way. Ian's the one who needs you right now. Sit down, put your shoes on." He laid a beefy palm on her shoulder and not so gently moved her to the couch. "Sit. I need to talk to Mike for a minute." He motioned Mike toward the door. "I've got a really bad feeling about this."

"Yeah, I agree." Michael's voice was just above a whisper. "The thing is, Ian reminds me of a buddy from my early days in the navy. The kid was lonely and pissed off, just like her brother." He glanced at Emily. "He ended all of it at the end of a needle. I hope I'm wrong, but my instincts are rarely off."

"I can hear you, you know," she said. *God. Some men.* Did they think she was completely in the dark about the possible result of shoving drugs up his nose?

Pat looked chastened and stepped through the door. "Sorry, honey. Just wanted him to know. Anyway, thanks for having her back, McCandlis. I'll check in with you soon as I get the bride and groom on their way. Any messages for your crew?"

"Nah, Jerry's their new boss. You can let him know I'll be calling with an update. Thanks, Mr. Evans." He pumped Pat's hand a couple of times, then followed Emily through the door.

"The name's Pat," the older man said gruffly. "You take care of our girl." He reached into his pocket and pulled out a business card. "If you need me, call my cell. It's on the back."

****

Hurrying through the lobby, headed for the parking garage, Emily fished in her bag for the keys to the Jeep. As she reached the bottom for the second time, a growl of frustration escaped her tightly held control. Damn

Ray Domenico to hell. Ian's drugs of choice used to be alcohol and sex, but cocaine had nearly killed him two years ago. Perhaps he'd raised the threat level of his substances. Regardless, every inhaled line and every depressed plunger slowly but surely sucked him deeper into the sewer of defeat and self-hatred. If it turned out he'd once again tried suicide, self-forgiveness would be in short supply. There was zero chance that Ian would've reached a conclusion like that if he believed he had any other choice.

She stumbled in her headlong dash for the parking deck. If Michael hadn't reached out with a steady grip to her elbow, her knees would have come to a painful landing on the unforgiving blacktop. She glanced at him apologetically. Christ, she was so freaked out she'd forgotten he was even there. He was right. She needed a driver, or the entire population of Denver was at risk with her behind the wheel of a car.

"Sorry, I wasn't watching where I was going. I...I can't find my damned keys! And I don't remember the way to the hospital clearly. They changed the name of the place. Can you believe that? All my life it's been Denver fucking General and now it's Denver Health. I hope Google Maps is working, or I might have to call a taxi or Uber because I'll never find it." The words tumbled out of her mouth at a breakneck pace. "I can't believe this is happening. Teddy can be a such a drama queen, but he'd never exaggerate a call about my brother. So I'm just...I'm..." Her breathless voice halted on a sob.

"Terrified?" Michael pulled her hand from her purse and kept drawing on her wrist till she was firmly wrapped in his arms. He rubbed comforting circles on her back and laid a soft kiss on the crown of her still-damp hair. "I know what you're feeling. Time goes into slow motion when shock sweeps in. Suddenly your steps feel lodged in cement, your normal reaction time is shot to hell, and bad things happen. We'll get there, beautiful. Don't worry about that. Don't worry about anything. I got you."

He rocked her briefly, then skillfully slipped her purse from her shoulder. The keys that had eluded her were peeking out of a side pocket. He scooped them out and pressed the lock button to activate the vehicle's horn. It beep-beeped in response, and he turned them toward the sound. "What color is your car?" he asked, moving her out of his embrace.

"Red." Her voice still as unsteady as her hands. She took several deep breaths and forced herself to calm down.

He flipped the hair off her shoulder and flashed her a grin. "Mmm, my favorite color." He held onto her hand and strode off in the direction of her Jeep.

****

From the street, Denver Health Medical Center had changed very little in the last two decades. It was still in the heart of old town Denver on 8th Avenue, and it took up a major part of the local floor space. Its red brick and slick, white, tile exterior was illuminated by the strobes of ambulance lights and the calmer washes of car lights. Emily, plastered against the glass inside her car, gave Michael cryptic directions to the parking structure. She tried like hell not to jump out of the door before he came to a complete stop. As it was, he had to jog to catch up with her as she sprinted to the nearest elevator out of the garage. Inside and across an immense lobby, they were directed to another wing on another floor.

She found Ted marching up and down the hall outside a family waiting room. He alternately tugged on his hair and stared daggers at his watch. Fear and impatience were a sickening taste in the air.

"Where's Ian? How is he?" Emily croaked as she reached him.

Ted blinked at her. "I tried to call you like a hundred times. He's in ICU, Em. They're doing checks or something for a while. They'll come to get us when they're done."

She gave a rough shove to open the waiting room door and whirled on him. "What the hell happened, Ted? I thought you were looking out for him." She instantly regretted the accusation dripping from her voice. Her hand slapped over her mouth, but it was too late to stop the words.

"I-I was." Ted's voice was rusty with his own tears. "I tried, but he-he… Oh, my God, Em, I'm so sorry." His tall, spare frame folded in on itself, and he collapsed to the floor.

She followed him down and gathered him, sobbing, into her arms. God, she could be such a bitch. "I know, I'm sorry too," she crooned. "I'm the one who's sorry, Teddy Bear. I shouldn't have let him leave without me. I should have kicked Ray's ass myself and taken Ian home. Not you, not you. I know you love him as much as I do. Don't cry, Teddy." She rocked back and wiped his tear-streaked face with her thumbs. He looked like she felt, robbed of anything approaching optimism and fearing the worst.

She took his arm and dragged him off the floor to a

chair. She shook off her sense of dread and forced him to look her in the eyes. "Now tell me what happened to my brother. Don't sugar coat it, just give me the facts. I've been through rehab with him more than once, so I figure I know the basics of what got him here." The authority in her voice surprised her. She was feeling anything but sure of her ground. Another lesson applied from the days of family visitation, "fake it till you make it."

Ted glanced at her, obviously still feeling her rebuke. "Twenty-five words or less? Are you counting or should I?"

"Ted…"

"Right, right. I wish it were that simple, is all." He gulped audibly. "He wasn't hurt badly by Domenico, just a banged-up nose and pissed off. Despondent one minute, raging the next. He was high when we got to the reception, and it didn't wear off when we got home. After he talked to you, he smoked a joint, drank the rest of a bottle of Jack, and finally passed out about one this morning. I was trying to keep him calm, watching him. Honest, I was. The apartment was clear. I searched it myself. He's been clean for nearly six months. I had such hopes that this would be the time it took. You know?"

He paused for a moment. Emily reached for his hands and gripped them, knowing the rest of the story would be the hardest to hear.

"I woke up a few hours later, and the bed was empty. The bathroom light was on, but he didn't answer. I p-pushed on the door with everything I had and couldn't get to him. Honey, I could see his arm, and there was b-blood. The smell. God, Em. I'll never forget the smell." His voice failed him. Emily tightened her grip on his hands, and they trembled together.

"I called the ambulance. When they got there, we had to remove the door to get to him. They worked on him for a long time. They...they wouldn't let me ride along with them. I nearly crashed twice on the way here." His fingers made tufts in his blond hair. "I can't believe he did this. He really tried to end it, end us. Why would he let that bastard push him so far that he would try to k-kill himself?"

Michael's deep voice made them jump. "Are you sure it wasn't an accident?"

Ted glanced at the big man, then shook his head. "No. Heroin is never accidental, too much prep involved."

"Heroin?" Emily whispered a startled gasp. He'd never traveled that far down before. "Maybe there's some mistake. Are they sure?" Images of seedy tenement rooms and dirty mattresses crowded her mind. Hollywood's version of hell on earth.

Ted nodded, his face bleak. "The doctor in ER said he had enough heroin and coke in his blood to kill a horse. They were amazed he'd made it to the hospital." He looked up at the clock. "They moved him from ER to ICU about two hours ago. He-he's on a ventilator. They put a tube down his windpipe to keep him breathing while they pump more drugs through his body." He looked up at the ceiling. "He may never come back, Em. What'll we do if he doesn't come back?"

He'd stepped from cocaine to the biggest cheat of all. Heroin. And she hadn't known. It was just another example of the voluntary disconnect between them.

"He'll come back, Teddy. He always comes back." She scrambled to find some scrap of light to cling to. She jostled his hands till he looked her in the eyes. She needed him to know that she didn't blame him for Ian's choices.

Ted nodded sadly. He looked defeated. "Yeah, of course. But you know how this works as well as I do. He's good for a while, then something happens, and he begins to spiral." He took a shuddering breath. "He won't accept the help he really needs. Won't listen to anyone, especially me. He's angry that he can't beat this on his own, sees it as confirmation of all the crap that Ray is so good at throwing at him. He's bound and determined to fight anyone who tries to help." He scrubbed his palms over his swollen eyes. "I guess last night was the straw that broke his back."

Emily shook her head, ready to dispute him, but he was right. They said the first attempt was a cry for help, a dry run. The second attempt was focused on the end result and more likely to be successful.

Ted stood and made a loop around the room. She watched as he plucked and fidgeted with his shirt, ran a hand through his hair, and grimaced. He examined his thumbnail. It was chewed to the quick and beyond. A tear joined the tracks of its predecessors. It ran down his cheek to drip off his chin and mix with the stains on his shirt. "God, I'm a mess." He shook back imaginary long hair and frowned at the darkness spoiling the bright lavender on his chest. "This rag used to be my favorite silk button down. I need to burn it, and the pants...and the underwear." He sighed heavily. "Might as well throw in the shoes. I'll never wear any of it again." He glanced at the clock on the wall. "I swear that thing is unplugged." He sighed and slumped back in the chair beside her.

Emily slipped her hand into his. "You should go home and take a shower, Teddy. You'll feel better with clean clothes. Maybe Mike wouldn't mind giving you a lift." She looked to Michael for confirmation.

He nodded. "Not sure you should be driving."

Ted shook his head vehemently. "Wish I could, but I can't go back there. The apartment is a wreck. We had to c-cut the door from the frame to get to him. And, God, Em, I can't handle it. The bathroom is covered in vomit and shit… There's no way I can face it. I-I just can't."

She didn't need to imagine it. She remembered all too well the scene in her own home the first time Ian had tried suicide. It had taken a cleaning crew to restore the damage he'd done that night. She hadn't been able to enter her own guest room for the rest of her time in the house without remembering the mingled scents of a body expelling all its waste and fluids at once. "Okay, we'll figure out something. Maybe you can get a room down the street. I think Park Place is nearest. Will that do?"

Ted nodded. "I want to wait for an update from the doctor, and my mother should be here soon. I called her a couple of hours ago. Everything is going in slow motion since they moved him out of Emergency and into a room. All any of them would say was that he was stable. And to get that much, I had to tell them we were engaged." He made a whimpering noise and covered his mouth with trembling fingers. "If only that were true."

Emily's ears perked up at the sound of sharp steps

in the corridor. The waiting room door suddenly filled with the thin frame of his mother. Blanche looked like Ted clearly felt, stressed and spare, frightened and ready to claw her way past anyone foolish enough to stand between her and her loved one.

"Mama." Ted's voice was rusty with the tears he'd swallowed and the dozen or so cigarettes he sucked down in the last few hours.

Blanche wrapped him in a hug. "Oh, my sweet boy."

"Sorry for getting you guys out of bed so early." His words hitched in his throat. "You didn't drive down here alone, did you?"

Blanche just held on and rocked and patted and rocked some more. "Now, now. Don't you worry about that. Billy's parking the truck, and then it'll probably take him the rest of the morning to find this waiting room." She leaned back and gave them all a stern look. "You about done letting this situation get the best of you?"

Ted hiccupped against her shoulder. "I'm tryin'. I know it's not doing any good. Ian can't hear me, and the nurses won't tell me anything useful. I've been here all night by myself. I stink so bad even I don't want to be around me."

"Yeah, that's quite the parfumey you got there." She chuckled and released her son. She swiveled on bony hips and turned to Emily. "This is a mess, huh?"

"Yeah. We just got here a bit ago. My stupid phone was dead." Emily cast a guilty glance at Michael. "We got the news through Pat."

Blanch narrowed her eyes and looked Michael over. "Well, well, well. I thought you looked familiar. I recognize you now—even without all that hair." She took in the bright flowered shirt hanging off Emily's shoulders like a tent. "Very small world."

Michael's jaw clenched, and he stared her down. "Mike McCandlis." He stuck out a wide hand.

Blanche grunted and shook it. "I'd really like to know how this"—she circled her finger between Emily and Michael—"came about, but you can tell me another time."

Emily frowned, confused, and gave Michael a quizzical look.

He shook his head. "Doesn't matter now. I'll tell you later," he mumbled.

Blanche rose and peeked out the door. She turned and dusted her palms together. "All right, let's get organized. When was the last update on Ian? And for Christ's sake, would you guys stop looking like the human version of the hear-no-evil, see-no-evil, speak-no-evil statue? They ain't pulled a sheet over the boy's face. In my book, that means there's hope."

Ted straightened in his seat. He looked at his mother, his gaze full of the need for certainty. "Right. That's right. Tough and positive. Nothing's gonna happen, and he's gonna be fine." Then he slumped like his newly acquired backbone was broken, and his lower lip began to quiver. "But what if this doesn't turn out like we want? W-what if he doesn't make it? What if he lives and is—never the same somehow? He could stroke out, have permanent brain damage, never be able to paint again. I've tried so hard to keep him safe and away from all the contaminated shit out there. I'm afraid all I really did was make it easier for this to happen." His eyes filled with tears again.

"Theodore Allen Reese," Blanche said sternly, "you listen to me. No one on this planet coulda done more to keep that young man from the path he took. His problems started a long time ago and have zip to do with you. Stop borrowing trouble, Teddy. You gotta assign blame? Lay it at his father's feet. He never gave that boy a chance to be anything but a failure. From the very beginning, Ray treated him like a mistake."

Emily got up and started pacing. "That's the twenty-four-thousand-dollar question, isn't it? Ian used to try so hard to be what the man wanted." The waiting room's cool sage-green walls felt like a cage to her. She cleared her throat and glanced at Michael. He sat tense and silent, a quiet solid presence. She was suddenly grateful he'd insisted on staying with her. This couldn't be easy for any outsider to endure. God knew she'd rather be back at the hotel, warming up the sheets beside him instead of plowing through yet another load of her family's dirty laundry. Yet he was still here.

She stopped in front of the smudged glass door to the hallway. Her reflection showed a woman with swollen eyes in a blotchy face. She looked older than was comfortable. "I understand why Ray hates me. I even understand why he hates Ted." She turned back to the group, to Ted in particular. "I mean you *are* the one who brought Ian into the open sexually, but Ray always treated Ian like used toilet paper. Necessary but disgusting, you know? When he bothered to pay attention at all, he crammed his idea of being a 'real man' down Ian's throat."

She hesitated, wondering how much it would take to finally chase Michael out the door. At a time like this, it shouldn't matter to her, but it did. "It was always about control for Ray. I tried to distract him. Figured if I caused a big enough shit storm, he'd focus on me. It never worked for long. He'd always zero back on Ian."

"You sure you want to get into this?" Michael asked.

She shrugged. "There's more than enough blame to go around. I'm just sayin' he learned early that it was easier to escape, however he could find it. It's always been the option he chose." She glanced at Michael. "We have that in common."

Blanche cleared her throat and looked at her son then Emily in turn. She closed her eyes for a moment, then stared up at the ceiling. "So you're sayin' Ray…what, abused you? Christ, Emily, why didn't you ever say anything? Pat would have been all over him. You've got to know that."

"He wasn't the law back then, and I did go to the cops. When I was eleven or twelve, I went to the sheriff. He made a show of talking to Ray, but nothing ever came of it. He probably bought the man off. I don't know. But Ray made his point, and it got worse for us. So I stopped wondering why he hated us, and we stopped looking for help." Saying it out loud brought back all the bleakness of those desolate days. She shook her arms loose from the protective wrap they had around her stomach.

Blanche shook her head sadly. "I'm so sorry. I swear to you that I didn't know how bad it was for you kids. If I had, I'd have moved heaven and earth to bring that man down." She dug into her jacket pocket and pulled out a pack of cigarettes. She tumbled the brightly colored package over and over in her hand. "There are things that you don't know. Things that happened a long time ago. I don't know if it will make a difference now or not."

She paused, frowning. "They might answer some of your questions. Maybe make things better once Ian wakes up, and I believe he will wake up. I shouldn't have kept this to myself, but I...well, I thought it was best left in the past." She spoke quietly, perched in one of the hard plastic chairs that populated the waiting room. "I think I know why the senator always hated Ian."

Chapter Seventeen

Emily's heart did a strange hip-hop in her chest. Suddenly the air got thinner in the tiny waiting room. Blanche's face was awash with guilt, as though she were responsible for all the ugliness that had been their childhood. She'd known Blanche Reese for as long as she could remember. If there was one thing that typified the woman, it was that she was stubborn and close-mouthed at the best of times. Blanche only revealed her feelings when she deigned to do so. The rest of the time, she clutched them close to her vest like a champion poker player. The same went for advice. Ask directly and heed the response, because it wouldn't be offered a second time. For her to volunteer information was a truly rare thing. Still, the thought that she'd withhold something that could have made "all the difference" in the life of her and Ian pissed her off. She wanted to leap at the woman, drag the story out of her, and then beat her with it.

"Is that right?" Emily's hands gripped the fabric of Michael's shirt at her hips. She stared Blanche down, willing her to get on with it. "What do you think you know? And why, for the love of God, did you keep quiet if it might have helped us? You only know the tiniest sliver of what we went through. What we desperately needed was to know that someone, anyone, cared. Don't you see that?" She took a step toward

Blanche, incensed that the woman had held back when she could have done...something, anything.

"Goddamn it, Mama," Ted said. "Say your piece, and it had better be more than 'the old man's an ass' because he's been one for as long as I can remember." He grabbed a handful of hair on each side of his head and pulled straight out, leaving him looking like a mad scientist.

Appearing guiltier by the second, Blanche grimaced. "The problem started before the boy was born." She glanced at her son, but her attention was on Emily. She huffed out a breath and stuck an unlit cigarette in her mouth. She closed her eyes and squared off her shoulders, then looked up at Emily with determination in her face. "I was friends with your ma way back in the day. You and Ted were maybe four or five years old. She used to drop by the diner, and we'd chat. She was a beauty, that girl. Talented too. A painter, no surprise you kids are both good with your hands. Creative souls all of you. But back then, she was new to the marriage, and it really brightened her spirit after losing Brent to the war." She stared off into a corner of the waiting room, a sad smile dusting her thin face.

"Brent? My father?" It had been many years since Emily had heard his name. A familiar empty feeling accompanied it. "She loved him. The best man she ever knew, she used to tell me. Ray said he was a coward and a fool for getting killed."

Blanche nodded in agreement. "Don't surprise me none. Ol' Ray, he hated to be reminded your mama belonged to anyone before him. Shocked everybody when he married her. I thought it was smart on his part.

Her looks and the fact she was a war widow with a cute little girl got him his second term in office. There was a while there when he couldn't do nothin' wrong in this state." She scrunched up her face, like anything to do with politics left a bad taste in her mouth. "Anyhow, like I said, they started out happy. Spent the time Congress was in session in DC, all very public, very shiny and clean. Then something happened in Washington. I'm not sure what it was, though I suppose it had something to do with the good senator's wandering zipper. Sarah never said. One day, she showed up at my counter and informed me she wanted to buy the old hardware store next to me. Said she wanted a place of her own to show her work. Said she'd decided to stay in Tamarack full time because you'd be better off in our small schools. I didn't question it. She was a painter, and I knew the store owner wanted to sell, so I helped her."

Ted threw his long body back in the chair. "What does this have to do with Ian, Mama? I wish you would just get to the point and stop the narrative."

"I'm gettin' to it. Anyway, like I said, she and Ray seemed happy enough together, but things changed about the time you guys started school." She fished out her lighter, looked disgustedly at the *No Smoking* sign on the wall, and jammed it back in her pocket. The cigarette continued to waggle between her lips as she spoke. "Sarah stopped following the senator around the country and used Emily as an excuse to stay home. The senator made obligatory visits, but he never stayed long. That seemed to suit Sarah just fine, so I didn't question the reasons behind it."

Blanche got up and did her own turn around the

waiting room. "Then one time, after a visit from Ray, she was sitting in a booth, nursing her third cup of coffee. I remember her looking up at me, all empty and blank-faced. She asked if I thought anyone would believe her if she told them about the kind of man she'd married." She slumped back into her chair and took a serrated breath of air that reeked of industrial cleaning products. She fished a tissue out of her sleeve, blew her nose, and wiped at her eyes. When she continued, her voice had lost some of its bravado. "I looked into her eyes, and there was a well of hopelessness the likes of which I'd only seen one other time. My mama had that look every time my ol' man beat her—and I knew. She didn't have to tell me. I knew what she was dealin' with." She leaned forward, plucked the smoke from her mouth. She rocked, elbows on her angular knees. "I told her not to waste any more breath on me, to take her story to the sheriff and get the hell out of the house."

She watched Emily. Looking for redemption, forgiveness? Emily had neither to offer; her body was a frozen, heartbroken statue.

Blanche shook her head. "She didn't of course. Like a lot of women, she stayed with him. Never brought it up again, never showed up with bruises that I could see. And I looked, I'll tell you that. Anyway, time passed, and she was smiling again, more relaxed, seemed to be making plans for her little gallery. She told me she was learning all kinds of things. Got a horse from Pat and loved it. Used to spend the whole day out on the trails above town while the both of you were in kindergarten.

"I thought for a while she had a lover, maybe one of the cowhands at the Evans ranch. But I never found out who. Then long about the time you and Teddy were in first grade, she up and agreed to go on the campaign trail with the senator. I remember telling her I thought she was nuts to be around him so much, but she insisted he'd asked her to be part of his bid for a third term. Finally, he needed her she said. A couple of months later, she was back in town with a big smile on her face. She told me she was pregnant and due in June or July." Blanche paused and drew a steady bead on Emily. She waited till their eyes met. "What I'm sayin' is, there was no way Honorable Senator Raymond Domenico could possibly be the father of the child she carried. The timing just don't work out."

Emily's mouth dropped open in shock. Seriously? An affair? Her mind spun. That would explain a lot of things. If it was true, it didn't bring as much relief as it should. Ian, not Ray's child? He must have known. She couldn't have hidden it from him, even back then. She jammed her hands in her hair and gathered twin handfuls at the scalp. The sting didn't register over the pounding of her heart. "This…this means Ian suffered his entire life for the sins of our mother?" Her next breath turned into a hitching sob. Her mother had the chance and the reason to get out from under Ray and didn't take it.

"Oh, honey, I wouldn't put it that way. Remember, we're talking Tamarack's golden boy here. Worse yet, the story would've been a huge scandal. She'd have had to leave town or the state to get away from it. Ray never woulda let that happen."

Suddenly on the defensive, Emily stepped forward. "That's not the woman I remember at all." At that moment, she wanted to throttle Blanche. "Aside from relieving Ian of the burden of carrying that bastard's DNA in his bloodstream, what possible difference does it make now?" Emily glared at her. Blanche was like the majority of Tamarack, willing to turn a blind eye to the "family business" of its precious native son. "Maybe you're looking for a reason not to feel guilty as shit for leaving us to the mercy of a sadist."

"You know, Mama?" Ted spoke up. "I can't even look at you right now. You kept this to yourself for over twenty years, and now you think it will help? You and the whole town stood by while he abused those kids, bent and twisted his son into a hollowed-out carcass of a man." His voice choked to a stop. He looked up at Emily and whispered, "Sorry. I shouldn't have said that."

Blanche looked at her son, regret and remorse pale on her face. "Yeah, I guess I did. I had my own to look out for." Ted jumped to his feet, ready to blast her again, but Blanche held up a bony hand to stay his anger. "I won't apologize for that, not to you, not to anyone."

Emily slumped down in a chair, her head heavy in her hands. No matter how she romanticized the ways it might've been different had her mother lived, she couldn't change the past. Sarah was human and had simply done the best she could. Not a champion, not a heroine. In the end, she was the lucky one. Death had taken her.

Michael laid a gentle hand on her shoulder, and she looked back at him. "The doc's here," he said, nodding to the door.

"Ms. Domenico? I'm Dr. Adams. I'd like to speak with you about Ian." The young doctor was tall and gaunt, his gaze direct.

Without realizing it, she was on her feet. "It's Converse, Emily Converse. Can I see my brother now?"

"After we talk, yes." The young doctor gestured to the hall, and she followed him out. Ted got up to follow them. The doctor stopped him. "Mr. Reese, you've been here long enough. There's no change in Ian's condition since the last check. I want you to go home and take a shower, get some food in you. You can come back later." His stern look brooked no argument. Emily was impressed.

"Come on Ted." Michael stood and put a hand on his shoulder. "I'll take you to a hotel, then come back for Emily. Okay?" He looked from Ted to Emily. They nodded in concert. He nudged Ted through the door and kissed Emily on the forehead before following him down the long green hall.

Blanche looked fragile as Emily turned back to her from the door. "You going with him?"

"No, if it's okay with you, I'll wait for Billy." She bit her lip as she gave Emily a look filled with remorse. "I wish I'd done things…differently."

Emily wasn't ready to make peace. "That bell can't be unrung." She turned and followed the doctor. She caught a glimpse of a man stepping hurriedly into the stairwell opposite the waiting room. *Eavesdropper.* He'd definitely gotten an earful. Hopefully it wouldn't be another headline in the papers.

Chapter Eighteen

Michael stood by, quietly watching Emily while she sat at her brother's bedside. She held Ian's hand and talked to him as if they were carrying on a regular conversation. He couldn't make out her words, but clearly she was doing more than praying for him. And she'd been at it for hours. He checked his watch, nearly twelve by his count.

He marveled at her ability to reign in her fear, marshal it into a net of care around a man who'd doubtlessly caused her countless heartaches. Where did that strength to love so consistently come from? It wasn't something he was familiar with. He'd experienced the support of his teammates, felt the dedication of the medical staffers who cared for him and other patients. He'd seen families come and go from the hospitals he'd been in over the years. Witnessed the tears of veterans, both fit and wounded.

But in his entire life, he'd never made a connection as strong as the one he witnessed here. He was always at a distance from them, always found a place inside himself where he could retreat from the barrage of feelings emotionally intense situations generated. Years of practice made his "one-man island" act easy to access when the need arose. Now would be a good time for that, but he wasn't able to step away.

He watched her push her love out to a brother who

had taken the path of least resistance all his life. What would it feel like to be loved so unconditionally, so unreservedly? With Emily, he found himself pulled into her emotions, affected by her struggle, softened by her presence. It wasn't a comfortable revelation. How, in just a few brief hours, had this woman managed to change him from a solitary creature into someone who recognized a deep-seated yearning for more than duty, service, and purpose? He was shocked by the revelation, frightened by the prospect that with very little effort, he could find himself in love, real love for the very first time in his lonely life.

Was it as simple as the fact that they fit together like cogs in meshing gears? The analogy certainly worked. All it took to keep the machine purring along was the oil of trust, the fuel of selflessness, and the spark of desire. Skip one element, and the relationship's engine broke down. Was that akin to the kind of addiction Ian felt? He wasn't in the least bit sure that it was a healthy thing. Love like that gave each party the ultimate weapon—the power to destroy the other. It was a frightening reality he both craved and was hesitant to touch.

He was coming to understand the feeling and her role in it. The time he'd spent taking the exhausted Ted to temporary lodging at The Park Place Hotel had been very illuminating. He'd even garnered an apology from the man for the bachelor party fiasco. Not that Mike was ready to forgive and forget that little tidbit of insanity. He figured everyone, including himself, was entitled to a monumental screw up once in a while. And that had been a fuck up of legendary proportions.

In a short period of time, Mike had learned a great

deal about this woman. The loss of her mother as a small child left her feeling abandoned and lonely. Then, as the step-child of an important figure in DC politics, she'd spent a lot of time in the public eye, jammed into the role of perfect daughter, surrogate mother, stand-in hostess, and campaign staffer when she was too young to fill the roles. Though most of her year was spent in Tamarack, she was under the constant supervision of a parade of nannies and housekeepers. Ted believed the caregivers came from a pool of illegals passed back and forth by agencies who specialized in undocumented help. Senator Domenico had tightly controlled Emily's life, even when he wasn't physically with the children.

Mike did his best to remain detached, but when Ted began to list the highlights of Domenico's idea of discipline, he found himself clutching the steering wheel in a white-knuckled grip. Anger and yearning for retribution pooled in his gut. According to Ted, the senator had carefully walked the line between abuse and lawfully accepted parental control by doling out scripted "training regimens." It didn't take a genius to see that, at an altitude of nearly eighty-five hundred feet, compliance would be quickly obtained. Ray's constantly evolving set of standards made it easy for the children to step over an invisible line that separated safety and punishable infraction. Then, of course, there had been the root cellar in the horse barn. "The Hole" they'd called it. The fucking place was modeled after WWII prison camp solitary. A chill dark space with a steel grate that bolted on the outside.

Mike's admiration for Emily spiked as he learned she'd become an expert at escape and evasion. She'd figured out a way to slide the bolt back from the inside and was the one who picked the padlock that replaced it. If she and Ian were in The Hole together, she'd gotten them out. If he was alone, she'd sneak down the stairs at night and free him till bed check in the morning.

"I remember the day she left town," Ted said. "Her full-ride scholarship to Northwestern was her ticket out. It would look bad to the public if the senator got in her way. So she hugged me and Mama both, sobbed goodbye to Noni, and beat feet out of town. I've only seen her a few times since she left. Every time it involved Ian and his problems.

"Emily's always been independent, smart, inventive. But that's not the same thing as being street smart. In spite of everything, she still leads with her heart. I can tell she likes you, sailor. Just don't be another asshole. Okay?"

Ted gave a shaky sigh and shook Mike's hand. "Anyway, thanks for the ride. Sorry again about the…well, you know. I hope you don't hold it against me." His mouth quirked up into a small smile as he stepped from Emily's Jeep. He leaned down and looked in the door before turning away toward the hotel's portico. He tossed a lascivious wink over his shoulder. "Unless you want to, of course, then we'll talk."

****

At the hospital, time crawled. The quiet movements of staff, the shifting of patients in and out of ICU, all blended into a blur as the hours passed.

Michael stepped to her side and said quietly, "Emily, I'm going to get you something to eat. I'll be back in a few minutes. Okay?"

She barely heard his voice but nodded and resumed

her vigil at Ian's side. He was ashen, hollow-cheeked, and limp, but his chest kept on moving. That was good. It proved he had the strength to fight his way back. She knew it, she believed it, and she wouldn't put up with anyone saying anything to the contrary. That included the doctor who'd tried to tell her chances were slim, the nurses who'd told her they agreed without saying a word. But they'd removed the ventilator a while ago, and he was still holding his own. No signs of consciousness yet. But it was coming.

"Come on, little brother. You need to wake up because we've got stuff to do. Like, hanging those paintings you promised me. I know just where they'll go. Cloud to Ground has a whole wall I'm going to dedicate to you." She squeezed his limp hand. "What the hell were you thinking, huh? You know I'm counting on you. How could you think this was any kind of answer? You know there's no shit too big for us to handle together. I'm sorry I wasn't there for you, Ian. Sorrier than you can imagine."

She'd been babbling for hours. Talking nonstop. Reminding him of funny things, imploring him to listen when she said she believed he had the strength to return to her, promising they would take it slow and do it right this time. No more meddling on her part, no more hiding on his. She tried to stop her thoughts from straying into dangerous territory and refused to let her words reflect them when she failed. She kept watching the numbers on his monitors change and tried to ignore the soft sounds of the staff going about the business of keeping everyone alive. They'd been kind to her, allowing her to stay at his bedside beyond the allotted time.

"Did I tell you about the guy from last night? Probably. I can't remember, but he's just…wow. Big and gorgeous, perfection on a stick, if there is such a thing. If I was looking for someone, which I'm totally not, he'd be the one I picked. We're good together. We proved that last night. I wonder if it'll still be true tomorrow. The whole power-mad stepfather, suicidal brother, one-night stand with a needy git might be enough to push him out the door. What do you think? Maybe? Probably." She sighed and stroked his hand. "Oh, well…it's *my* luck to find the guy who fits me just right and feels just perfect; then the whole world blows up around me. Can't win for losing these days.

"Do you think, in the real world, it's possible for strangers to find each other, fit each other in ways that only seem real in romance novels? That would be cool, wouldn't it?" She sighed and stroked the cool skin above his IV. "It's more likely that you and I are so damaged there'll never be a Happily Ever After for either of us. Maybe we'll just grow old together, painting and designing things that will never be seen outside our studios. I'd take that over the alternative, though. You know, the one where I'm found alone, frozen to death in my apartment, half eaten by the neighbor's cat."

Jesus, enough of that. She was supposed to be coaxing him back, not making it sound better to float off into the soft darkness he currently clung to. She shook her head and stretched her back, aware of muscles atrophied stiff by holding Ian's hand for the last few hours. She stood slowly and smiled down at him, remembering for a moment how solidly he used to sleep as a child. How she wished this was the same kind of rest.

She leaned forward and swept her fingers through her brother's hair, letting the long, soft strands sift past her fingertips. The color an exact match to hers. She brushed a soft finger along his hairline. The silky texture felt much as it had when he was a child; the gesture was the same one she'd used a million times in the dark of night when their monster came out to play.

She hesitated when she felt the rough edge of a scar beneath the hairline. Her focus sharpened as she traced its progress from high above his temple to the side of his head. The puckered line was nearly the length of her hand. She frowned and lifted his hair to get a better look.

She parted the hair and looked closely at the scar. The three-inch-long track looked as if it had never been stitched closed. She'd never seen this gruesome mark, so plain in the harsh light of the overheads. When the hell had that happened? Why hadn't he told her? If he'd hidden an injury severe enough to cause this kind of a scar, what other unseen, untended, and horrific things was he keeping from her? Carefully, she arranged his hair back on the pillow and took a fortifying breath before she moved to invade what was left of his privacy.

The cotton tie at the back of his neck pulled free easily. "Sorry, honey. I've got to take a look." She pulled away Ian's gown to study the lavish ink that covered his shoulder and swept halfway across his chest. The swirling lines and concentric circles had a vaguely Celtic flair. It was a beautiful piece of art, one that Ian had doubtlessly designed himself.

She traced the intricate detail of his design with a

shaking finger. The knots of intersecting lines were densely colored. Her gasp of shock filled the room as she realized they worked as a highly effective mask over a network of scars. The cleverly shaded strokes of darkness covered a wealth of small nicks and thin slices long since healed. Her touch froze when she reached the first circular depression. Bile rolled up the back of her throat. It was a—burn mark, the diameter of her thumb.

"Son of a bitch!" Emily gasped aloud. She pulled up on Ian's shoulder and rolled him to his side. He was so limp and unresponsive it was like moving a slab of meat. She tried to swallow away the analogy, but it stuck in her mind. Her brother had been turned into a cheap side of beef with the same casual panache of a butcher with a knife in hand. Domenico's sick prints were all over the weapon.

On his back, she found faint lines, both parallel and crossing. Marks of a whip or a crop of some kind, again painted over with an intricate, clever spread of ink. Vivid color captured the deceptive depiction of a waterfall. A landmark she was all too familiar with. Angel Falls remained the turning point in both their lives. The scars—proof of the things Ian had gone through alone, young, and too traumatized to fight back.

She swallowed heavily. Her mind spun with the implications. When had he gotten the first tattoo? Chicago, while she was in college. At fifteen, the kid had disappeared from the military school Ray swore would finally get through to his rebellious son. The waiting had been torture. Ray's public appeal had been so compelling she was nearly persuaded that he cared.

No ransom demand was ever made, and the police were convinced Ian was just another runaway kid. While Emily worried and prayed, Ray basked in the light of another family tragedy.

Six weeks later, out of the blue, Ian showed up at her dorm in the middle of the night. He refused to tell her where he'd been or what he'd done. Swore if she tried to force him back into the school, he'd disappear, and she'd never see him again. She believed him. They'd been through too much together not to. The ink started soon after. He said if he was supposed to be such a bad boy, he might as well look the part.

Ray played on public sympathy and asked the networks for privacy in dealing with a delicate family situation. In other words, "nothing to see here but a screwed-up kid. Don't make it worse."

Logically, the cuts preceded the ink. The window of opportunity for the kind of evidence he wore shrank to his time in school and his weeks as a runaway. Was it possible Ray had him all along? Not only possible…it was probable. It all lined up in her head, and forgotten puzzle pieces dropped into place. And she knew. She'd left him vulnerable to the senator by convincing herself he'd be safe at school.

She understood now why he'd pushed back against her attempts at counseling with ruthless abandon. The drinking, the drugs, and the erratic behavior had all been designed to keep her at arm's length. Ian's two-fold method to keep this a secret, keep Ray away with a threat of exposure and her off the scent by ensuring she stayed busy keeping him sober.

"My God…my God," she whispered. "Oh, honey, I'm sorry. I'm so, so sorry." Pure, distilled hatred for

Ray swept through her like a mineral purified by fire.

It was time to put an end to the brutal bastard and his masquerade. "Man of the people and paragon of virtue, my ass." Her lips pulled back in a feral sneer. "I hope you get a good night's sleep, Ray, because it's gonna be your last."

"Is he coming to?" Michael's warm hand circled her elbow, and her back stiffened.

Silently, she shook her head.

His grip tightened as he leaned past her shoulder and got a clear look at the scars. "Wha...damn." He gulped loudly.

Her splayed hands moved to protect the things she'd uncovered. Beneath her fingers was the outline of another circle of raised flesh.

"You gonna tell me what this means? How this happened?"

"No. I'm not," she said sharply.

His quick intake of air let her know her dart had hit home.

"Guess you two weren't as close as you thought if this is news to you," he struck back.

"Not that it's any of your business. But you're right, I didn't know anything about the reasons for the ink. I'm his sister, not his lover." Shame swamped her. She should have known. It was like she'd thrown him to the damn wolves. Her fingers clenched into fists on the cotton of his gown. She forced them to relax into gentleness and settled him against the mattress. Carefully, she straightened the blankets into place over his chest.

She tried to step back but only came up against Michael's chest. The firm pressure of his palms rubbed up and down her arms, a warm attempt at comfort. For a heartbeat, she was sorely tempted to lean into him. Beg him to make all this go away, remove her obligation to—to murder the son of a bitch who had done this. Her breath sawed in and out; she struggled to lock up the fury and pain. If she let it out, she wouldn't stop screaming, not until she was strapped in a hospital bed beside Ian.

She shook off Michael's grip on her arms and sidestepped along the bed. "You're not part of this." She couldn't look at him directly. He'd see more than she wanted him to see. "You can leave now. I have things to do that don't involve you." She didn't want or need the overgrown boy scout beside her to get in her way. She turned away from his tacit haven and took a step toward the door.

"Hey, just stop a minute." The note of command in Michael's tone didn't slow her down. "Where do you think you're going?"

She spun back to him so fast the hair whipped across her face. "Excuse me? Where do you think? Should be pretty damn plain I need to see a man about a whip."

His eyes narrowed on her, and he stared her down, his jaw flexing with tension. "Yeah, well, I'm not gonna let that happen."

Of all the nerve. "And how do you plan to stop me? Are you going to tie me to this bed? Get a doctor to give me a shot to calm me down?"

Her bravado wobbled for a moment. He could probably make both those things happen, and then where would she be? Right back in The Hole unable to make a difference for Ian. She needed Michael to get out of her way, and she needed him to see the truth about her responsibility in this debacle.

"I'm sorry, but you don't get to take the moral high ground here. You need to get this crystal clear. This whole thing?" She swept her hand to take in the still form, so pale in the bed. "It's my fault. Ian is here because of *me* and what I never had the courage to do. I know you don't understand, and I don't have the time to tell you everything. Besides, really—why should you care? No one ever has." How could he possibly know what this revelation was doing to her? Like he'd understand the self-loathing, the rage, she felt. Finding those scars stripped her whole life bare. Every time she'd held Ian as a boy, every harm she'd tried to soothe, every lonely moment she'd tried to fill—wasted. Every single time she'd promised to protect him—scrubbed of its reason for being. "No one ever cared but me, because no one was there except me."

"Em, I just—"

She cut him off. Her anger, her failure, lashed at the most available target. "You think I should, what...let this go? No. Not one more second." Her voice was like broken glass underfoot. "I'm gonna put an end to that man once and for all." She glared at him, wide-eyed and stiff-backed.

"I *do* get it. You want to feel Domenico's blood on your hands. I've been there." He stepped toward her, his palms out. He paused, and his voice softened. "Look. You're freaked out right now, exhausted, and incapable of doing anything other than getting yourself hurt. Take it from me. Hatred only gets you so far. It won't accomplish your endgame. Whatever that might be."

"Endgame? There's only one end I can see that will make things right. Don't you understand? Those aren't new scars, Michael. Ian may be an addict, but he's not a masochist. And I don't need your permission before I do what needs doing. Besides, what's it to you? Why are you still here?"

"Why am I...?" A look of surprised disappointment crossed his face, and then he scowled at her. "Why do you think?"

She felt bad about hurting him, no matter how necessary it was. She needed to push him back. Stop his white-knight tendency before it manifested, and he physically stopped her from leaving.

"Nice to know our night together had such an enduring effect on you, Emily." His frown deepened, and she felt the sting of remorse.

Since she was holding a metaphorical knife, she might as well make the final slice through the connection she'd felt so strongly mere hours ago. It would serve her right. "Yeah, it was just great, and now it's over. So don't pretend this thing with us"—she swirled a long finger between them—"was anything more than a wham-bam little vacation from your life as a big bad SEAL."

To her shock, he smiled at her with what looked like pity. "You can tell yourself all the lies you want, Em. I know what last night was, and now you're trying to push me out. I'm not about to let that happen either." He hauled in a big breath and let out a loud sigh. "Look, I'm not stupid, and remorse is written all over your face. You think if you'd been a better sister, a more capable stand-in parent, Ian wouldn't have been fodder for Domenico. I get that, but Emily, going off half-cocked is never the answer. You need to stop and think. There's more than one way to handle this."

"Don't try to talk me down, Michael. I'm not into your 'voice of reason' routine. There isn't any justification for this to be on a list of things that matter to you. *We've* never mattered. Sorry, but really there's no reason for you to be involved."

"Oh, really? And you plan on doing what exactly, storming the castle on your own? Dragging the senator out and striping his back like he did Ian?" He reached for her.

She stepped back out of his range. Her shoulders slumped for a second, then she straightened and stuck out her stubborn chin. "I don't know…yes…maybe… Damn it, I have to do *something*. I'll never forgive myself if I don't. Look!" She waved a hand at Ian. Her vision became wavy with tears, and her dam nearly cracked. "Those marks come from torture, pure and simple. See, I thought I'd helped us avoid something irreversible. But no, I didn't. I couldn't. The damage happened anyway. He still got to us. That monster stamped a permanent mark on my brother. Body *and* soul." Her voice rose with each statement. Her face reddened with each labored breath until she was nearly hyperventilating.

Michael shook his head and made a visible effort not to crowd her. He dropped his hands to his hips, and for a second, she thought he was going to stop arguing. "Okay." He glanced at the bed. "You're right about one thing. I haven't known you long enough to be up in your business, but I *am* here, and I want to help. Regardless of whether you think we were nothing more than a mindless hookup."

Emily's derisive huff caused his nostrils to flare in temper. She folded her arms over her chest defensively.

He made a frustrated sound. "You don't think I can relate. I can't even count the number of times I've wanted to come out guns blazing and blow the ass off some fucker who took out an innocent civilian or one of my guys. But, Em, if I had? The only satisfaction would have been mine. Or maybe I wouldn't have been around to make a difference later. Isn't that what would mean the most to Ian? That you're here to help him in a way that counts? Later, when he can see it happen?"

"Of course I'll be here. Ian knows that about me if he knows nothing else."

"Damn, you're stubborn."

They glared at each other for a heartbeat.

"Not if you're in jail, you won't. I'm just guessing here, but I think Ian didn't *want* you to know what happened. He didn't want you hurt, so he did what a lot of us do. He kept his injuries quiet and dealt with it the best he could. He should have stepped up a long time ago, and he knows it. It's not your job to fight this battle anymore." His voice was calm and oh, so reasonable.

He should know better than to poke the bear.

"N-not my job? He's my brother! Of course it's my job. It's always been my job. Obviously, one I'm a colossal failure at. But not now, not anymore. I'm done letting Domenico get away with this. Letting him parade around the country like God's gift to family values. I had the chance to put an end to this when I was a kid, and I didn't make it happen. But now"—she pointed a shaky finger at Ian—"I have the living proof right there. He drove my brother down this road, and

I've got to stop him. Once and for all. Don't you see that?"

"No, I don't. I'm not about to step aside and let you do something you're not fully equipped for. So just settle down and think—"

"Settle down?" she shouted at him. "Don't you tell me to settle down. Who the hell do you think you are? You think because you fucked me you have a claim on me? You don't own any part of me. You don't even know me. You sure as shit don't tell me what to do." Some of her tears escaped, and she used the tail of his garish shirt to scrub them away. She held on to her momentum by a slender thread.

She dragged a hand through her hair and stooped to grab her purse off the table next to the door. Frustrated, she thrust out a palm. "Give me my damn keys. Right now, Michael McCandlis. You've got no right to dictate to me. You're nothing to me but a great lay. That's where we started, and that's where we end." She tried to look as certain as she wanted to be.

He raised his palms in surrender. The look of hurt on his face was nearly her undoing. "Your keys are somewhere in that backpack you call a purse," he said quietly, the words rough with unspoken loss, resignation.

Emily released a hollow breath. Her indigent anger deflated a touch when she saw the effect her jab had on him. "That came out meaner than I meant it to. I'm sorry." She pulled open the door, then looked back at him. "Have a nice life, Michael. I hope you find what you're looking for."

"What if it's you?" His voice was empty as the door closed behind her.

Chapter Nineteen

Before she cleared the congestion of the inner city, Emily thought she'd tear her hair out. Denver had never been easy to navigate, especially difficult when fired-up on hours of caffeine, adrenaline, and rage. It was a true miracle she made it to I-25 without killing anyone, including herself.

Cold air poured in through the car window and cleared her head while her heart pounded out a rhythm matching the hum of tires on the asphalt. She glanced at her speedometer and nudged the Jeep up to eighty mph. If she didn't get popped for speeding, it would be another miracle but a risk worth taking. The way she figured it, she had a slim chance she could achieve the kind of closure Ian could truly get behind, and she wasn't stupid enough to believe putting a gun to Ray Domenico's head was the answer.

From deep in the sullen part of her heart, she muttered, "Why aren't you here with me, Ian? Where do you get off, huh? Always running to your bottle or your lover and doing fuck all to make a difference other than changing your drug of choice. I'm so mad at you I could spit. Goddamn it, Ian. I shouldn't be doing this alone."

As much as she hated to admit it, Michael was right. She couldn't go blasting into the senator's home. She'd been in a type of prison all her life. The idea of trading one jail for another brought bile to the back of her mouth. Not a choice at all.

She was halfway to Tamarack when she slapped a hand on her head. How stupid could she be? This was the reason Ian had drunk-called her the other night. The diaries. They were the coup de grâce.

Her mother's words filled her mind. *Write it all down, honey. All your wishes, all your dreams, all your tears. Don't leave out a thing.* The first book a leather-bound gift from her mother on her seventh birthday. A week later, the first entry had been about death.

Recording her life was a practice she'd continued right up until she charged down the mountain and made her break for freedom. She'd listed every slight, every punishment, every angst-ridden thought, and tirade-filled incident until the single volume became two and then three. Each book was choked with entries detailing their life inside the sadistic Domenico household.

If what Ian said was true, the journals were still buried in the wall of The Hole. Making good on this final step into freedom meant she'd have to get them back. There was no other choice in the matter. She'd have to sneak up to the compound and lay hands on them without waking the dragon.

The miles sped beneath her as her plan took shape. The diaries might be the key pieces to the plan, but she needed Noni's husband, Bob Sears, to put it in motion. His contacts at the Rocky Mountain Examiner would be critical to stamping *paid* on the debt owed to both her mother and brother. If there was a way to link the senator to more than the assault of her and Ian, then so much the better. For now, it had to be enough that she plastered every news organization in the country with an exposé big enough to destroy Ray's career and reputation in the same breath.

Emily reached for her "backpack." Damn Michael McCandlis anyway, he kept leaking into her thoughts. Her phone, of course, was at the very bottom and still turned off. She grappled with the charger cord attached to her console and plugged it in. The device connected immediately to her car speakers, and she voice dialed Noni Sears.

"Em, where the hell have you been? I've left about a hundred messages. Daddy told me about Ian. I'm so, so sorry. Are you still at the hospital? Will he be okay? Where the hell are you?" Noni's penchant for rapid-fire interrogation was a familiar balm to Emily's fragile bravado. It was good that some things never changed.

"Christ, take a breath. I'm in the car headed back to Tamarack. Ian is holding his own, and I'll tell you more when I see you. Is Bob home? I need to talk to him right away. It's important, Noni. Really important."

"He's just putting his stuff in the car for a business trip. Should I get him? He's supposed to be in Tulsa tomorrow afternoon."

"I've got to talk with him. I need his help."

Noni's phone clattered against a hard surface, and the sound of a door slamming followed it. She waited impatiently till she heard the deep voice of Bob Sears, former senior investigative reporter for the newspaper she hoped would make revenge possible.

"This had better be good." He sounded winded; she could just imagine tiny Noni hustling him up the steps and back into the house.

"Bob. Thank God, I need you. I've got a story that could win you a Pulitzer."

He laughed derisively. "Christ, Emily, if I had a dollar for every time I've heard that line, I wouldn't be hocking my ass on the freelance circuit."

She imagined him rolling his eyes to Heaven for patience.

"Okay, I'll bite. What story? And please don't mention puppies or the environment. I can't do another one of those; the puke factor is just too high."

"How would you feel about a political bombshell exposing one of the biggest names in the US Senate? Would that be worth your time?" Emily paused for impact. "The story is mine, Bob. Mine and Ian's. You can guess who the bad guy is." A panicky laugh bubbled out of her throat. She was really going to do this. No more hiding, no more couching her cowardice in the guise of protecting Ian. Finally, the possibility of living out loud was within her reach.

There was silence on the other end of the phone, then Bob said, "Tell me where and when to meet you, and I'll be there."

"In the morning, my apartment, ten o'clock. I'll give you all the details and the evidence. Will that be good enough?"

"Seriously?" His tone changed from skeptical to intrigued. "If what you're saying is that you're finally coming forward with the details of your childhood, and you believe it will be weighty enough to knock that bastard off his pedestal permanently, I'm all in. The media will be all over this. Just be sure, Emily, because let me tell you, he's got some big ugly friends. If you do this, you've got to go for his balls and not back down."

"I've never been surer of anything in my life. I'm

ready to do this." If her heart didn't explode first. She squeezed her fist to her chest and took a few cleansing breaths.

"I'll contact a friend at CNN who's looking for a reason to ramp up the investigation into the good senator's ejection from the Armed Services Committee. Not that the two are related, but where there's smoke…as they say, there's probably a huge inferno waiting for a gust of wind. I for one would love to see you blow on that flame."

Emily breathed the first easy air she'd had in an eternity. "I'll see you then. And Bob—thank you."

****

Michael stared at the closed hospital room door, his heart thudding, his thoughts a swirling cloud of indecision. And that was a whole new thing for him. He should go after Emily, stop her headlong gallop toward a confrontation that would get her nothing but hurt. The question was, would he be doing more harm than good if he went roaring in on his white horse? It was his SOP: rescue the damsel, take down the bad guy, and restore order. It's what he had done for the last fifteen years. He was good at it, a fucking expert as a matter of fact. So why hesitate now? He scrubbed a frustrated hand over his face. The answer came as quickly as the question.

Because this thing with Emily Converse mattered more than any mission he'd ever been on. Her parting shot was so unexpected he felt each word acutely. It was like a knife in his chest and a sucker punch to his guts rolled into one. He was blindsided by her tirade and didn't understand why she, all of a sudden, had begun to see him as a controlling asshole.

He *did* feel as though they'd come to mean more to each other than a casual hookup. From the beginning, their time together had been charged with emotional landmines. Somewhere along the line, he'd started to believe they'd begun to forge ties. Ties that reminded him of his time on the battlefield. But this kind of arena was new to him. This combat was emotional, not physical, and the stakes were higher than he'd ever faced. He didn't want to let her go, didn't want to see her in harm's way. He wanted her safe.

In spite of everything, he had to admit she was right. He had no claim on her, no right to assign action and dictate behavior. He was out of his depth, and Emily was completely out of his reach. Damn it to hell.

Before he'd left the navy, outcomes were always dictated for him. Parameters were set: infiltrate, extract the victim, make the kill if necessary, never leave a man behind, get the hell out, and do it all over again the next time around. This time he wasn't familiar with the terrain. He didn't have a concise set of orders, a plan, or a team to back him up. He'd left all that behind him along with his sense of direction. And apparently, his goddamn mind.

He looked over his shoulder at the still form on the bed behind him. He truly felt sorry for the guy. He couldn't imagine the degree of despondency it took to cause a person to attempt suicide, though he'd known plenty of men who had tried it. Some of them more successfully than Ian Domenico. He could relate to one thing—the scars on the guy's body. A gorge of coffee and fatigue washed up and filled his mouth with a taste as bitter as hatred. He knew well how it felt to bear the pain of a hundred small wounds. Shrapnel left a lasting memory in a man's mind. The ceaseless itchy tautness of skin constantly pulled and reinjured by simple movement. It was agony. Add to that the weight of constant humiliation and abuse at such a vulnerable age. It was some kind of miracle her brother had gone so long without courting death on some front. His own or the senator's. There was no semblance of normal that didn't include pain for Ian. Michael's anger spiked. Fury replaced hatred, edging his vision with the craving for bloody retribution.

If Emily were still with him, all she'd have to do was ask him to take out Senator Ray Domenico, and he would've done it. Gladly. Slowly.

Michael straightened his stance and gave Ian a silent salute. He pushed away his concerns about Emily's reaction to him continuing to insert himself in her life. She could hate him if she needed to. He didn't have it in him to step away from either one of them. Ian may be the one in the hospital, but Emily was the walking wounded, and Michael McCandlis, Senior Master Chief, never left anyone behind.

His phone was in his hand before he pushed the elevator button. He pulled up a number for a local cab company and told them to meet him at the curb in front of Denver Health. If Emily thought she could slap him hard enough to drive him off, she was sadly mistaken. "Stubborn damn woman anyway," he mumbled as he stepped off the elevator and rushed across the chrome and glass lobby to the massive sliding doors. "Stubborn, blind, and mine."

The school-bus yellow of the approaching cab was a welcome sight when it rolled through the pools of light cast by the street lamps. He barely waited for it to stop before he jerked open the passenger door and gave instructions to the driver. He glanced at his watch. It was scraping eight in the evening, and the way he figured it, he'd be nearly an hour behind Emily by the time he collected his bike at the DoubleTree. Another hour and a half from Tamarack, less with the way his big, sweet Harley ate up the miles, and then he'd be within reach of her.

If, and it was a big if, he could find the senator's compound, he was going to need help. The only man he knew of with the authority to both protect Domenico from Emily and Emily from herself was Pat Evans. If she managed to get past them, God only knew what chaos might ensue.

As the cab rolled through traffic and they finally reached I-70 heading east toward the hotel, Mike had the Sierra County Sheriff's card in his hand and was dialing the number on the back.

"Evans." The gruff answer came on the second ring.

"It's Mike McCandlis, sir. We've got a problem."

"Of course we do." Pat gave a frustrated growl. "Let me guess. Emmy handed you your nuts and kicked you to the curb."

"That's just the beginning of it, but yeah, she did." He swept a tired hand over his face. "How'd you know?"

"Emmy's been a tough nut since she was a kid. You're used to people doing what they're told and were dumb enough to start issuing orders where her brother was concerned. Right?"

"Dead on, sir." Once again, he was reminded of his father. This old man had the same way of cutting directly to the chase. "I sort of forgot I wasn't in charge. I pushed; she pushed back. She ditched me at the hospital and is headed to Tamarack. I believe she's headed to Domenico's to do something really stupid, like confront the man on her own. I think that's a really bad idea, don't you?"

"She's taken on the world for her kid brother before. I ain't surprised she's doin' it again. He's the only thing she's ever taken a stand over, and you're right—a really bad idea." Pat was silent for a moment. "All right, listen. I'm all the way out in the backside of beyond right now, but I'll radio my deputy and get him on the road up to Domenico's compound. He'll keep an eye out for her and head her off. There aren't many ways around the main road, but there are some. We'll do our best. I take it you're headed this way too?"

"I am, sir. Look, I'll give you another call when I'm outside of Tamarack, and we'll recon the situation. That work for you? I got no idea where the bastard's place is, so I'm flying blind. And Sheriff, thanks for agreeing with me. I don't want her to get hurt, that's all. Though why I'm feeling so protective is a mystery to me."

"Ain't no surprise to me, son. Call me when you're closer, and maybe I'll have some news for you."

"Will do, sir." Michael blew out a breath and rocked his head against the tired muscles in his shoulders. His back ached like a motherfucker. Just another reminder that he wasn't Superman after all.

He focused again on his phone and scrolled through his contacts until he found Jerry's stupid nickname. "Smooth Talker" but it fit him to a T. Michael smiled to himself, remembering the day Jerry had decided they all needed call signs like the pussies in *Top Gun* and then refused to answer to his real name till they all got on board. He needed Jerry's help. But this time a text would definitely have to do.

Iron Mike: *Meet me @ my bike in 20. Bring keys, helmet, & jacket.*

Smooth Talker: *You taking off? Thought we were going fishing?*

Iron Mike: *Nope, got something to do. Be there, K?*

Smooth Talker: *Yeah, will do. Need company?*

Iron Mike: *Nope. Thx.*

Smooth Talker: *K. C U 20 min.*

He leaned back in the taxi seat and watched the industrial landscape fly by. It didn't fit the postcard view of the state capitol. Flanking both sides of I-70's march out of Denver were blue-white pools of the light coming from arc lamps. They illuminated acres of warehouse silhouettes with more roof than green space. Not an attractive aspect to the city. He was looking forward to putting this part of his introduction to Colorado behind the wheels of his Harley.

Eventually, the city gave way to the open skies of the planes and then to the turnoff advertising Denver International Airport and the DoubleTree convention center. His heartbeat picked up as he planned his trek north and the interception of one Emily Converse. She wouldn't be happy to see him, but he couldn't wait to feel her warmth pressed against his chest again. Crazy, just fucking crazy, the way he needed that.

The cab dropped him at the entrance to the parking garage. He jogged through the gate and down the row of cars that held his bike. He stopped abruptly at the sight in front of him. Four of his former teammates were leaning casually against the side of Jerry's red pickup.

He scowled at them. "This is not happening."

"What?" Jerry spoke up. "We were feeling kind of left out. So we decided to come along."

"Absolutely not. I don't need you guys playing soldier in the civilian arena." And that was more info than he'd intended to let loose. "Nobody's going anywhere, and that's an order."

"Well then, good thing you're no longer in command." Jerry's drawl was deceptively jovial. He smirked, but his eyes were deadly serious. The rest remained silent and watched the showdown.

Mike was annoyed the man picked this moment to assert his leadership of their band of brothers. It had to happen sometime. But damn, now? "Just let it lie, all of you. I've got some business to take care of up north of here. That's all."

"Up north? Like that tiny ass mountain town you're intimately familiar with? Yeah, I hear that little redhead you're following around is from up that way. So's her big-deal daddy. This business wouldn't have anything to do with the stupid shit that went down last night, would it? I gotta to say, that man's a real asshole." Jerry reached into the pickup bed and fisted the jacket and helmet. He strolled across the distance and thumped them into Mike's chest hard enough to cause a grunt. He reached into his pocket and tossed the bike keys straight up.

Mike snatched them out of the air. "This is *my* business, not an op for you guys. You can't afford to do anything that will put your asses under scrutiny. You know that. Just let me handle it."

"What? We're just goin' fishin'. Ain't that right, guys?" There was a murmur of agreement from the crew, and they scattered to their respective vehicles.

He shook his head in resignation. Looked like there would be a fucking convoy headed to Tamarack. He stuffed his helmet between his knees and pulled on his leather jacket. "As you pointed out, I'm not in command anymore." He jerked his helmet down on his head and slammed back the visor. "All I've got to say is, you'd best keep up."

"Ha!" Jerry barked a laugh. "And all I want to know is, how the hell did you lose your other boot?"

If Wishes Were Horses

Chapter Twenty

Senator Ray Domenico's snore jerked him out of the dream. It took him a second to pull himself back to the present. The dream was a familiar one, and its insidious head had been popping up regularly since Emily blew back into Tamarack. It didn't take a genius to see the reason. If they were putting their heads together to destroy him, why wait so long to grow the balls to make a move? Did they know more than he thought? He gave a regretful huff. It probably would've been smart to simply hire someone to get rid of both perfidious brats. It wasn't like the world would truly miss a loud-mouthed broad or a degenerate painter. And now that they'd made their animosity public—he'd be stupid to give them more time to plot their next move.

Like they'd be able to prove any of it. Not Ian's tale of woe and damn sure not his hand in Sarah's little trip over the falls. He snorted and scrubbed a hand over his face. He swallowed another Percocet with the dregs of the scotch in a glass at his elbow. They had no direct evidence to tie him to Sarah's death, none whatsoever. He was certain of that.

It had happened thirty plus years ago, for Christ's sake. Ian was two years old, too young to remember the fight that erupted before Sarah ran. Emily was away for the night. It was just the three of them, completely isolated inside their little family drama.

Sarah was strong for a woman. He'd admired that about her. She lasted longer than he'd expected before she stopped fighting back and took her punishment like a good girl. Though the last fuck had been lackluster. When she finally gave up, she was only a series of limp, unresponsive holes.

It was her fault really. She was so stubborn. He prided himself on his ability to maintain his temper, dish out his edicts and demands with a cool sense of deliberation. He was, he thought, an expert on how she would react to any given stimuli, and had spent countless hours training her to be exactly what he needed her to be. He hadn't expected her ability to *act* the part and not actually *be* the part. He was surprised by her ingenuity and her spark of life when she woke him up via a golf club to the head. If her aim had been better, she would have gotten away with it. As it was, she only managed to slow him down enough to grab her keys and her kid and beat him to the car by a moment or so.

Hadn't he spent hours going over it? There were no witnesses. No one to see the fear and abject terror on her face as she stuffed the boy into his car seat. No one to watch her hands shake and her tears fall as she'd slammed her car into gear and roared down the road to the highway.

His memories of that night produced a grim sense of satisfaction. His smile was a cold flattening of the lips as he recalled the excitement, the rush of the hunt when he'd fired up his truck and followed her onto the road. She'd been foolish to think she could get away from him. His vehicle was bigger, faster, and better equipped for the chase than hers. Poor little rabbit, nowhere to go. Her brake lights drew him along behind her until he was breathing her exhaust, and then—it took no effort to tap her bumper with enough force to set the spin in motion. The road was wet, and her tires screamed for purchase but found only the loose gravel at the roadside. He watched in satisfaction as the car plunged over the verge and through the bracken at the drop-off to the falls. He didn't bother to stop or get out of the truck. Gravity did the work for him.

He covered his tracks like a master. Thanks to the deer guard protecting the grill, his truck showed no damage that a brush of spray paint couldn't cover. A thorough going over of the house, a few applications of bleach on a blood stain in the bedroom, a small fire for the bedclothes and his favorite zip ties—and it was as if nothing had happened. An instant widower, brave single father soldiering on through tragedy. All he had to do was wait for the phone to ring when they found the bodies. It had been deliriously simple.

He grasped a cold pack in one hand and pressed it to his throat. His doctor had said he needed to keep the area cold if he hoped to avoid the spread of bruises that were inching across his neck. The drugs he'd been eating like candy did little to ease the pulled muscles in his back or the stitches holding his scalp together. The little prick's antics had once again provided him with more than just a headache. There were more important things to do than lie around here nursing injuries that shouldn't belong to him in the first place.

He growled at his empty glass and stumbled to his desk for a refill when the doorbell rang. He was five miles outside Tamarack for a reason; only invited guests were welcome. The home's remote nature was perhaps its most attractive feature.

The October light was waning. The room's darkly paneled walls and rich burgundy carpet did an effective job of pulling it into the dimness of evening. He struggled to focus on the computer monitor, but it was still in sleep mode. Nothing had triggered the system into operation. It showed no breaches of the perimeter. He frowned and swiped the control pad to pull up the camera for his front door. He sucked in a deep breath and concentrated. His hands were almost steady when he tapped the keyboard to switch settings and view all his cameras in a split grid. The live-feed, high-resolution cameras gave him a sweeping view of the wide plank porch and the empty expanse of the spruce-dotted yard. All were empty save the one covering a corner of cleared land edged by dense forest. Just a flicker of movement but definitely there. Someone on foot, slipping from the tree cover, moving toward the old barn at the rear of the open space.

Adrenaline jolted him into sobriety. He jerked open his desk drawer, grabbed his pistol. He strode down the long hall, across the towering great room, to the wide double doors. They were heavily carved oak that at one time had graced the entry of a California mission. The precision, balanced hardware from which they hung allowed for a smooth pull and a silent open as he cracked the portal and stepped onto the porch. The house was clear, the cameras told him that, but whoever paid him a visit was crazy if they thought he'd simply dismiss the threat to his security. This place was as safe as he could make it without fencing the entire fifty acres in electrified chain link and razor wire.

He carefully surveyed the perimeter. The only movement came from the ever-present wind that swept the tree branches and murmured through the bracken beneath them. It was a deceptively peaceful sound. His visitor was nowhere to be seen. The chill that chased up his spine lingered as his eyes swept the porch. The intruder had to have some reason for being here. He was certainly no kid playing pranks. Not all the way out here. Not with the measures he'd taken to ensure nothing like this happened.

He hitched up his grip on the Colt and turned back to the door when a flutter of paper caught his eye. A single page, printed with a photo, was pinned to one of the porch columns.

His hand began to tremble as he recognized the grainy black and white image. The woman was young, her stringy hair swept away from her shoulder to reveal bruises encircling her neck. Cuts and scratches ran from her shoulder up the side of her face. Her blank eyes were both blackened, her jaw clenched. The remnant of a sob stretched her mouth. A sheet lay across her chest to shield what dignity she had left. Her hands, resting beside her, resembled claws. The colorless skin was mottled with bruises and abrasions from the things she'd suffered before her death. Her corpse, forever preserved in the stark relief of the police photo, told it all.

The notation at the bottom read:
Sarah Converse Domenico
Age: Thirty-five, Deceased
TOD: 8:00 p.m. (approx.) 5/4/83
COD: Drowning
Ray crumpled the photo in his fist, then threw it to

the ground. He turned away from the house and stepped back till he could plant his back against the solid oak of the front doors. The sting of pain caused him to suck air through his teeth. The pistol was slim comfort in his grip.

"Who's out there?" His voice was steady, challenging, in spite of the fear trying to crawl its way to the surface. "What do you want? This is private property, and you're trespassing." He waited for a beat, then shouted, "I'm calling the sheriff."

He reached behind him and groped for the door handle. His fingers brushed it as the first bullet smashed a crater into the wood just above his head. The sound of the shot echoed off the trees. He ducked and fell to the plank surface of the porch. Two more rounds plowed into the door, following him down. He smelled gunpowder on the wind; the rough planks beneath him dug into his cheek.

"You bastard!" he shouted. "What do you want?" Ray's voice came out in gusts, his mouth dry with terror. His heartbeat filled his ears, and he tried to push his body closer to the deck. Air rushed in and out of lungs compressed by fear as he tried to make himself as small as possible. His brain froze in indecision. Should he try to scramble for the cover of the bushes surrounding the porch foundations? Fire back? Should he get to his knees and try to slip back inside or…shit. There was no *or*. He was pinned down. No matter what he tried, he'd be an open target.

"I want you dead." A man's rough voice sounded off to his right. "On my terms. In my time."

The gunman's voice sounded familiar. Gruff, demanding, and thankfully distant. Ray rotated his shoulders, trying to get a look at the man. His hand clutched the grip on his gun. He thumbed off the safety. Silently, he cursed himself for not chambering a round before he stepped outside.

"I see you got my note." The gunman's voice was closer. "You didn't study the picture very long. Guess you already knew what she looked like, huh, Senator? You didn't need it to remember what you did to her. But then you never cared about her to begin with. Not like I did." The disembodied voice got louder, closer, with each question. "Did you put those bruises on her neck? Did you beat her black and blue? Was she running from you when she died?"

"I don't know what you're talking about," Ray cried, his voice high and defensive. "Sarah ran her car off the road. It was raining. It was an accident. Read the report!" Over his shoulder, there was the snap of a breaking twig, then the creak of a plank. Suddenly the acrid scent of spent powder and gun oil clogged his throat. The hot, hard press of a gun barrel punched behind his ear.

"I don't need any report," the gunman sneered. "Answer my question, Senator. Was she running from you when she died? When she nearly killed *my son*?"

Ray clenched his jaw against the painful pressure of the steel against his skull. "Y-your son?"

The gunman planted his boot solidly on the muzzle of Ray's gun, forcing his fingers into the porch. He hissed and jerked his hand away from the weapon.

"That's right," the man snarled. "My son, the one you pushed over the edge last night. The one who's barely holding on in the hospital right now because you made his life a living hell."

"Who are you? D-do I know you?"

"Oh, you know me, all right. I was the one who found her car. I pulled our boy from the water. Me." He delivered a crushing kick to Ray's side.

The senator yelped like a wounded dog and rolled into a ball.

"I know who you are. What you really are." The gunman punctuated his words with a second bruising kick. "Now get up, you stinkin' coward. I want to see your face when I tell you what I have in mind for you." This time the man's toe connected with Ray's balls, and the contents of the senator's bladder spilled onto the wooden porch.

****

Ray struggled to open his eyes, not that it did any good. Not a sliver of light pierced the darkness of the place his son called The Hole. It had been constructed as a makeshift bomb shelter back in the 1950s by his parents in case the Ruskies attacked. By the time LBJ put the Red Menace to rest, the space had been turned into a root cellar. Over the years it had lain empty till he'd found a new use for it. The Hole had been a very effective training tool in the education of his children. Oh, wait, not his children at all. Emily and Ian were the gets of two different men. One dead and one dead set on killing him.

He didn't know how long he'd been down here. The passage of time outside the haze of his pain meant little. All was blackness save the bright flare of sharp agony that was his every breath. At least he was still breathing, for that he should be grateful, but he couldn't drum up the strength to draw hope from it. He supposed it was possible he was going to die in the place he'd inflicted so much damage of his own. There was a sort of cosmic justice in that, not that he believed in anything so mundane as God.

So the boy was in the hospital. Figured that he'd try to off himself. Weak. He'd always been too much of a weakling to stand on his own feet. Never had the guts to be a man. Took after his father apparently, Ray thought with a wry twist of his mouth. The damn fag was the spawn of the idiot who thought he could get away with offing a US senator. Moron. Like father like son.

His hands and arms had long since lost all feeling, bound as they were behind his back. He was a slab of meat. Soon the butcher would finish him off with the swing of an ax or the sharp bite of a blade to the throat. If he was lucky, maybe a bullet.

His captor had been gone a long while. "Give you some time to reflect," he'd said, in a voice like whiskey-soaked gravel. Then he'd delivered another blow with the sharp toe of his boot. The excruciating result was the broken ribs that turned each inhalation to fire. And he stunk like piss. The loss of his dignity hurt nearly as bad as the beating.

He tried to marshal his scattered thoughts, tried to find a scrap of hope, a way out. He'd done everything he could think of. Reasoning, pointing out that his political office would be reason enough for the law to come searching for him. Bartering for the wad of cash in his safe. Pleading a heart condition that didn't exist. Anything to get his captor to back off.

Billy freaking Strauss. Who would believe it? It proved the old adage, never overlook the quiet ones or some such crap. But the man had no desires outside revenge. No amount of threats, bribery, or begging had any effect on the insane course Strauss had set for him. It was clear that he didn't expect to get away with it either. All the man wanted was redress for the wrong done to the woman he loved. Simple as that. Crime, then…punishment.

The quiet fell away from the dank interior of his tomb as something dragged across the floor above him. The slithering sound, long and sinuous, grated along the rough boards. It echoed uncomfortably like the noise he imagined a huge python would make as it hunted its victim. Ray tried to suppress his moan of terror, but the pain made his fear ever sharper. He would have cowered in a corner if he could have moved, but the stubborn beating of his heart kept him anchored, waiting for Billy's next onslaught.

The steel door at the top of the stairs opened, and the bright beam of a flashlight swept across his body. The shivering that had left him returned with a vengeance.

"I thought you might be thirsty," Billy said in a friendly tone. He jerked on the length of hose in his hand and dragged it to a stop in front of his captive. "Are you? Thirsty?" He tilted his head and smiled affably. Water dripped slowly from the nozzle he held.

Ray's imagination fired to life, fueled by scenes of CIA waterboarding. "Oh, Christ. Don't. Please don't." His strangled whisper made Billy smile in satisfaction.

"What? Do you think I'm gonna cram this down your throat? Crank up the pressure till you suffocate? Watch your belly bloat and your face turn blue? Tempting, I gotta admit. But I've got bigger things in store for you. A big important guy like you deserves the best, don't you think?" Billy dropped the hose to the floor and adjusted Ray's Colt in his belt. "See, I think you need to feel what Sarah must have felt, some of it anyway. The trapped part, the drowning part. You get to feel both of those because I've already made you feel the fear." He leaned the gun against the wall and reached to his belt. A wicked-looking hunting knife glinted in the cold beam of the flashlight. He skated the glittering blade along the side of the senator's face, down his throat, and paused at the thick vein of his neck. He smiled and nicked the thin skin. Ray felt the sting and then a trickle of something warm and wet soak into his collar.

Billy sheathed the knife and pushed him to his side. The senator toppled like an overstuffed gunny sack. He pulled on Ray's arms and ankles, laying him curved back in an arch on the cement floor of the cellar. He smoothly passed a braided, leather tie-down over and around the ankles and pulled until they met the wrists. He looped them all, once, twice, and secured them with a quick knot. He pulled the connection tight and threw up his hands in a signal that his hog-tie was complete. "The crowd goes wild." He cupped his hands around his mouth and mimicked the sound of adoring fans. "Ladies and gentlemen, Billy Strauss, World Champion All-Around Cowboy!" He stood and dusted his hands. "Damn I'm good."

He bent, picked up the hose, cracked open the valve, and let water flow over the floor. Its icy tide swept up the senator's legs and coated his side in freezing wetness.

Billy backed up and sat heavily on the steps. His jacket pocket produced a flask that Ray recognized from his home office. He tipped it back and pulled hard on the mouth, then swallowed deeply and reclined back against the cold, rough steps. He studied the slow and steady rise of the water as it picked up years of forgotten dust and mouse droppings from the old abandoned cellar.

He stretched out his legs and got more comfortable. "Way back then, I nearly made it, you know. All the way to World Champion. I ended my career on the wrong end of a bull called Bone Crusher. Went to work for a pool company that belonged to a buddy of Pat Evans. Did you know that? Yup, had to find some way to make a living while I healed up from that last ride. I was pretty tore up, couldn't do nothin'. Damn sure couldn't help Pat at the ranch. He found me a job carting parts around. Good man, Pat Evans. And Sarah, she looked after me too. Brought me homemade soup and loving kindness, she did." He tipped back the flask again and smacked his lips in appreciation. "That's fine liquor you got there, Senator. My tax dollars at work, no doubt."

He wiped his mouth with the back of a dirty hand and adjusted the direction of the hose so its spray washed closer to Ray's head. "Anyway, like I was sayin', I learned all kinds of interesting stuff working for the pool guy. Like how long it takes to fill up a pool with a hose. Now a hole like this? Ought to take, oh, say twenty-five maybe thirty hours. 'Course we don't have to go that deep to get the job done, now do we?" He kicked Ray's foot with the toe of his boot. "I asked you a question, Senator. Thought you might like to know how long you got left. Thought I'd give you time to unburden your soul, make your peace with God, and all that. Not that you gave Sarah that option. Unlike you, I ain't no monster, and I'm inclined to hear your story while we wait for the water to do its job. I'll be your father confessor. How 'bout that?"

Ray struggled with his bonds and tried to organize his thoughts, figure a way out of this death chamber. "Why should I tell you anything, you fucking psycho? You're going to let me drown just the same, right? Then you know what'll happen? They'll track you down. When they catch you, they'll inject you with enough poison to put an end to your miserable life. Thank God for capital punishment, because that's what's waiting for you unless you let me go."

"That ain't happenin'," Billy scoffed. "'Sides, don't much care at this point. I figure you already got me on two first-degree counts for what we've been up to so far. They can only kill me once, not that I'm gonna give them the chance. I got me a date with the end of your pretty little Colt here, just as soon as we're done chewing the fat."

"You're certifiable. You plan on watching it all happen? You're the monster here, not me. What happened between Sarah and me could have happened to anybody. Do you think it's easy serving the damned people *and* a wife who can't stand the look of you or the touch of your hands? You think that wouldn't drive you to extremes just to get a reaction?"

He was tired, exhausted from the pain, the fear. Beaten down by the relentless focus of a man he'd always considered one step above a street corner bum. All the while, the frigid water inched its way up his body. There had to be a way to fight the inevitable. At least slow it down till someone came looking for him.

He'd scheduled his driver to pick him up at noon for his return to DC. Could he hold on that long? Not likely. He'd always thought that staying aloof and separated played into his importance as a public figure. He'd foolishly thought it best to keep his distance, both physically and emotionally. Isolation from his neighbors meant he paid in real time for his arrogance.

Maybe the fool was right. A back-handed confession would slow him down. He'd lead Billy to think he was resigned to his fate and had decided to admit to all the things the man pegged him for. What harm could it do now? It was a story he'd clutched inside the confines of his memory for a long time. It might even convince the lunatic that the law would hold him accountable for Sarah, for Ian. If nothing else, it would assure that Billy would use the first bullet on him instead of letting the icy water do its work. Besides, the idea of goading the bastard was really pleasing. Provoking the man was freeing in a twisted way.

Ray struggled to lift his head to see his oppressor. "You think you knew Sarah? I'm the one who knew her the best. That first term we went to DC together? She loved it. Never had any of the things I gave her before. The best hotels, the clothes, the people. I thought I'd hit the goddamned mother lode with her. She was a cat in heat, that girl, a great piece of ass. But then she stopped loving it, the women that were always hanging on me, the parties, the receptions, always in the public eye. She said I was using her as a prop, like a trophy of war to puff myself up in the media. And she was right. She was good for my image. Then she started pushing back, stopped putting out altogether. At least not willingly. Funny, I never knew resistance could be so…stimulating."

The flashlight's beam reflected off the ceiling of the cellar, giving just enough light for Ray to detect a muscle jumping in Billy's jaw. Yes, a reaction.

"I used to get harder when she slammed those delicate hands against my chest, trying to get me to stop plowing her. See, it didn't matter if she liked it. She *needed* me to take her. It turned her on. And she stayed despite everything. I figured she wouldn't have continued to hang around if she didn't secretly love what I was handing out."

He took a deep breath and despite the vicious pain, rolled to his back, his hands flat on the water-washed floor. The cold mud on the concrete collected on the hobbles. For a moment, he lay there, waiting for the pain to abate, the water to soothe his flesh. And then he felt it. Just the slightest give in the leather straps of the hobbles. His heart rate picked up, and he smiled. Ray took a steadying breath. He'd waited as long as he could. He collapsed his thumbs into his palms to make his hands as small as possible and kicked out with his legs. The wet leather dug into his flesh but slipped toward his fingers. With a sickening squelch of viscous fibers, they slithered across his skin. The hobbles vibrated against the pressure as he used his legs to drag on the section connecting his hands to his boots. His muscles trembled with the effort. The adrenaline of possible victory swept his body.

"I know what you're doin'." Billy's words slurred. "You're tryin' to get me riled up. You think that if you talk filthy about her, I'll give you the easy way out. It don't matter what you say." Billy waggled the Colt in the light, then let it clatter to the step beside him. "I knew the real Sarah, and she was good and kind and loved her kids more than anything. Including me. You're wasting your breath, and that's something you're gonna need, Senator. 'Cause you and me? We're gonna stay right here till the water does its job and you feel the cold, the pressure. Just like Sarah did. Remember? That's the way this is gonna go."

Ray made a contemptuous grunt and stretched his legs; the wet leather gave a bit more. "As I said before, you just *think* you knew the real woman. Maybe she thought I'd get tired of the fight and move on to her little cunt of a daughter. I could have, but I'm not a pervert. I just wanted what was mine by law and by right. And she needed to get that through her head." He paused for breath and raised his head a bit more. The water slowly inched up the back of his neck. Why stop now? "Sarah was my wife, and she owed me. Owed me big time for taking her in when she was living hand to mouth with a kid to feed. Owed me even bigger for pretending that little bastard she popped out was mine when I knew he wasn't."

His eyes must have drifted closed as his mind called up his feelings from thirty-seven years in the past. He jumped awake as Billy cocked the pistol. The cold slide of steel on steel filled The Hole.

Chapter Twenty-One

Emily shivered and cursed under her breath. Few things were lonelier than an isolated mountain road in the middle of a moon-drenched night. This Forestry Service road was no exception. It'd been many seasons since anyone had been down it; the weeds and the buck brush had done their best to reclaim it for the forest it bisected. That was the beauty of being a girl who'd learned to drive in a four by four. The hard-learned lessons on navigating the way past axle-breaking ruts and oil-pan-piercing boulders lasted forever. Of course, it was easier done in the daylight. That's what God made long-range, off-road lights for. Emily was grateful she'd indulged the whim to install them on the Jeep. Besides, they looked cool. She'd never anticipated actually *needing* them to keep from killing herself while trying to sneak up behind her stepfather's property.

She found a relatively flat spot, set her emergency brake, and shut down the engine. She thanked her lucky stars she'd managed to get this close to the senator's compound without doing any major damage to the one thing she had left that might make getting away with this crazy stunt possible.

It had sounded simple and scary exciting while she plotted her covert mission, but now it seemed like a totally stupid, crackpot idea. What made her think it would be possible to drive undetected around the backside of the rise separating the house from the property line? Then change her clothes in the woods for the ones in her emergency box, which she hadn't opened or refreshed for the better part of two years. She'd have to hike a mile plus through the woods in the dark and slip past his security lights into the barn. Try to find the place in The Hole where she'd stashed the diaries twenty years ago. Get the hell out the way she'd come. Most importantly, *not get caught.*

She glared at the size thirteen mystery boot resting on top of her box of supplies and tossed it over the back seat. "Maybe I should have taken advantage of the big bad SEAL while I had him," she grumbled as she snugged the laces on her own hiking boots, glad they were part of her emergency preparedness plan. Boots, a flashlight that thankfully still had power, a pair of jeans, and a flannel shirt, all standard issue for a mountain girl no matter how far from the hills she got. At least she wouldn't be needing the crinkly, foil survival blanket or the energy bars…well, maybe the bars. It had been a few years since she'd done any hiking. She stuffed them in the side of her backpack and jammed her arms through the shoulder straps. Its soft leather shell may have been intended for trekking through a city packed with commuters, but it did the job for cross-country burglary well.

She swept the intense beam of her flashlight over the brush surrounding her Jeep and hitched her pack higher on her back. There was no going back now. If she chickened out of this recovery plan, there was no way she would be able to make her story concrete enough for Bob or the people he'd promised to contact. She couldn't leave it up to chance—her previous actions had done nothing to change Ian's life. She obviously couldn't change the past, but she could damn sure do things differently in the future. Starting with bringing an end to Ray Domenico's lifelong reign of terror. Regardless of whether he was a constant presence in their sphere or not, he was like cancer, hiding quiet and deadly in the background. He was waiting for the right combination of ingredients to awaken his special brand of lethality. There would be work to do, hard work. Ian was worth it. Hell, she was worth it. That would be the biggest win of all, wouldn't it? To be able to say, "This is what happened to us, and I'm done being ashamed. We didn't deserve what he did."

If the only thing that came of this was blowing Ray's cover, then bring on the fucking dynamite. One way or another he would pay for his crimes.

Her pep talk withered a hundred yards from her starting point when there was a loud crash and an answering squeal in the darkness that stretched beyond the focused brightness of her flashlight. She yelped in response and dropped the light. It wavered and blinked out. Emily froze in place. "Holy shit! Please…oh, please," she whispered a desperate prayer, "don't let that be anything larger than an owl or a starving chipmunk. I'm not in any shape to run uphill away from a bear, or God forbid, a wolf."

There were a few scuffling noises and a muffled squeak, doubtlessly signaling the death of some innocent woodland creature, and then silence. She squeezed her eyes shut and hoped her night vision would return quickly because without that light, she might as well put a cap on this little adventure right now.

She pried her eyes open one at a time and was rewarded by the glint of moonlight on metal. The flashlight lay at her feet. She said another prayer, this one of thanks, when a good shake and a threat brought a searing stream of light right into her face. For a few seconds, all she could see was bright orange light traces. The humor of the situation struck her, and she laughed at the memory of the night she'd met Cinderella and Enrique's guttering Zippo.

She wished she could turn back the clock and wipe out everything that had happened since then. Everything except that kiss and her night with Michael, master of the multiple orgasms. Holy crow, that was some technique he had there. And why was her mind running down those paths, when the only thing she *should* be paying attention to was this overgrown game trail? Self-preservation no doubt, like staring past a nurse's shoulder so the needle she knew was coming didn't hurt so much. This needle, however, would still hurt. Hopefully, there would be an end to her disease on the other end.

She shook her head at her own foolishness. She had a long way to go. The longer she delayed, the better the chance she'd talk herself out of finally growing a pair of lady balls. She laughed at that. Boy, wouldn't Michael be surprised as hell he'd missed those last night? If he was still around when this was over.

The rest of her midnight hike was uneventful, no broken bones, no bears, no hungry chipmunks. Best of all, her flashlight was still burning when she saw the first glimpse of Ray's house. She quickly shut down her light and tucked herself behind the last bank of trees on the edge of his house yard.

The place looked deceptively welcoming; warm amber light washed over the log exterior. The yard appeared just as she remembered, broad expanses of grass broken by tasteful flowerbeds surrounding specimen evergreens. Again, the quintessential picture of hearth and home. It had a camera-ready—nothing but wholesome here—veneer. Just like her childhood, smoke and mirrors, public facades and private terror.

Emily slipped from tree to tree, bush to bush. She skirted the yard and the cameras that watched the perimeter. They provided an invisible net of warning around the island of light that was the house. As a kid, she'd learned the art of walking softly, to leave no trace of her passing. She and Ian used to make a game out of sneaking around, getting as close to the housekeeper or the parade of nannies as they could, then slipping away. They got good at fading into the background and disappearing into the pines. It became one of their best strategies. The only way they had to exercise control over their time while the senator was out of state. Aside from those times they were closely structured while he was gone. Scheduled, reported on, and watched twenty-four/seven. So what the guards didn't know couldn't hurt them.

Nighttime forays became the times they lived for—and paid for whenever they made a mistake. Misbehavior sponsored their introduction to the "training" regimes that became a way of life when the senator returned home. The staff always managed to be unavailable during those brutal times. They'd been well paid and completely disposable, she supposed. Or it'd seemed that way. The only caring going on inside the

Domenico household had been between brother and sister. No one had ever voiced an opinion to call attention to their plight. If they dared to notice, they'd disappeared.

The barn's dark shadow loomed up out of the moonlight at the side of the house yard. Its weathered facade was the same hulking, dark presence it had been when she last roared past it on her way to college. The wide door still reminded her of a frightful maw, like the wide-open mouth of a scream trapped in silent terror. An apt metaphor for the times spent inside its dusty interior. The Hole, home of both nightmare and redemption, lay down its broad center in the rear corner, beneath a steel door. The one that had replaced its wooden counterpart. Wood could be whittled apart, bolts removed, hinges disassembled, locks picked, and escapes made. She smiled, a flat drawing of her lips, as she remembered.

Sticking to the shadows, she slipped up to its darkest side. A few feet more and she leaned back against the last inky corner of the barn. The weathered siding slid rough and raspy against the palms of her hands. Her backpack cushioned her as she pressed against it. She wished suddenly that her shirt was a darker color and for a skull cap pulled down over her hair. It was too late to worry about wardrobe changes now. Still, if she'd been thinking more like a cat burglar instead of a would-be trespasser, she'd be dressed like a ninja instead of a lumberjack.

She peeked, one-eyed, around the corner and breathed a relieved sigh when she found a wedge of shadow behind the canted door. Its tall planking was the only cover available on the moon-washed front of the building. Carefully, from her spot undercover, she watched the house. No lights and no shadows moving behind drapes watched the darkened yard. All was quiet. A hysterical giggle burbled up her throat. This was without a doubt the craziest—in a long line of crazy—things she had ever attempted.

Emily filled her lungs and let it out slowly. She'd come this far. She wouldn't invent a reason to retreat now. The senator had zero call to be watching a distant patch of darkness at well after midnight. She gained nothing by crouching in the shadows. One last peek around the corner and she vaulted toward the edge of the barn door.

Her heart beat a thundering tattoo in her ears when the shadows behind the door washed over her. She fanned her heated face and leaned her forehead on the creaky surface of the door. The cedar still held the scent born to it a hundred years before. A few steps more and she'd be in the relative safety of the cavernous barn. Once inside she could risk the shielded beam of her light and get this the hell over with.

She waited and listened. The only sound was the brush of the wind and the blood rushing in her ears. She was stalling. Stalling was good. Stalling had worked for her most of her life. Dealing by refusing to acknowledge the reality, the gravity, and the danger of the situation was her default setting. Running instead of confronting? Check. Misplaced trust? Check. Codependent caretaking instead of self-care? Check. Pretending she was *actually* capable of pulling off this midnight caper? Check and double check. If her goal was to shove her monster into the light and rob him of his power over both her and Ian, then she had to "act as if" she could do it till it was done. No new bones were growing under her skin. "Get the damn diaries and run like hell," she whispered into the shadows.

The time wouldn't ever be any better. She shoved hard on the door and slipped along behind its width till her hand found the opening's interior edge. The door's weight creaked alarmingly on the track at the top, and dry debris peppered her hair. Hopefully, no spiders were involved. She gave the house one last careful look, then slipped into the dim interior of the barn.

Deep stalls flanked both sides of the center's plank floor. Even after all these years, the smell of hay and horses clung to the air. Her hand went to her flashlight, but she hesitated. It would be best to wait until she was shielded by the door to The Hole before she gave in to the luxury of light. The beam would stand out like a spotlight on a battlefield. No need to risk it; the way to The Hole was something that would never leave her. Fifty feet, turn at the last stall, and past the tack room door. The raised edge of the slanted door would be directly in front of her.

She nearly ran the length of the stalls and twisted around the last upright corner post. She froze for a moment. Breathing hard, she did her best to listen past the pounding of her heart. Nothing but the fluttering of wings in the rafters somewhere above her, probably an owl like the one that used to make its home here. Many were the times she and Ian found the discarded pellets it left in the wake of a successful hunt. The ghoulish glee they shared in dissecting those desiccated packets of bones and matted fur caused her skin to prickle with gooseflesh. She peered up into the dark above her and prayed the feathered hunter would spare her an appearance.

"Jesus Christ, Emily. Get it together," she whispered to herself. She couldn't afford to let her imagination make this any more frightening than it already was. "It's just a cellar, just an empty hole in the ground. You've come this far. Just do it."

Her toes contacted the cement edge of the old cellar, and she bent to sweep her hand over the surface, searching for the handle near the center seam of the heavy double door. It didn't occur to her it might be locked. There hadn't been any prisoners to occupy its depth in a long time.

All she found was a void, an empty space where the heavy door should be. "What the hell?" She froze, fumbled for her light, and pushed the glass lens against her thigh. Her thumb trembled as she pushed the button. A halo of halogen brightness escaped around the edges.

Her hand clutched the flashlight more tightly, and she tilted it to open the gap against her leg. Brightness spilled into the blackness of The Hole, and she froze again. Her head spun with flashes of cold nights clutching Ian for warmth, inventing stories to keep him calm, struggling to find ways to comfort them both, find some way past the fear that the door would never open again, and they would die. Forgotten—in the dark. She still tasted that fear.

She bent, clasped the frame of the door for support, and forced herself to take the first step down. Her foot landed on something hard and round. She teetered back and forth, looking for balance and fumbling her flashlight to chase away the specters that were rushing at her from every deep corner. When she dared crack open a thin sliver of light against her jeans, her eyes found the round contour of a green hose. Its length disappeared into what should have been the darkness of The Hole. Instead, weak, reflected light and the undeniable sound of splashing.

"What the hell?" she whispered. The words were covered by the cold, unmistakable echo of a gun chambering a round.

****

Michael tapped the speaker embedded in the side of his helmet. He waited for just a second before giving the voice command to dial Pat Evans. The speaker next to his ear crackled, and the signal connected. The tech making a hands-free call from a moving motorcycle possible was a true miracle.

"Evans." The answer came through loud and clear. "How close are you to town, Mike?"

"I'm ten minutes out. Where should I meet you?"

"That's the problem. There's been an accident on the highway between you and Tamarack. Some drunk idiot hit a deer and damn near killed himself. My deputies are tied up on the scene." The sheriff cleared his throat, then swore under his breath. "The highway is blocked about a mile out of town. That'll hold you up. They know to pass you through, but it'll still slow you down, and I don't think we should wait around to rendezvous. I'm up the pass road above Domenico's. Looks like I'll beat you to the compound by let's say ten minutes."

The sheriff's tires on crunching gravel covered his voice for a moment. "Listen, Mike. I was hopin' this was all a wild goose chase, but a few minutes ago, I got a call from Noni's husband, Bob Sears. He said he'd talked to Emmy, and he believes she's going to make a play for some kind of evidence she thinks will put Ray away for good. He didn't know what for sure but thinks it's still on Domenico's compound."

Mike groaned his frustration. Damn it anyway. Emily was more than likely at the compound by now, and the Lord only knew what she'd do. Something foolhardy, no doubt. Like get herself hurt or worse. Ray Domenico was capable of more than bluster and vitriol. He might take her threat seriously, and Emily wasn't prepared to defend herself against a desperate man.

"Well, shit. That's not good." He glanced in his side mirror. His posse was still intact, keeping pace with his breakneck speed. They'd covered the distance from Denver in record time, under the radar all the way. Another miracle, no speeding tickets. He needed a new plan. "Sounds just like something she'd do. I agree we can't wait. You go ahead to Domenico's and give me directions. We'll be there quick as we can."

"We?" Pat barked. "Don't tell me you brought the whole damn crew. Not that we couldn't use the backup. I don't want a parade of badasses rolling through my town in the middle of the night."

"About that, I couldn't stop them from coming. Even tried to outrun them. Problem is, I'm the one who taught them all the tricks I used to dump them. I must've done a really good job too because they're still on my ass."

Evans harrumphed his dissatisfaction and gave Michael a concise set of directions as well as assurances his deputies would wave the convoy through the accident site. "Once you reach the gate to the compound, come in quiet. You're about a quarter mile or so from the house. No sense advertising your presence till we know what's going down. You'll see my Bronco on the road. The gate is probably hot. Go around it. Ray's a little paranoid. That work for you?"

"I guess it's the best we've got. See you in a few."

A short trip down the two-lane blacktop that masqueraded as US36, and the strobing red and blue lights of cop cars stopped them.

He took off his helmet as the deputy stepped up to his bike. The kid looked to be no more than twenty years old. Way too young to entrust with the job of public safety.

Mike made short work of introductions, expecting the officious deputy to wave them through, but he insisted the traffic stay at a standstill. Mike groaned with frustrated impatience.

The young deputy was polite but stiff-necked in his refusal to let the posse through. Mike hated to pull rank, but this needed to end. He slapped his phone against the kid's chest and told him to talk to Pat Evans. The kid visibly snapped to attention and glowered at him while stammering his hurried reply. He handed the phone back, and the highway magically became passable. Fucking midnight and the convoy was finally rolling uphill toward the entrance to Tamarack.

He downshifted his bike and slowed as he rolled past the Mexican restaurant that had been his inauspicious introduction to the town. The parking lot he'd crawled into was dark and empty. Like the place in the center of his chest used to be, before he'd come to Colorado. Before he'd run up against a redhead with a sinfully sexy mouth and a temper hot enough to strip paint. Damn, but she was fiery, smart and funny and wounded and confused and…his. He had yet to convince her of that.

Had it only been a short thirty-four hours ago when he'd first seen her? Yeah, he'd counted the hours. She'd been so lovely fighting her nervousness at his attention. Of course, she'd masked it like a trooper, all *backoff and don't crowd me*. At the same time, she'd let him know their attraction was an unexpected plus in a day that was challenge laden at best. Just over one rotation around the sun and his crappy little world had tilted on its ear. If he concentrated, he could still taste her, hear the exquisite sounds she made when they came. He was so gone on her he had to laugh.

He wasn't even sure how it'd happened. First, he was alone and struggling to find his…something. Then—blam. He was no longer lost. Sometime between fighting with her in the hospital and busting ass to this wide spot on a mountain highway, his axis had come back to vertical. That space in his chest, left vacant by the loss of his command, magically filled in. His purpose shifted, solidified. He stopped drifting and found his course. His reason.

Find Emily and keep her safe. Even if it meant pissing her off. Even if it meant having to win her all over again.

The night on the other side of the little town stretched with blue-black intensity beyond the reach of his headlamp. The two trucks behind him did little to reveal anything more than an occasional glimpse of a lake shore. The drop off at the edge of the pavement slid past in a blur. They began the climb up the backside of the canyon, taking the turns faster than the highway department ever intended. The solid yellow line in the center gave him all the direction he needed to cut the curves down to size and straighten out the serpentine route of the road.

Look for the Angel Falls sign, Pat's instructions told him. *The senator's compound was three miles up and on the left. Fancy ass rock pillars and a gated entry. Look for the Sierra County Sheriff's Department Bronco. Go in on foot.* After that, they'd have to wing it.

Suddenly the road veered sharply to the left, and the green and white sign for the falls whizzed past him. His Harley became a beast that clawed traction out of thin air when the switchback tried to toss him to the asphalt. Adrenaline punched his heart into his throat until he got the bike back on the flat of its wheels. Maybe slowing down a bit would be the best way to make it the last few miles to his destination and his woman.

A short ride farther had them pulling up behind the Bronco. His teammates crowded the center of the road, flashlights in hand, faces serious with mission-ready concentration.

"Damn, it's dark up here. And cold," Jerry grumbled and blew into his cupped hands. "What's the plan, Mike?"

"Thought we might need these." Alec stepped around the back of his truck and slapped a pair of night-vision goggles against Mike's chest, then passed out the same to the others.

Rico dropped a heavy pack in their midst and handed out a bevy of side arms. "And these." He shrugged when Mike started to protest. "What? I was a Boy Scout. Always prepared and shit."

"Fuck," Mike said. "I'm not going to ask why in

hell you have those with you." Not like this was a firefight, not even close. "Right. Tell me later. You got com units in that bag? Might as well pass them out too."

He shook his head as Alec bent again to his bag of tricks. He flipped the switch on his flashlight and swept it over the area on either side of the gate onto Domenico's property. "The fence is hot, Jerry. Make sure we don't get fried. Then a quarter klick up the drive. Spread out around the house. We'll do a search of the main structure. For fuck's sake, don't shoot the sheriff, because he's ahead of us. Locate Emily, grab her, and hold her. Find and secure the senator. Quick and quiet, boys. Just like we've done a thousand times."

Chapter Twenty-Two

Emily stood frozen on the steps leading down into The Hole. She stopped breathing. The remembered noise from a thousand TV cop shows filled her ears. Not something a girl ever expected to show up in the real world. But in this trip into Noir drama? It fit. The thought that the business end of that same gun was probably pointing at her chest caused the muscle beating beneath its target to jump like it was trying to flee. She had no cover, no place to hide, and a huge freaking floodlight in her hands. If the person in charge pulled the trigger, she was absolutely a dead woman.

"Shit," she heard from below her. "Emily?" The voice sounded eerily familiar. Again, not what she expected.

Without thought, she whipped the light away from its shielded spot on her thigh, down the stairs, to the floor of The Hole. Before her was a tableau straight out of one of those cop shows. Billy Strauss stood, legs spread, pistol in hand, pointing down at the prone body of…Ray Domenico.

Her light swept him head to foot, paused on the gun barrel that moved from her stepfather to her. "What the hell. Billy?" She blinked in disbelief.

Incongruous, the floor appeared to be several inches deep in pooling water. Both men stared up at her, shocked looks on their faces.

"W-what's going on? Is he tied up?" The words stuttered out in disbelief. "God, Billy. Did you do this?"

"Yes," Ray cried. "He's gonna kill me. Emily, run! Get help!" His voice made her jump. She juggled the flashlight, and it rolled down the stone steps. The light bounced and swung, rippling shadows moved against the ceiling, and reflections lit the walls. The effect was dizzying, surreal. Her palm slapped on a damp stone wall, searching for solid ground.

"Don't even think about it, Em." Billy's voice was dark, heavy with threat.

The light finally stopped its wild trip down the steps, landing at his feet. The water-covered lens poured into the pool's debris-covered surface, illuminating the room with murky amber highlights. The muzzle of the gun moved from her to Ray and back to her. The muscles of her whole body locked up.

"Why don't you join us," he said. The muzzle of the pistol waved her down the steps.

Would he really shoot her? Was he crazy enough to pull the trigger? Take her life? She wasn't prepared to find out. She swallowed a mouthful of fear and forced a tentative step down and then another. She froze, freedom at her back, terror in front of her. Both fitting for the scene. She needed to inject some sense into what looked like a bad dream in the making.

Slowly she raised her hands in surrender and her gaze from the yawning mouth of the gun to Billy's eyes. Even from the distance of a few yards, she could see the twitchy tick of a muscle in one lid and the grim set of his mouth. He looked nothing like the affable, occasionally drunken cowboy she knew as Blanche's boyfriend. He was someone different now, focused, hate-filled, and teetering on a dangerous ledge.

"Think I'll stay right here if it's all the same to you," she said. "Wanna tell me why you're doin' this, Bill? Thought I was the one with a grudge against the good senator." *Get him talking.* Stave off the whole shooting thing till the rescue party she *hoped* was hot on her heels arrived to save the day. That's what the hero was supposed to do. Right?

"I guess you was wrong about that." Billy sneered and beckoned her farther into the scene.

With terrified eyes, she took in Ray, hog-tied in the water. In spite of her hatred for him, she didn't want to watch him die. "What's the plan here, Billy? There's no way you're going to get away with this. What you gonna do, kill me too?"

His breath hitched on a sob. "You weren't s'posed to be here," he shouted. "Just him, the man who stole my family from me. *My* family. The one I never got the chance to have." His voice trembled, and the hand gripping the pistol shook along with it. "I put the pieces together, you see. Ian—he's my son. Mine and your mama's." He slumped for a moment, like the weight was too heavy to hold any longer. "This bastard punished my Sarah till she ran, and when that wasn't good enough, he chased her off a cliff." Anguish clenched his jaw as he forced out his words. "He still wasn't satisfied, so he pushed my boy right over the edge behind her. They didn't deserve any of the things he did to them." He looked back to Emily, and his eyes were bleak, empty. "This is justice. Ain't it? This is me, finally doin' what's right."

He looked down at his captive and took aim. He tightened his grip on the gun. "This is the only thing I can do to make it right." His gaze became focused. He spat in Ray's face and jammed the muzzle against his temple.

"Good Christ, Billy. Stop. Don't, please don't," she pleaded. "You're not thinking straight... Wait!"

Billy shoved Ray's head to the side. Ray made a gasping try to avoid going under the churning surface.

"He's crazy, Emily." Ray's strained words struggled through the relentless wash of dirty water. "He brought me down here and beat me. Tried to get me to confess to something I didn't do. Your mother died in a car accident. I swear I didn't kill her." He pushed with his heels, trying to wriggle away from the gun. "You got to believe me. I loved her. She was my wife."

His pleading words brought a wash of emotion up her throat. Her head reeled with memories, the wreck, the funeral, the loss of gravity she felt when her mother was ripped away. All of it crashed over her.

"Shut up!" Billy screamed, shrill and tragic. "Shut up! You lying bastard." The gun vibrated in his grip as he leaned forward to track his target. "You ran her off that road, chased her over that cliff! You did it, I know you did it. This is for Sarah!"

The world erupted into chaos. Billy shrieking his intent, Ray ripping his hands from the water and grabbing the gun. Emily launching herself toward them with all the force left in her legs. The wild swing of a kicked flashlight and the swirling arcs of light reflected on the cold stone walls. A scream of impotent rage from Bill as Ray's frigid hands suddenly gripped the gun. The sickening crunch of the impact as her shoulder slammed into Billy's side. The stinging lash of the wet leather as it became a whip to Emily's terrified face. The flashing roar of the gun.

****

Mike stood quiet and invisible in the shadows of the big log house. He watched as Pat Evans stepped out of the senator's front door and down onto the blacktop of the circular driveway. Behind him the house was silent. The only evidence that something unnatural was going on was the wraithlike presence of the men in the forest surrounding it.

The sheriff bent to pick up a white scrap of paper off the ground. He flattened it out and then shook his head. Sadness radiated off him in palpable waves. He creased the paper and slipped it into his shirt pocket next to his heart. His hand rested there for a long moment.

"What you got there, Sheriff?"

"Jesus Christ!" Pat spun and found Mike standing beside him. "Damn it, you nearly gave me a coronary."

Mike was unsuccessful at hiding his grin. "Sorry about that, you said to come in quiet. We did." He held up a fist, and four other shadows stepped from cover around the perimeter of the yard. Silent and focused.

Pat shook his head and pulled out his find. Mike's flashlight lit up the copy of a 1983 morgue photo of Sarah Converse Domenico.

"Emily's mama," Pat said and cleared his throat. "Somebody's making a point, I'd say."

"Not Emily, though." Mike frowned into the darkness. It didn't seem like her to carry around something so gruesome. "Someone beat her to the punch I think."

"Yeah. I agree. There were a lot of unanswered

questions about Sarah's accident. Some folks, including me, thought she'd been forced off the road. But I wasn't sheriff back then, and Domenico was a very popular guy. The judge in the case closed it without a lot of fuss."

Mike's mind went to the obvious conclusion. Someone besides Emily had come looking for revenge. "You find anything in the house?"

"I found three bullet holes in the door, but the house is empty. No signs of a struggle. No blood. No body. Glass of liquor left on the desk. The computer system's in sleep mode. I didn't take the time to check for security footage."

"Right, we're on it. Alec?" One of the men stepped forward. "Check the senator's system for shots of the last few hours." The man slipped past them into the house. "Let's clear the area. Doyle, scout the rear. Jer, Rico, the outbuildings. Pat and I'll take the barn." He paused to make eye contact with each man and got nods in return. "Go." The men melted away as quietly as they'd appeared.

"That's frickin' scary." Pat swallowed.

"No, that's my team. Now let's go find my woman."

They'd gone ten yards when the roar of a gunshot split the night.

****

Emily didn't remember landing on top of Billy, but the sting of the icy water snapped her back to consciousness. There was grating pain in her forehead, like she'd been kicked by a horse. Her eyes came into focus slowly, and for a sickening moment, she wished she'd stayed out cold.

Beneath her hands, the wet slip of a denim-covered pant leg. The muscle inside it trembled and contracted as Billy struggled to stand. He pulled himself to standing, and she slithered down into water tinged red in the flashlight's halo. Not breathing, waiting for the pain to register, she shook her head, hoping hearing returned to replace the ringing sting of the shot.

Slowly, she unfurled her body and pushed up against the stone wall. The smell of the spent shot filled the room. Beneath that, the coppery scent of blood. She took a step back and reached out for Billy's arm. As her trembling fingers made contact, big hands jerked her backward and dragged her body up against a solid chest. Michael.

"Drop the gun, Billy," Pat echoed from the darkness behind them. The Hole lit with another larger light, throwing the chamber into stark relief. She wished it had remained dark. Michael spun her around, but not before the scene cemented itself inside her head.

Billy stood statue still. Then slowly opened his hand and let the gun splash to the floor. The water wrapped a ripple of crimson up into the light. Beside him, the inside of Ray Domenico's skull jumped into view in excruciating detail. A gruesome mash of bone and hair and bloody debris floated alongside his corpse.

Emily tried to force her eyes not to see the horror show below her. She tried to force the acrid smell from her lungs and her throat. Nothing worked the way it should. Her balance took a spin around the inside of her head. She threw up and passed out. In that order.

****

She woke up in the house, held close by arms as warm and strong as she remembered them to be. And then the tears started. He began a slow rocking motion and settled her head in the heated skin of his neck. *Home*. There was no place safer or more wanted on earth.

The room was quiet, the lights dim, but beyond the windows, the searing strobe of light from emergency vehicles filled the night. For Billy, she guessed. For the body...and the tears got heavier.

Michael held her closer. Dropped a kiss on the crown of her head and tucked a tissue in her hand.

"I'm getting you all snotty," she murmured into his shirt.

"A little snot never hurt anybody." His voice rumbled from his chest and into hers. "Better than barf any day."

"Oh, my God. I threw up on your feet, didn't I?" She raised her head and glanced to his toes. "I'm so sorry. They'll wash, though. Or I'll buy you another pair. I...I'd never seen anything like..." Her words jammed up in her throat.

"Don't think about it, honey. Just let it fade, don't replay it." He kissed her forehead. "And don't worry about my shoes. I might have been upset if it'd been on my favorite boots. I used to have a great pair. But these? Naw."

She pushed away from his chest and wiped her eyes with the tissue. She cocked her head when his words seeped through to her soggy brain. "Boots, like size thirteen, scruffy, black."

"Yeah, they were." He frowned, looking at her curiously. "I loved those things. Just got 'em good and broken in and lost one. Wanna help me pick out a new pair or what?"

A smile as wide as her cheeks broke out on her face. "Don't need to, sailor. I think I found your not-so-glass slipper."

Michael looked puzzled for a minute. His face lightened with relief and clarity. "Well, I'll be damned." He hugged her tight. "Did you ever have a night that changed everything?"

She nodded. The events of the last few hours fit that bill.

"I've been looking for a way to tell you how I landed in Tamarack. But there never seemed to be a good time to tell the tale. The damnedest things happen to me. The bachelor party, the ride with the girl who wasn't. An embarrassing case of drunken stupidity. Then a kiss from a red-haired angel." He wiped a thumb across her cheek. "You seemed so familiar to me right from the first. I just didn't put it together. Guess that makes you my handsome princess, huh?"

He moved to kiss her lips, and she put up a hand.

"Not on your life, buddy. Not till I find some toothpaste."

He smiled seductively. "S'okay, beautiful. You'll be my last frog. Or am I mixing fairy tales?" He pushed her back against the cushions and stole what was left of her breath.

Chapter Twenty-Three

Blanche's Diner was quiet for the first time in almost three weeks. The news crews had finally cleared out of town. The news cycle had moved on to another scandal, this time featuring the nation's president and his propensity for hookers. It was a relief, really it was. Emily took a long sip of her coffee and pushed the *huevos rancheros* around on her plate. Her appetite wasn't very good these days.

Her grand plan to be the hero hadn't played out the way she thought it would. Not even close. Michael had kissed her goodbye and returned to Coronado to make sure the team didn't suffer any fallout from their involvement in the final scene of Ray Domenico's downfall. There would still be Billy's trial to face. The murder would be food for the sharks for weeks to come.

The only bright spot was Ian. He'd been released from Denver Health and was currently back in rehab. He'd declined her offer to blast the news with their history. Too much scrutiny would only make his recovery harder, he'd said. Perhaps that would change. Bob Sears was hopeful that he'd eventually write the book anyway. He'd digitized Emily's diaries and returned the originals. They were back in their box, this time in the bedroom closet above Cloud to Ground.

She rocked back in her booth and closed her eyes. She did that a lot lately. A vague sense of fatigue and emptiness would pull her eyes closed and her shoulders down with unseen pressure. Depression. She wondered if she should get that looked at. Probably. Maybe tomorrow.

The metallic jangle of something hitting her table jerked her eyelids open, and she jumped upright.

Michael McCandlis stood above her, hands on slim hips and a huge grin on his face. "Hey, wake up, beautiful. I've been looking for you."

Her heart did a tumble in her chest. "Hey yourself, sailor. Thought you'd be back on a surfboard by now."

"Nope. I decided to stay landlocked for a while. Got a job instead." He nudged the black leather rectangle laying on the table in front of her.

"That right? You figure you can make a living doing leather work?" She picked it up and was surprised by the weight. She smiled up at him and flipped it over. Her breath stalled in her throat.

A gold star surrounded by a solid rim of silver sparkled from her palm. *Sierra County Deputy Sheriff.*

The lettering wavered in the tears that sprang to her eyes. "You're st-staying?"

"I am."

And she was in his arms before her next breath.

A word from the author…

I've been an avid reader and sometime writer all of my life. I've never been able to resist the draw of a good story, and that has been true in my professional life as well.

I was raised as the third of three children in the Colorado high country. Early on, I discovered the joy of creating handcrafted jewelry, which led to a forty-five-year career as a professional jeweler. Every customer, every piece has its own story. I've collected them like pearls in a strand, and I often use them as a jumping-off point for the tales I tell.

If you're looking for me, you'll find me on the shores of a northern lake, hammering away on my latest story of love and life in the modern world.

~*~

Find Jayne online at:
http://www.JayneYork.com

Thank you for purchasing
this publication of The Wild Rose Press, Inc.

For questions or more information
contact us at
info@thewildrosepress.com.

The Wild Rose Press, Inc.
www.thewildrosepress.com

To visit with authors of
The Wild Rose Press, Inc.
join our yahoo loop at
http://groups.yahoo.com/group/thewildrosepress/

Milton Keynes UK
Ingram Content Group UK Ltd.
UKHW020759250224
438379UK00013B/1375